Theft of the Seven Scriptures

Meg Price

ISBN-10: 0-9972506-5-8
ISBN-13: 978-0-9972506-5-7

CONTENTS

CHAPTER I

Thunder growled as I ran through the deserted streets. Rain dumped down and my boots splashed puddles of murky water onto my legs. The buildings rose tall, and as I ran through the back alleys my heart pumped and churned blood vigorously. I walked up a set of uneven rock steps and stood on a square porch. My shoes clicked as I paced back and forth, then I finally took hold of the doorknocker and tapped over and over. It was now midnight and lightning struck just beyond the village. The hollow knocks echoed in the cold like a heartbeat, and Mayor Elchyard himself opened the door. We quickly walked through the mansion to a tiny library. His voice was old and scratchy as he ushered me to a circular, mahogany table where a group of councilmen in charcoal black suits had already congregated.

"What's going on?" I asked wearily.

"It's your father," said Elchyard, "he is gone, merely disappeared along with the scripture."

"Do you have any information on where he might have gone, where the scripture is?" One of the men said as he lunged across the table towards me.

"No," I said flatly.

"We need to know!"

I was frustrated, and I too wondered where my dad had disappeared. "My father wouldn't have taken it!" I stormed to the door, but one of the men stopped me from leaving.

"We will need to ask you a few more questions if you don't mind."

"Your father was the last one with the scripture before it disappeared, and before it was separated back into its seven pieces."

"He wouldn't have done that! He is the protector!"

The men kept on with their questioning, as if they didn't even register what I had already told them.

"Pages had been mysteriously disappearing when it was in his possession. That is not the sign of a protector, Zach."

"Now he is gone, the scripture is gone and some pages may be lost forever! You do realize what happens when a page goes missing, don't you?" The man grimaced.

"A Charmer goes missing. I know that already!"

"Where is he?"

"I don't know. Do you really think I would still be in this damn village, being accused, if I knew where he was?"

"We have insight that you met with him two moons ago. Did he bring up anything suspicious?"

"He mentioned none of this to me."

"We need more information."

"I don't have any more!"

The council looked to Elchyard and he subtly nodded back to them.

"We want to keep you here until we find him. You are the closest thing to him, without you we might not ever see him again."

I knew then that I was meant to be kept prisoner until my father was found and I had no time to be held captive; I needed to get to him before he was killed. I slowly looked up from the floor. Another cluster of men had let themselves into the room. I squirmed in my seat, trying to pull my scepter out of the air, but I didn't have enough concentration. Without my scepter I was nothing, weak compared to the other men in the room. Before anyone could grab hold of me I ran to the window and jumped.

"My father is innocent!" I yelled out before hurdling all my body weight forward, hoping I could reach the roof of the building adjacent. I could hear the others coming. I needed time to stop and think for a moment. I knew I didn't have anywhere safe to go. I was a fugitive now.

"Get him!" I heard Elchyard bellow from the library above as I lowered myself down a fire escape ladder and made my way to the fishing docks at the edge of the island. I was panting as I looked over my shoulder to see if any of the men had caught up to me. I could hear them shouting in the distance and I knew that if they found me now, they might try to kill me.

I saw a little wooden rowboat tied to a steel pole, crashing into the barge with waves pouring inside of it, slowly sinking it under the water. I paddled out to sea in no apparent direction; all I knew was that if I stayed on the island I didn't stand a chance.

I was finally out far enough in the ocean that Elchyard and his men wouldn't be able to spot me. I relaxed my grip on the oars and floated further out to sea. I reached my hand into my pocket and pulled out the note my dad had written for me right before his disappearance. I hadn't dared to show it to the council.

"My boy, I know I have been distant from you lately, but it is for your own good. I fear that I may be in danger; you are safer with me not around. Duchura has gained her strength back as many fail to recognize. She is going after the scripture. I have no way of knowing what is yet to come, but you must send for Sable Writhm. She will be of help to us now. Stay safe."

I was scared. I didn't know what I was doing. I never thought that any of the rumors of Duchura were really true; but now I was alone, and the realization of everything began to settle in. I crouched down in the boat, trying to stay dry from the increasing intensity of the waves. If I didn't come across a neighboring island by the time the full-fledged storm hit, I would be subject to the monsoon.

As the storm grew stronger, I grew weaker. Fighting the waves in an attempt to keep my boat afloat seemed nearly impossible. I drew out my scepter with a thought to use a spell to calm the waves around me. It worked, and I slipped into a light sleep as the boat drifted onward.

I woke later to a sharp jolt from below the boat. I saw one of my oars slipping into the water. I lunged to grab it and as I did I felt something grab me by the arm. I lost my balance and was pulled into the water. Their vise was strong and I reached out, grabbing at the boat with my free hand, restlessly trying to free myself.

I lost concentration of the spell and the waves began to grow in size. I struggled for one last gulp of air before I was dragged below the surface of the water. I opened my eyes and my heart jumped. There in front of me was a man with stone black eyes. He attempted to force me deeper into the water as I fought my way to the surface. I grabbed him by the throat, trying to choke him, to weaken him, to make him lose his grip, but he was strong.

Duchura was already one step ahead of me. She knew where I was and she had already sent a Boggele to kill me. I dragged the man up with me towards the surface with the last of my energy and forced him above the water. I reached for my scepter in the boat and cast a spell at the man. Rage surged through my body as I looked into his cold eyes, the windows to his cruel, lifeless soul. He screamed in agony. He became limp and I flung him into the boat as he gave up his fight.

I had no idea Duchura had accumulated so much power already. I hadn't fully believed that she was even still alive; but she was, and she really did plan on getting back the scripture.

I frantically searched the boat for the oars and

couldn't find them. I looked overboard into the water. There was nothing, but I needed to keep moving. There were few ways to hide, especially now, and little more I could do on my own. I needed help.

The storm was picking up and without my oars I could only sit and hope for shore. I screamed out in frustration. Sable Writhm would not know how to help, but that was the only option I had left. I drew out my scepter and sent a bolt of lightning through the air, calling for the girl.

The man beside me appeared dead and I wanted him out of my boat. I picked him up and cast him into the ocean. I had my scepter at the ready in case he was still alive; but I watched as his body sank down into the water. His eyes were still open and staring at me, his hands appeared frozen in a craggy position as if he was still reaching out for me, and a green eye necklace that I had not noticed before, wrapped tightly around his neck, floated down after him.

All of the sudden, a wave hit my boat, sending me against the wood planks. I reached up to my head and felt something wet. I dabbed at it and brought my hand to my face. I was bleeding, badly, and I felt my consciousness quickly slip away from me.

My eyes finally fluttered open and I became aware of a stinging sensation on my forehead. My boat had been flooded and the gash on my head had been soaking in saltwater. I had briefly forgotten where I was. I looked around and realized if I didn't start paddling my boat would soon run into a cliff of rocks. Then I remembered that my oars were gone, but I couldn't force myself to flee the boat for fear of another Boggele.

"Jump!" I heard a faint voice say from the distance. I looked around to see where it was coming from. "Jump!" I heard it again.

There was the girl; there was Sable -- I was sure of it -- standing on the shore. She started making her way out into the water and I waved my arms frantically to get her to stop. But she came.

I had no option but to jump now and head for shore. I couldn't let her risk coming into the water. The storm created the allusion of a deep, abyssal darkness below the water. I couldn't see anything that lay below the surface. I noticed the girl had begun to turn back to shore now. Possibly because she saw there was no need to rescue me now. Possibly because she had seen something out there.

I swam faster. My feet touched sand and I drudged through the water and towards where the girl was. We sat together in a blistering silence.

The girl wiped blood from her legs and pulled her long brown hair away from her face with shaking hands. "It was rocky out there."

"Let me help you." I took my scepter out and held it to the lacerations on her leg.

She jumped back in surprise, looking up at me with piercing blue eyes.

"What are you doing?"

I had forgotten she knew nothing of magic. She believed she was human.

"I was just going to get rid of those gashes." I held

my scepter up to her one more time and she drew away again. "Let me at least…"

"I'm okay," she said.

She was lying. The blood flow refused to stop. I took my shirt off and wrapped it tightly around one of the deeper cuts.

"Thanks," she said quietly.

I nodded.

"Where are we?" she asked, looking idly out at the ocean.

The storm was starting to die down and I looked back at the island, wondering if I could notice anything familiar now that I could see through the sheets of rain.

"I don't know." I knew I had a concussion, my sight was blurry and my thinking was slow.

"You don't know where we are?" She sounded out of breath, perhaps worried, but I couldn't tell for sure.

"No," I was lost for words. "I'm Zach." She reached out to shake hands and when we touched I could feel an energy being channeled inside myself from me to her. We both pulled back and stared at each other in silence.

CHAPTER II

We both stayed quiet, seeming to think the other would provide some sort of answer as to what was happening.

I inhaled deeply, taking in the air and the ocean and the island. With my exhale my chest shook with fear. I turned back to the boy, he was still silent. "What is happening?"

"I don't know." He said with an edge of discomfort. "I was given instructions to summon you."

"You brought me here? How did we get here, when did we get here? I don't remember anything." I racked my brain, trying to understand, to make sense of everything that was happening.

"I was told you could help me, us." He stuttered.

"I don't know anything that is going on. How would I be able to help you!" I was panicking.

Zach began to answer my questions, "it was a summon, you were brought here instantaneously. As for what you are here to help with, I am not entirely sure myself."

Before Zach could say anything more I heard a noise coming from the forest. Zach whipped his head around in the direction of the noise and pulled me to my feet.

"We have to hide."

I ran much slower than him, especially with the gashes on my legs.

"Hold on." Zach stopped running and squatted down for me to get on his back.

"I can make it by myself, really," I said; but he refused.

He started sprinting down the beach and I was amazed at how fast he could go with me on his back. He was strong and I could feel his muscles moving as he ran. I looked behind me as the sounds grew louder. My heart immediately started pounding, a group of men, all with stone cold, black eyes, was following close behind us. I couldn't help but gasp.

Zach must have sensed my fear.

"I will find us somewhere safe to hide," he said panting; I was unsure if it was from running or out of fear. He quickly let me off of his back as he slashed through the bushes where the sand turned to forestry.

Something grabbed hold of me from inside the bushes and I screamed as I was pulled from my feet, falling hard onto the sand. A hand clasped over my mouth. The only noise I could make was a muffled scream.

Zach was quick to notice. He tore through the bushes after me and pulled out some sort of wand.

He shouted out what I assumed had to be a spell. The man that had grabbed me was thrust back. Zach approached him. The man didn't move, but his eyes stayed open, and stared back at us expressionless.

Zach knelt down to let me on his back again, but I refused. It would be better for both of us if I ran too. I looked up at him and he silently ushered me deeper into the forest. I could hear the men yelling in the distance. They were closing in on us. Zach suddenly switched paths and their voices began to grow fainter. The forest began to thin once more and we made it back onto the beach.

My voice was shaking, "what was that about?"

"They were sent by Duchura. She must know you are here. I should have never sent for you." He seemed to be talking more so to himself.

"Who is Duchura?" I asked, still breathing heavily.

"I'll explain. I promise, but not here. There's no time."

I listened for the men. We still had a moment; they weren't within earshot yet. "Where are we going to go?"

Zach seemed to be thinking, but I was too impatient to wait. "Who is Duchura?"

"We have to get off the island, and find a cave."

"To hide?" I nearly begged him to answer at least one of my questions now.

"We'll use it as a gateway to get out of here." He explained, walking back into the forest. "I'm so sorry Sable, I should have never brought you here."

Suddenly Zach stopped. I had been following close behind and ran into him. "What is it?"

"I thought I heard something." He stared at me peculiarly and reached up to touch my forehead, "your bleeding."

My adrenaline had been pumping, keeping me from

feeling an pain, but when he brought it to my attention I began to feel a warm trickle of blood sliding down my face.

"I can help you, if you'll let me." Zach offered.

"What exactly is that?"

"A scepter." Zach said as he touched it to my skin. I didn't stop him this time. He said something to himself and I could feel the same energy rushing into me that I had felt when Zach and I first touched. Only this time stronger. Much stronger.

Zach lowered his scepter and looked up surprised.

"What is it?" I asked, feeling my forehead. It was completely smooth, the blood gone, no sign of the cut.

"You syphoned my energy." He stumbled back, holding himself up by a tree trunk. "A lot of it."

I looked at him concerned, his face was pale and gaunt.

"We'll have to look for the cave tomorrow. I can't keep moving right now." He slid down to the base of the trunk and sat in the sand.

I looked around, listening for the men. If they came now, we would be no match. "Okay." I sat down next to him, still worried.

His hand shook as he reached for the same peculiar object that he had been using earlier, the scepter. I handed it to him. When I touched it, it shocked me, but I pretended as though nothing had happened.

"Thanks." He breathed. I nodded back to him. "We can't stay down here, the men will find us." I was relieved, he had been thinking the same thing as me.

He pulled himself back to his feet and leaned all his

weight against the tree. I watched silently. He looked up to the trees as he spoke to himself. I stared with my head craned back, looking into the branches; they were moving, contorting to form something. The leaves rustled and a light rumbling noise resonated all around. I looked back to Zach, but he was too focused on something up above to notice. Then all at once everything was quiet.

"We'll stay here for the night." Exhaustion had completely taken over him.

"What do you mean?" I asked, confused.

Zach only pointed. Vines has wrapped themselves around the trunk of the tree, creating rungs just large enough to climb up, and at the top of them laid a twisted platform of branches.

I looked to Zach, about to speak, amazed at what he had just done, but he did not notice. He was hunched over with his hands on his knees, drawing air deep into his lungs. "Go, I'll be right behind you." He said between breaths. He must have sensed I was watching him.

I took hold of the vine, my feet were still planted on the ground. Its thick, spindly body was hard to grip.

My foot was now wedged between the vine and the tree and my body was pressed tightly against the trunk. I was almost to the platform. My arms were beginning to tire and as I reached my hand out, ready to hoist myself further up, I could see it shaking. I pulled back and clung to the tree. I needed to rest for just a moment.

I took a deep breath, gripping the vine tighter and resting my head against the bark of the tree, collecting myself. Then I reached for the vine above once more. My fingers slipped and in the same moment I lost my footing. Hands from below almost immediately wrapped themselves around my waist to steady me. My shouldered tensed in surprise. Zach had started climbing, and he was already right below me. I looked at him thankfully.

He nodded back.

I helped pull Zach onto the platform after I made it up. He immediately fell against the limbs and rolled onto his back. I still didn't understand what he had meant earlier, that I had taken his energy, but I didn't ask. I watched him as his chest moved up and down. He crossed his hands over his stomach and looked up into the trees, staying completely silent.

I sat up for a long time, my eyes wandering from Zach to the surrounding scenery. Everything was visible from the platform. I looked out to the ocean, to the far side of the island, above the tree top line, and to the ground below. The men from earlier seemed nonexistent from above. Nothing seemed real. Everything had to be a dream. I lied down next to Zach and closed my eyes.

"Sable." I felt a slight nudge against my shoulder. I jolted upright, breathing hard. It was already dark and I was disoriented. I was still on the platform. It wasn't a dream. "You were having a nightmare."

He was right. I had been having a nightmare, and it hadn't ended. I was living in it.

I had been dreaming of the island, and the men, and now too, a woman. "You have to explain this to me." I demanded.

Zach seemed to think hard about something. Then

he began to speak. "My father went missing a while back and I believe it is because of a set of spells that he was in charge of protecting. Together the spells make up a scripture that protects my kind."

"I don't understand." I sniveled.

"The Charmers," he explained, "and the others are the Boggeles. They are after the scripture. Only one of the two can maintain control in this world at a time -- whoever has the scripture. Many people think that my father is working for the Boggeles and that the government wanted him imprisoned, so he vanished. Others think that he really was trying to protect the scripture and that the Boggeles took him. Sable, I know that my father is trying to protect it, but either way he is gone and I have to bring him back. The Boggeles are gaining strength; they were able to separate the scripture back into seven pieces. It's worse than I ever imagined."

He grew quiet again, allowing the darkness to consume us from all around. It still didn't make sense. Why was I here? I opened my mouth to speak, but I didn't know what to say.

"I don't know much more about what's going on myself," Zach broke the silence. His eyes were all I could make out in the darkness. They reflected against the black of the night, appearing sad, yearning for some abstract thing that I did not yet comprehend. I feared that whatever it was, it would inevitably become a worry of my own as well. There was more to all this than getting his father back, I knew it, but he did not explain any further and I allowed him to remain silent.

My eyes adjusted to the darkness and the soft lines of Zach's face were now visible against the night sky. He looked back at me, still quiet, so mysteriously. I bit my lip and turned away from his gaze. "We should go back to sleep."

Each time I closed my eyes an image of the woman from my dream appeared. I had no recollection of who she was, and each time I thought of her a feeling of unease took hold of me.

The night felt long, and lonely. Zach had fallen asleep, leaving me alone in the darkness for hours on end. A light rain trickled down and dripped from the leaves to the platform. Faint noises kept me alert. The sound of soft earth being crushed below wandering feet was constants through the night. I couldn't help but wonder if it was the men. The platform seemed less of a sanctuary now.

The early morning finally set in and Zach started to stir. He then held completely still, moving only his eyes back and forth, seeming to look for something.

"What is it?"

"I'm not sure. The Boggeles could have caught up to us by now. We should get out of here as soon as we can."

Zach was starting to scare me. He still wasn't making any sudden moves. I strained my ears to hear what he was hearing, but the noises present throughout the night had suddenly all subsided.

"We've got to get to a cave." he said, lowering himself back to the beach. I quickly caught up to him and stayed close to his side.

"Zach," I whispered. He didn't hear. "Zach," I said again.

He finally looked up and we both stood completely still, facing one of the Boggeles. The man quickly slipped behind a bush and I was unable to figure out where he had gone. Then Zach shot a spell out from behind me.

"Sable, run!" he said, turning around and bumping into me.

I was facing yet another one of the men. As I looked around I noticed more of them, moving in on us from all sides. Zach was now pressed up against me as the Boggeles cornered us.

Zach stood frozen and for one slight moment everything was still, then is one swift motion Zach cast a spell at the men, they stammered back, giving us just enough time to push past them.

"How does she knows we're here!" Zach appeared on-edge. "She's not going to stop until she finds us," he said to himself.

"Who knows where we are?" I panted.

She. I thought to myself. The woman from my dream was the only thing I could think of.

"Duchura, the Boggele leader." Zach explained.

He beat through the bushes moving away from the men as fast as he could. Then he abruptly stopped and pulled out his scepter, shooting a spell out towards nothing.

"Zach, calm down."

He breathed in deeply and lowered his scepter. "I'm sorry. I just need to get us away from here."

"Your right, let's keep moving." I said calmly.

Before Zach continued to walk he reached for his scepter one last time, shouting out a spell I had not yet heard him use. A faint ball of light appeared, suspended in the still in air for a only a moment before it started to move. Zach followed it with no explanation.

The light gradually began to dim, leaving us alone in a clearing just a few yards away from the beach.

He pointed to something in front of us. I looked and then turned back to face Zach once more, smiling contently. The light had taken us to a cave.

Zach wasted no time in walking up to the cave's entrance. I followed close behind.

The cave started to fill with a heavy fog, and I realized I had grabbed Zach's hand instinctually out of fear. I could no longer see him standing next to me and I began to sweat from an intense heat.

Finally I felt the cool air once more, and slowly I began to see the outline of Zach's face as the fog dissipated. I quickly let go of his hand and looked to the mouth of the cave.

Zach wiped water from his face and slowly approached the exit. Then he motioned for me to come forward.

"We can't let anyone see us," he told me. "People are looking for me here."

"No one believes you and your father are innocent?" I asked.

He shook his head. "I'm sure by now the council has made up some sort of story about the whole thing."

"The council?"

"They are the head chairmen of the government here, they have a lot of leverage with the villagers. They trust the council too much to turn against them and side with my father and me." he explained.

I nodded that I understood. I had just noticed that it was dark as I looked out into the village. We must have been in a different time zone than the island.

Everything looked old and primitive here. Tiny shops lined the streets and rundown houses with missing shingles and uneven roofs filled the hillside.

"Okay, ready?"

"Yeah," I whispered.

"We have to keep quiet. Luckily there shouldn't be too many people out at this hour."

The cave was up on hilltop overlooking the village. Zach constantly glanced behind him as we made our way down to the edge of the town. He kept up a brisk walk into an alleyway.

I didn't want to follow. The alleys were eerie; shadows passed over the back walls of the buildings as we walked even though they appeared empty, I felt watched. A dog ran by and knocked a can out from a pile of garbage. I jumped. It must have startled Zach too, he started to walk faster and constantly checked for anyone who might be following us. Finally he stopped in front of the back door to one of the shops. A little, splintery sign with paint flaking off the sides read: Etan's Place.

Zach took his scepter out of his pocket and poked it through the mail slot. I saw a burst of fluorescent color light up the building inside. Zach peeked over his shoulder one last time before pushing the door open.

It must have been a general store because a hodgepodge of items overflowed the counters. Barrels of candy lined the cash register, advertisements were plastered on the doors and walls, and in the back of the store what looked to be a lizard was sitting in a large glass tank.

"What is this place?" I asked.

"It's my Dad's store. We'll need a few things before we leave again," he said as he opened up the register.

"I thought he protected the scripture?"

"He does. This store has been in the family for decades though; he runs it just for the historic link."

While Zach busied himself gathering supplies I went over to the glass tank in the back of the store. I peered over the case and looked at the animal that now stared back. It opened its mouth and breathed out a tiny cloud of water vapor. I leaned in further to watch as it opened its mouth to do it again and Zach suddenly pulled me back.

"Damn," he said, looking around.

"What is it?"

"That's a toxin it just breathed out. I don't know why it did that to you; it should only do that to a Boggele, but it's going to set off an alarm," he said as he quickly pulled a glass lid over the tank.

It had been so quiet outside, but the toxins in the air soon became pervasive through the store and an alarm started to blare.

"Hide," Zach whispered as he scrambled for a place out of sight. I managed to maneuver behind a stack of dusty carpets and conceal myself on a shelf behind them.

Suddenly I heard the front doors of the shop open and footsteps flooding inside. I peered around the side of the carpets and saw a group of policemen standing in the room.

"Find him," one of them said to the crowd that now began to congregate at the store's entrance. My heart was racing. I wondered what would happen if they saw me. I wondered what would happen if I breathed in the toxins.

The villagers started tearing apart the store, overturning tables and dumping out barrels of supplies. I heard footsteps coming towards me, but when they came closer in my direction, I heard violent coughing and the sound of them turning away. It was the toxins, I knew it. They were drifting closer to me.

I started to faintly smell a pungent scent, and I held my breath, doing anything not to breathe in the smell. I started to sweat until I finally couldn't take it any longer. I breathed in the air and felt a choking sensation. In a fit of coughing I accidentally knocked over an enormous rug in front of me. I was able to see a group of people, scepters held in the air, staring at me.

"Where is the boy?" a policeman demanded.

I was coughing profusely and unable to stop.

The police looked at the villagers, expecting them to do something.

"Bring her with us," one of them said as a few of the braver villagers approached my hiding place. As they got closer to me, and attempted to walk past the animal's tank I could see their eyes start to water and their faces turn pale as they breathed in. Before they were able to make it over to me they turned back. We were separated by a cloud of toxins that slowly crept deeper into the store.

The villagers were the only ones with a clear route out of the building; I was trapped in between the back wall of the store and the noxious air. The policemen seemed to know that sooner or later I would have to move to their side of the store to get away from the air. They waited, watching me patiently.

I saw a figure, working his way up through the crowd of people. He was going to cross through the room, over to my side -- I could tell by his quick, unwavering movement. The figure emerged at the front of the crowd; I saw that it was Zach. As he pushed past the remaining officers in the front of the group, people started to recognize him. He ran over to me right before an officer was able to grab his shirt and pull him back.

Red veins took over the whites of his eyes and he had trouble breathing, heaving in a bent over position. He cast a spell to the wall behind us and I watched, thinking that something would happen. Then he cast it again and grabbed one of the carpets beside me, pulling me onto it with him. My eyes started to water too, and I became disoriented, feeling unstable, and falling to my knees.

As I regained my balance, I noticed I was able to breath better; I wiped the tears from the toxin away from my eyes and realized we were no longer on the ground; we were about to fly right into the back wall of the store. I screamed, and braced myself for the collision, holding onto Zach's waist.

Zach yelled out after me, with his scepter pointed

against the wall; we were moving fast now, about to hit it. "Zach!"

Right before we slammed into the sheetrock a hole in the wall started to emerge; Zach turned the carpet completely sideways and we managed to fit through the opening.

I loosened my grip on Zach and looked back down at the shop.

"There's another island nearby -- I'm not exactly sure which way, but my dad has friends there that may be able to help us," Zach said, seeming rather panicked about what we had just done.

My whole body quivered as I breathed. "How are we going to find it?"

"We will have to stop in the next nearest town and buy a map. We need to rest somewhere for the night anyway."

I could tell Zach was still nervous; his hands were shaking and the rug would occasionally drop a few feet down in the air before jolting back upward. We kept a lookout for another city. All I was able to see now was ocean. Finally I noticed another island, barely visible in the distance. We dove down closer and I realized that it was a small city. Buildings rose in the foreground and behind them, on the outskirts, was a cluster of smaller shops. We made our way to the edge of the city and landed swiftly on a quiet gravel road.

"We should be safe here for the night. I don't think Duchura will be able to find us; we've already been on three different islands today. There's no way she could track us that quickly."

We started walking further into the city, looking for a map store. There were hundreds of people gathering around us, all trying to talk to us and trying to sell us something, or give us a sample of something. I looked to Zach in surprise.

"We have to ignore them," he said as we pushed past the crowd. "We don't want anyone to know we are here."

We stopped by an old Victorian house on the corner of the street where traffic was light. I saw a girl peer out through one of the windows on the second story and a moment later she was walking out the front door, headed over to us.

"Do you need a place to stay?" she purred. Zach and I both looked up. I didn't say anything.

"Yes, is there space here to rest for the night?" Zach asked. I nudged his shoulder and glared at him. I had a strange feeling about this place.

"Perfect," she answered. She opened a wrought iron gate and led us to the front door. We followed her into a lavish sitting room and sat across from the girl on a sunken leather couch. "I'm Scarlette Lule," the girl extended her arm out to shake hands. Her grip was much tighter than I expected. I attempted to pull away from her, but she held her grip, looking into my eyes for another moment before finally letting go.

A fire was crackling and made the room feel hot and stuffy, with a lingering smell of smoke. A man walked in and whispered something in Scarlette's ear.

"Thank you Henry," she said.

"We have a place for you two to stay." Scarlette led us to a marble foyer and up a winding staircase. It was dark outside and the moon illuminated the night sky with a dingy glow through a thick haze.

Scarlette's heels tapped against each stair as we walked to the second floor. We followed her down a long corridor and a dark hall lit by sconces. She finally paused in front of two adjacent double-door rooms.

"Here we are," she said, looking at Zach, opening the door for him. Without another word she disappeared back down the hall. The fires in the sconces went out one-by-one as she walked by them, leaving us alone in the dark.

"Zach, I don't think we should stay here," I whispered.

"Why not?"

"I just have a weird feeling about this place."

"Sable, this looks like a bed and breakfast; we're not doing anything wrong."

"Zach, it doesn't seem like that at all to me. This is someone's house, it's weird. I don't like it here."

"It will be fine. It's just for the night; we'll leave early tomorrow."

I couldn't help but feel like we were being watched. It was beginning to become a regular paranoia. I knew this was not a bed and breakfast, but there was no sense in arguing, it was late already.

"Goodnight," I said as I walked into my room.

I closed my eyes, trying to get some rest, but every time I was about to fall asleep something jolted me awake once more. Something seemed familiar about this place, like I had dreamt of it before perhaps. I lay in bed, stiff, not wanting to move, not feeling welcomed. Something still didn't feel right. I wondered if Zach was still awake, too.

I crawled out of bed and left the room, walking over to Zach's door and quietly knocking. He didn't come to open it. I held my ear to the door and heard nothing. He was asleep and I was all alone.

I didn't go back to my room; instead I went to look around the house. I opened each door as I went down the hall and found a variety of spare bedrooms. If this was a bed and breakfast, we seemed to be the only guests.

A small green door at the base of the staircase caught my attention. The paint was chipped and tarnished, and it looked nothing like the rest of the house. It creaked when I opened it and I jumped back to make sure no one heard. I crouched down to step inside. It looked like a library. I walked over to one of the shelves and removed a scripture. It had a strange cover, with a green eye depiction on it.

A ladder led up to more rows of scriptures and one in particular caught my attention. I carefully rolled the ladder over to where the scripture was and climbed up. The last step was too wobbly to step on so I had to lean. My fingers barely touched the scripture as I eased it off the shelf. I knew this scripture, it was in my dream. I started to remember more, pieces, fuzzy pieces of the dream. We had been in a cellar, in this very house, Zach and I.

I reached for another scripture on the shelf, flipping through the pages. Every single scripture I grabbed had the same insignia somewhere on the cover: a green eye. I couldn't read any of the scripture, it was in some other language. I put it back on the shelf and looked around a moment longer. I kept the scripture from the dream with me; it was the only one I was unable to open.

I hugged the scripture tight to my chest, remembering more. There was a lady in the cellar with us, the same peculiar lady from all the other dreams. Zach was in chains and I was being dragged away from him.

I grabbed one last scripture before I left the library. I flipped through it, trying to take my mind off of the dream. I couldn't control my thoughts; I was scared; I was hyperventilating.

I stopped on one of the pages, only able to understand one of the foreign words: Duchura.

My heart pounded faster now and my hands grew cold and clammy. The lady in the cellar, the lady in all my dreams -- she was Duchura.

I had to get Zach and myself out of here. I slammed the door to the library, quickly running back to our rooms. Then I heard a mumbling from downstairs and I stopped. It sounded like Scarlette and Henry. I couldn't make out what they were saying. I got closer, slinking down one more stair at a time.

I was now right outside of the sitting room entrance.

"Tomorrow we'll move them to the castle's dungeon and wait for Duchura to come." I froze. I was sure the sound of my heart beat could be heard allowed. "Go make sure they are still there." Henry obeyed Scarlette's orders and took a gulp of tea before getting up. I bolted up the stairs. Right before I got to my room, I tripped and landed on the floor.

"Who's there?" Henry's voice snapped as he ran in my direction. It was too dark for him see who it was so I threw open the door to my room and leaped onto the bed. Right as he walked in I pretended to be asleep. Then I heard him leave, probably to go into Zach's room.

I waited a few minutes, lying flat against the bed, listening to the rhythm of my heartbeat before I went back to Zach's door. I jiggled the knob and realized that it was locked from the outside. I knocked again, louder than before. I waited for a few seconds but he didn't come.

I couldn't think of any other plan. I was going to break Zach's window and go in to get him. I eased myself onto the steep roof and made my way over to the outside of his room. I kicked at the window, but it didn't even crack, and Zach hadn't seemed to hear a thing -- I could see him through the window, still asleep.

Rain was now pouring down in icy sheets on the already slippery roof and I was completely drenched. I crawled back to my window and my foot slipped, only to be caught by the gutter. I wrenched my foot back out and when it finally came free I lost my balance, dropping the scripture. It slid down the side of the roof and I stretched my arm as far out as I could to grab it. My fingertips barely touched it and as I tried to get a better grip it fell from the roof and onto the ground below.

I slid back into the room empty-handed and frantically searched for something that would break the window. I saw nothing.

The only other plan left was to find Henry. He had to have keys to get inside. I left my room once more and listened for him and Scarlette. I was running out of time. Soon it would be light and Zach and I would be stuck here.

He was nowhere to be found upstairs. I managed to slip down to the first floor to look for him there. I found myself in a dining room, with utensils, plates, and cloth napkins already set for breakfast; but no sign of the greasy-haired butler.

I heard a faint sound of voices and followed the noise over to the foyer, just in front of the staircase. There was a sound of rock scratching against the floor, and I saw a space in the wall start to slide to the side, giving way to a tunnel. The voices grew louder and I could hear Scarlette and Henry's conversation now.

"Do you have the second scripture?" Scarlette barked.

"It's in the library," Henry said back.

"Well go and get it!" She snapped.

I could hear Henry briskly walking by me and I ducked behind an antique oak table. When he passed I heard his keys jingling. A few minutes later he passed by me again and a strong smell of cologne lingered in the air. He came hustling back to Scarlette empty-handed.

"Where is it?"

"It was gone." Henry looked panicked, "I looked through the entire library." It must have been the scripture I took with me, that was now sitting on the lawn outside.

Scarlette took a deep breath and tried to keep from yelling. "Well, where did you move it? You can be so stupid! Find it tomorrow," she yelled, "or else I'll have to notify Duchura of what you have done."

"No! No, I'll find it. I must have moved it when those children came this morning."

"Those children?" Scarlette spat at him. "Those children are links to getting the Boggeles back into power! The son of Auckmonrahado is upstairs, Zach Etan -- and Sable! Sable Writhm is in this house as we speak! Do you know how powerful she is? Do you not remember our orders from Duchura!"

I wondered how she knew who we both were, especially me. Henry now seemed interested in what Scarlette was saying, as was I. There was something special about me, but I had no idea what it was.

"Do you think Sable really is..?"

Scarlette cut him off. "Yes! Of course she is! Do you know how valuable she is to us! If we can get her to Duchura with the complete scripture we will be on good terms with her for eternity and when she comes back to power again we will never have to be servants again. Henry, there is so much riding on this, you have no idea."

"Yes, master. Shall I bring the other scripture with us tonight?" he asked.

"I have already told Duchura we secured two of the scriptures; if we only show up with one she will be furious. We leave them both; that's the safest way to attend at this point."

"I will get them both tomorrow, do not worry."

"Oh, Henry," Scarlette said, dragging her scepter across his neck, "I am not the one who should be worried.

If you don't get me those scriptures tomorrow I will only have one choice. I am not afraid to give you over to Duchura," she warned in rage.

Henry and Scarlette made their way to the front door. I peered through the window by the entrance after they had closed the door and ran after them, staying a distance behind them as they walked miles in the darkness. Finally they stopped under a street lamp at the corner of two intercepting roads. I watched the strange scene curiously. Scarlette took her scepter out and held it up to the light. The orb-shaped bulb floated down and Henry caught it, handing it over to her. She held it tightly with both hands as it grew brighter. Suddenly she dropped it and screamed in pain, looking at the burn marks on her hands. I wondered if that was supposed to happen. The ball hit the ground and shattered into hundreds of pieces.

Scarlette and Henry's figures started to become translucent, and then they were gone. I sat on the curb in the darkness, not having any idea when they would return.

If I turned back to get Zach now I wouldn't have to worry about keeping quiet, but I would have to walk all alone in the dark. I wasn't even sure which way I would have gone to get back. I grabbed one of the pieces from the bulb and looked at it; it was still hot. I could see images moving around on it. They were blurry, but I was able to tell that they were people. As they moved around I could see their images jump from piece to piece.

I saw two pieces that looked like they would fit together and tried to stick them into place. They fit, and seemed to glue themselves back together. There was one last piece to complete the bulb, but I couldn't find it.

I could faintly hear people talking now and then I saw Scarlette walk by and slam her hands down on the table. I held my ear up closer to hear the conversation better.

"When we bring the girl and Auck's son to you tomorrow we can work on removing the spells on the scriptures we already have. We haven't made any progress so far."

"How will we get them to do that?" someone else said.

"The girl hasn't chosen a side; I doubt she even knows the legend. She will be easy to convince."

"Why would we want the Etans there? They are going to try and change her mind."

"Auck has to be there, he will have to help open the scriptures, and he is already in the dungeon anyway. He has been growing weaker; it will be hard for him to put up a fight. The timing is good, but we need to act fast."

"As for you," someone said, looking to the figure at the head of table -- that was the only person I was unable to see because of the missing piece -- "they trust you, you will have to help convince them."

"Of course."

The conversation seemed to be dying down and I felt the bulb start to get hot again. I quickly ran to the bushes and waited for Scarlette and Henry to emerge.

They were completely silent when they returned. As their figures became more defined, the bulb secured itself together tighter and the last piece was back in its place. The bulb floated back up to the street lamp and Henry and Scarlette made the walk home. I followed behind them in the darkness.

Scarlette dropped something and I froze, thinking she would turn around and see me. Henry was the one to notice and went back to pick it up. It was an eye necklace, the same as the ones I had seen on the scriptures back in the library. He bent down to grab it and gasped.

"What Henry!"

"Master, you, you…"

Scarlette snatched the necklace and put it back on in a hurry. Henry didn't seem to notice that when he bent down, he dropped his keys. As he walked further away I grabbed them, holding on tightly so that they would not hit one another and make any noise.

I made it through the door before Scarlette and Henry and ran to Zach's room. We had to at least hide before Scarlette and Henry came. The sun was starting to rise, and there was little time left to get out of this place.

"Zach?" I whispered.

He didn't answer. I went over to the bed and saw that it was empty. "Zach!" I yelled as I pulled all of the covers back. He was gone. I had to hold onto the side of the bed for support, I was so anxious that I felt dizzy.

"Oh, my God." I whispered to myself.

I left the room and ran down the stairs, Scarlette and Henry were inside, but there was no way they would have been able to get to Zach's room before I had.

I heard footsteps and realized that Scarlette was at the top of the stairs.

"They're gone."

"What do you mean?" I hadn't realized Henry was so close to me. I heard him only a few feet away from where I was standing, on the other side of a grandfather clock.

"They are gone!" She yelled.

I heard Henry run up the stairs towards her. "They couldn't be *gone*."

Scarlette screamed. "Henry they are not here! Look for yourself!"

I heard them both quickly walk down the hall on the second story. This was the only chance I had to find Zach; they were going to start looking for us soon.

I heard the same sound I had earlier of rock grating against the floor. The entrance to the concealed tunnel was opening up. I pressed myself against the wall staying out of sight from the tunnel's entrance, waiting to see what would happen.

I heard the noise stop; the tunnel must have been entirely open by now. I didn't hear anything so I leaned around the corner to see who had just come out.

"Sable," it was Zach's voice.

I turned around and ran back towards him. "Zach, you're here, thank goodness."

"Where have *you* been?"

"Looking for you; trying to find a way to get inside your room. We've got to get out of here before morning, Zach."

"I know, I should never have let us stay here."

"Come on then, let's go!" He didn't seem to be

moving.

"We need to get something first," he said, turning back to go into the tunnel.

"Zach, we don't have time. Scarlette and Henry are looking for us!"

"Part of the scripture is here."

"What?" I said, confused.

"The scripture, one of the scriptures, it's in here. We can't leave without it."

I looked back to make sure Scarlette and Henry weren't coming back down the stairs, and then I followed him into the tunnel.

"Sable, I'm pretty sure that they are Boggeles. They are working for Duchura."

"I know."

"What? How do you know that?" he said, confused.

"I heard Scarlette and Henry talking and then I followed them."

"Did they see you?"

"No, but they are planning on taking us to Duchura tomorrow, Zach. They want us to help them remove spells from the scriptures."

"We will be out of here soon, don't worry; but we can't leave without this scripture."

The tunnel finally ended and we were in a small room. In the center of the room there was a pedestal, and on top of it, the scripture, encased in glass. Zach was fixated on it; he wasn't listening to anything I was saying. "Zach!"

"We have to get it, we can't go without it!" he said as he shot spell after spell out at the glass case.

I just realized that Henry's keys were still in my pocket. "Look what I have," I said, dangling the keys.

"Where did you get these?" I handed him the key ring and he started trying each and every one of the keys until there was only one left.

"Last one," he said as he turned the key. The case opened and we both stepped back, thinking that something else was about to happen. When nothing did, he grabbed the scripture and we ran for the front doors of the house. We were about to leave when Zach stopped.

"The carpet," he said, "it's still in there; I've got to get it." He ran back down the tunnel, leaving me waiting by the stairs in the foyer with the scripture.

I waited. It was completely silent, but if Scarlette or Henry were to walk by the staircase from the story above they would see me. Finally I heard him coming back down the tunnel.

"Good," I sighed with relief.

I heard someone clear their throat and looked up, the footsteps had been Scarlette's, from the second floor, right by the staircase.

I looked up at her; she had definitely seen me. "Zach!" I yelled.

Then Scarlette yelled for Henry.

Both of them came rushing forward at the same time. Zach came dragging the carpet behind him.

Scarlette was screaming at Henry to do something and Zach was frantically unrolling the carpet.

Henry shot out a bright light towards Zach and I pushed him aside. He aimed for Zach again and this time I was unable to do anything, Henry was too fast.

Zach rolled onto his side in pain.

"Sable, get us out of here," he said, as he tried to reach for his scepter. He was hit again by Henry and yelled out.

"Zach, what do I do?"

He was in too much pain to answer. I grabbed the tassels to the rug and pulled. We lurched forward and hit the door. Zach managed to reach up to the handle and open it. We escaped.

Zach sat back up and held his scepter up to his side where he was hit.

"Are you okay?" I asked.

He cast a spell where he was hit before saying anything back. "I'm fine. Here, switch places," he said, reaching for the tassels.

As we got further away from the house I remembered the scripture I had found earlier that night.

"Zach, turn back."

"What?"

"I know where another of the scriptures is."

Zach seemed reluctant but he went back to the house and we searched the side lawn for the scripture. It was wet and muddy and when I reached for it, something grabbed hold of my leg and I screamed.

"Henry!" It was Scarlette. Cold sweat formed on the brow of my forehead. "Give me the scripture."

"No," I screamed. She tightened her grip on me and I screamed again, "Zach!"

"Let go of her!" Zach pulled out his scepter.

Scarlette cackled and drew out hers in response. I kicked at her and tried to pull away but she was strong. Zach yanked up on the rug in one fast jerk and Scarlette lost her grip, but the scripture went tumbling down with her.

"Go!" I yelled at Zach. Instead he flew straight towards Scarlette and grabbed the scripture back from her. He managed to fly past her, through the window and back into the house. The front doors were still open and we flew back out through them again.

"We made it," he sighed in relief.

I was too shaken to say anything, I just nodded in agreement.

"Will you hand me the scriptures?"

I gave them to him and he pulled out his scepter.

"I need to secure these two scriptures." He said something under his breath and the scriptures disappeared.

"What did you do with them?" I asked.

"They are hidden now. I can get them back when we need them, but for now they are safe," he said, letting go of the tassels and turning around to face me.

CHAPTER III

I had been thinking about what Scarlette had said and I needed to ask Zach about it all.

"Remember what I told you about Scarlette earlier?"

"What about her?" he asked.

"How I followed her and Henry last night and they…I don't know how to explain what I saw, it makes no sense."

"What were they doing?" he asked curiously.

"It was weird. They took this bulb from a street lamp and I don't know if they were inside of it, or…"

Zach smiled, "Ahh, light travel," he said.

"Yeah, I guess," I said.

"You saw them doing that?" Zach asked. "What were they doing, could you hear them?"

"They were talking about the scriptures. They said that they wanted us to open the ones that they already have," I started.

"How many scriptures do they have?"

"I don't know." I was thinking of a way to explain what I had heard them saying about me choosing a side, and about his father. How could I tell Zach that his father has been tortured in a dungeon room all this time? "Zach, they said something else, too."

"What?"

"They said they needed me to choose their side. Scarlette kept talking about how I was powerful, and Henry, he kept asking if 'it was really true,' what does that all mean?"

"I don't know. The Charmers knew that *you* in particular needed to be the one to help us, and for some reason the Boggeles must think that too. I don't know why though."

"They mentioned a ledgend." I added.

Zach seemed interested. "A legend?"

"They just mentioned it when they were talking about the scriptures."

A look of astonishment took over Zach's face. "It couldn't be." He said under his breath, so quietly that I wasn't even certain that's what he had said.

"What's the legend?"

"I'm not completely sure." He suddenly acted oblivious.

I looked at him confused. I didn't think too much of it though, because in the back of my mind I knew I still needed to find a way to tell him about his father.

"Do you think Auck knows?" I asked.

Zach looked back at me curiously. "My father? How do you know his name?"

I didn't say anything.

"Did they mention him? Do you know where he is?"

I looked at him sympathetically. I knew I couldn't

keep this from him. "He's in Duchura's dungeon." I finally answered.

Zach was silent. He nodded his head and turned away from me. I put my arm around him and we sat for what seemed like a long time before either of us said anything more. "They're going to kill him, Sable," he sniffed.

"Zach, they can't do that. They need him to help remove spells from the scriptures."

"We have to get him out of there."

"We will."

The carpet was still moving fast across the ocean and I was able to see another island in the distance now.

"We'll get a map here and try to find my father's friends. They might know what to do, or at least be able to tell us where Duchura's castle is. Then we can get my Dad."

Zach landed the carpet on the beach and rolled it up as we walked into the old city. Everyone seemed to be in a hurry and we were shoved and pushed as we entered the mix of people who had congregated in the streets.

I thought Zach was right behind me, but I looked around and saw no sign of him. "Zach!" I kept getting pushed forward and people started to glare at me as I walked.

"Watch it!" a lady yelled as I bumped into her.

A horse carriage with a load full of people came barreling through the street and stopped for no one. "Out of the way!" a man hollered to everyone as he used his whip to fight through the crowd.

"Zach!" I was so overwhelmed.

All of the sudden I saw someone sprinting through the crowd. There were people chasing after him and I realized it was Zach. I ran towards him and finally caught up to him.

"Sable we have to hurry," he panted. "Someone recognized me. There are wanted posters of me everywhere, I had no idea."

We ran through the crowd back out to the beach and quickly got on the rug.

"I got a map. I had to steal it, that crowd of people was already chasing me by the time I found one."

We wasted no time. I read out the directions to Zach and we made our way towards the next island. It took little time to get there, maybe an hour at the most. I didn't want to worry Zach, but if there were more wanted posters here I wasn't sure what we would do. This was our only chance to get information on Auck and the rest of the scriptures.

The very first thing we saw when we walked into the village was a wanted poster. Luckily there seemed to be few people moseying through the streets.

"Do you know where they live?" I asked.

"They've lived in the same houses their entire lives," Zach said as he tore down the poster. Then he started making his way through the streets. The village seemed to be built on one enormous hill where hundreds of narrow streets intertwined with one another.

Zach approached a house far upon the hillside of the island. He knocked on the door and took a step back. A little old lady came rushing towards the door. "Zachary!

It's been so long, darling! I saw you walking up through the window!"

"Mrs. Maples, it's so good to see you!" I stood a few steps back on the porch and watched the two of them greet each other. "This is Sable," Zach said, looking back at me.

The old lady came rushing over and hugged me. "This your girlfriend, Zachary?"

"This is Sable Writhm."

The lady stared at me and her eyes got wide. Then she quickly wiped away the expression, "Well, she is a beautiful young thing now isn't she."

Mrs. Maples peered around the corner of her house and quickly let us inside. "Let me go get James," she said as we sat down on the couch.

"Well, if it isn't Auck's little boy! Finally decided to visit us -- did ya?" a man said as he walked through the entrance to the room. Zach stood up to hug him.

We all sat in silence for a moment. I assumed they knew the real reason why we had come. Mrs. Maple's smile all the sudden went away as she started to speak. "The posters, they have them everywhere now."

"I know," said Zach. "We came to talk to you about the Boggeles."

"There isn't much that we know." Mrs. Maples said grimly.

"The scripture has been separated into seven scriptures. We think we may have found two of them, but there are still five more," Zach paused, "and my father..."

Mrs. Maple started to tear up. "They took him,

didn't they?"

"He's in Duchura's dungeon."

James was quiet. He still hadn't spoken a word since we had sat.

"They have him alive?" he finally asked.

"They have to keep him alive; they need him to help remove the spells from the scriptures, otherwise they are all worthless the Boggeles. Except, now they know that Sable is here, I don't know what will happen if we don't get him out of there soon."

"Anything you need, we can get for you," said Mrs. Maple.

"We just need to know how to get to Duchura's Castle, and where we could start searching for the rest of the scriptures. I've never crossed over to the Boggele territory, I don't even know how to," Zach said.

"I am afraid we wouldn't be of much help," James said, "but Mr. Winters, he may know more."

"Thank you, James."

Zach made his way to the door as he said goodbye. "Zach, wait! Winters isn't on the island anymore."

"Why? Where did he go? This has been his home for years."

"He's in the human world now: Santorini."

"Greece?"

"The government was starting to go after him; they thought he knew too much. They thought he was a spy for the Boggeles, so he fled."

"Greece. He's really in Greece!"

"I'm afraid so, but we know just the place there, he

gave us this." James handed Zach an envelope. "This is his address."

"Thank you," Zach said.

We walked out the door and the Maples yelled their goodbyes down the street until we were out of sight.

"Sable, where do you live?"

I started reading off my address.

"No, what country?"

"Upstate New York."

"We will have to stop there so that you can pack, I can tell James to send us tickets to Greece from there."

"I don't need to pack, you're not," I said.

"Sable, I have never been to your world. We have to seem as normal as possible. I need to adjust before we go out in public. I need you to show me how to blend in before we are around too many people."

"Zach, no one has any idea about this world. You will be fine."

He seemed skeptical, "I don't know. I don't want to make a scene or anything."

I didn't argue any further. We planned on getting one-way tickets to Greece and deciding what to do from there after we had talked to Winters. The Maples would send the plane tickets to my house and we would do everything just as a human would from there.

We walked back down the street and Zach stopped to look at one of the wanted signs of himself. He stood there for a moment and then tore it from the wall and threw it into the street.

"It's just so weird seeing yourself on something like

that."

I didn't know what to say. Zach kicked the poster down the road as we walked. "How are we going to get back?" I asked. I realized that I didn't know how I had gotten here in the first place.

"There are three ways to travel between worlds, diving through the deepest part of the ocean and flying past the highest place in the sky, or being summoned, like you."

"How does this all work?"

"I've never actually done it before, but its supposedly possible to go through the ocean and once you have swum down far enough you technically have swum up and into another world's ocean. Or, you can do the same thing through the sky. Once you fly high enough and at a fast enough speed, you will have merged worlds and gotten into the next."

"Which one are we going to do?"

"I've been told that traveling through the sky is much easier."

I nodded in agreement, but I was nervous.

"When do we have to leave?"

"The best time is at sunset during the flash. Right as the sun starts to set there will be a green flash. That signals the switch of light from one world to the next. We will leave then."

Zach and I ran back towards the beach to make sure we didn't miss the flash. He quickly rolled out the rug and we sat waiting.

I never did end up seeing any green flash of light, but the moment Zach did we left. Our takeoff only seemed to last a few moments before I heard a loud ear-shattering thud as we broke the sound barrier; we were traveling faster than noise itself. Then it was all over. We were back in the human world.

We landed hard and the carpet skidded to a halt.

"Is this it?" Zach's eyes wandered in amazement.

"Is this what?"

"The human world."

I looked around, I didn't know where we were, but everything seemed normal, like home. "I think so."

Zach let out a sigh of relief. "Good." He picked up the carpet and threw it over his shoulder. "I should have landed us a few miles out from your house if this is the right place. Let's just see if anything looks familiar to you." He seemed nervous, looking around as if we were in some strange, alien world. I guess for him we really were.

We started walking and I saw a town spread across the hillside below, my town. I was back. "This is it."

It was early in the morning here, maybe three a.m. The light really had switched from his world to mine.

"We will just have to wait at your house for the tickets, and then we can leave." He began to walk with the carpet over his shoulder as if nothing was out of the ordinary. I didn't say anything until we got closer to town. "Zach, you've got to get rid of the carpet, it looks suspicious."

Before I could say anything more he threw the carpet to the ground and drew out his scepter. He said something and the rug folded itself up and disappeared. It was all very dramatic.

"Sorry." He looked paranoid.

"Zach, its fine. No one is going to think anything different of you here, you just have to stay calm."

He relaxed his shoulders slightly and breathed deeply, "You're right. I've just never been here before, I don't know what to expect."

"We'll be fine." I promised, but as we approached my house a feeling of uneasiness settled in all around. Something didn't seem right. The back door had been left slightly ajar. I looked back to Zach, slightly worried now. We both listened for a moment, everything was silent. Zach lightly pushed the door open and we both froze, waiting for something to happen. Nothing did, and we both stepped inside.

"Oh my god." I looked around the room, swallowing hard, breathing heavily. Someone had been here. The entire house had been left overturned.

"They've been here already." Zach shook his head, pulling me back to the door.

"Whose been here?" I asked panicked.

"The Boggeles."

We stood in the doorway for another moment in silence, taking in the destruction.

"They are hunting you, Sable. They need you."

"For what!" I yelled. I was losing my patients, and too scared to act at all sane.

"For power," was all he answered.

"This needs to end Zach." I was so confused, so scared. "If my parents had been here," I paused, "If my parents had been here I don't know what would have happened. This *has* to end."

"It will. One way or another, it will." He mumbled.

I didn't say anything back to him, at that moment I was too overwhelmed, completely lost for words.

"Where are your parents, Sable?" Zach seemed to understand the gravity of the situation.

"Turkey, to watch a meteor shower."

Zach looked calmer now. "They will be safe then."

"How do you know that?" I said coldly, scanning the room in front of me over and over.

"Those meteors are pieces of our world sent here by the Charmers. It's how they watch over the humans, and protect them."

"What do you mean?"

"Charmers sympathize for those with no magical capabilities. There are many who try to take control of the humans because of their lack of power, but the Charmers are able to stop them. The meteors give off a presence of magic and deter those who are looking to overrun your world. The shower should keep them protected."

I began to walk back inside, but Zach put his hand on my shoulder to stop me. I looked up at him, wondering what was wrong.

"We can't stay here."

"We don't have a choice. This is where the tickets are being sent."

I saw Zach clench his jaw as he thought for a moment, "I guess we do have to stay."

He didn't stop me from walking inside this time. I lifted a chair up from off the floor and sat at the kitchen table. Zach hesitated a moment longer, still lingering at the door. There was something outside he was fixated on.

"Zach?" I leaned forward in my seat to get a glimpse at what he was looking at. Too many shadows from the trees covered the lawn to be able to see anything.

He turned his attention back to me now, double checking that the door had been fully closed and locked before taking a seat next to me.

"Is there something wrong?" I questioned.

"No, I don't think so." He tapped his fingers anxiously against the table. We both sat silently, waiting for something else to happen.

The doorbell rang, finally breaking the silence, and made me jump. I caught a glimpse of a man in the window. It had to be our tickets.

Zach and I both went to the front door. When I opened it there was no one there, the man had disappeared. I looked down and saw a small package lying on the doormat.

I picked it up and looked at it. The back side read "First Class Mail" and underneath in tiny letters it read *World Imports*. It was stamped in huge letters with red ink: "Human." I flipped it over and my name was on the front.

I tore open the top and pulled out a parchment paper. The Maples had sent us a letter along with the tickets.

"Best of luck. Hobart Winters should know what to do, but there is more than just knowledge that resides with him." The two airline tickets were enclosed at the bottom.

"What does this mean?" I handed Zach the letter.

"I don't know." His interest in the side lawn suddenly came back and he quickly opened the door to the house back up for me to go inside. "We should leave now."

"Okay," I agreed, peering through the window, curious what kept getting his attention, "I'll call for a cab."

We only waited what seemed to be a few moments before a cab pulled up to the curb outside. "That was fast."

"You ready then?" Zach was overly anxious to leave. He opened both the front door and car door for me before climbing into the cab himself.

"We're headed to the airport," I told the driver. He nodded without saying a word and started driving.

Zach and I sat close together in the cramped backseat. The driver hadn't said a word, but I could see him constantly glancing through the rearview mirror at us, once making eye contact with me before quickly looking away.

"What was back at the house that you were so interested in?" I finally whispered to Zach through the silence.

He continued to look forward, but whispered back quietly, "A Boggele. I didn't want to worry you. He was alone. I think he knew he wouldn't be strong enough to fight us on his own, but I knew he was sending for others. We had to leave before they came."

"How fast are we going?" Zach asked a moment later. I hadn't noticed until he pointed it out, but when I looked at the speedometer it read almost ninety miles per hour. "Could you slow down a bit?" He said almost angrily, after hearing no reply from the driver. The driver scowled at us through the rear view mirror now, but did as we asked and slowed back to the speed limit.

I saw Zach slide his scepter out of his pocket and looked at him concerned. I knew what he was thinking. This was a Boggele, but if Zach killed him now there would be no one driving the car. I shook my head in disagreement.

Before either of us could do anything, the man grabbed Zach's scepter without even turning around. Zach unbuckled and leaned over the driver's seat, lashing out to get it back. The man took his hand off the wheel and grabbed for Zach's neck. He had his foot now pressed flat against the gas pedal and the car was drifting from lane to lane as it gained speed. Cars honked from all around us as we slammed into the side of a semi-truck, jolting the man back, forcing him to loosen his grip on Zach.

Zach was able to grab his scepter back from the man. I reached over the seat for the steering wheel as he shot out a spell at the man, killing him instantly.

I screamed. I didn't know what else to do.

The man fell to the side, on top of my arm that was attempting to steer the car, and I let go. His foot still pushed down on the gas and we continued forward, straight into the median. Zach pulled me back right before the collision and shot out one last spell, making the impact less severe.

My vision was blurred and the noises around me were muffled. I felt something wet on my forehead. I touched it and blood dripped on my fingers. "Zach," I said groggily, picking my head up off the ground to look for him.

"Sable! Sable, it's okay." I hadn't noticed that he was kneeling down right beside me.

Cars were piled up all around us and there was a complete stop in traffic. Zach looked around and discreetly drew out his scepter.

"Zach, you can't do that here, people are going to see you," I said, pushing his hand back down.

"It doesn't matter."

He held his scepter up to me, quickly healing my wounds. I was able to sit up now and I looked around to see who had been watching. "We've got to get out of here." People were starting to get out of their cars and make their ways towards us. We couldn't risk getting held up.

"Are you sure you're okay?"

"I'm fine." I promised. Zach pulled me to my feet and we fled the scene. "How many people do you think saw that?" He asked.

"A lot." I was in no mood to lie to make him feel better. "You shouldn't have done that."

"I had no choice." He argued.

We stood outside of a sandwich shop trying to think of what to do. "What time is it?" I asked a lady walking by. Neither Zach nor I had a watch.

"Eight-forty," she said as she walked by.

"Our flight leaves in half an hour."

"We'll make it." Zach looked around to see if anyone was watching us. He took out his scepter again and held it up to a man who had just walked out of the store in front of us. I looked at Zach contemptuously. He had gotten hold of the man's car keys.

Zach set the alarm off for the car to find it faster, but the owner must has recognized the noise. He turned back and noticed that it indeed was his car. "Go, go!" I yelled at Zach.

The man started to run towards us, "hey!" he shouted, "hey! Someone stop them!"

Zach struggled to get the key into the ignition fast enough. He pressed down on the gas and we launched over a curb before getting away.

I couldn't help but to let out a slight laugh. We had actually managed to get away from everyone. Zach looked over and laughed too, sighing with relief.

"Are there more, you think?" I asked as we continued forward.

"More of what?"

"Boggeles, do you think there are still others here?"

"I'm sure. We have to get to Mr. Winters quickly; we're safer in my world. There are more Charmers to protect us there."

Zach abruptly stopped the car once we made it to the airport and came around to open my door.

"What time is it?" Zach yelled to a man across the dingy parking structure.

"Eight fifty-five," he said before stepping into the elevator.

"We have five minutes, Sable."

We took the stairs down and into the airport. Waiting for the elevator to come back up again was taking too much time. We pushed past a tour group that was headed to the security check-in and I lost sight of Zach.

Then I heard one of the security guards at the front of the line yelling, and a metal detector going off.

"'Scuse me, sorry," I said, pushing my way to the front of the line.

I saw Zach underneath one of the metal detectors with TSA security guards hovering around him, trying to pat him down.

"Sir, you're going to need to step aside."

"I'm just trying to make my flight, get off of me!"

"Zach! He's with me!" I yelled as I fought my way closer.

"Ma'am! Both of you! You are going to need to get to the back of the line," a security guard told us, pushing us away.

As we were pushed into the crowd of people, they started to nudge us further back until we were at the end of the line.

"We don't have time for this. What are they doing up there!" Zach said, reconfiguring himself after the pat down.

"We'll just have to get another flight."

"How? I don't have any money. Why are we all stopped here?"

"It's security, we have to get checked in. Calm down."

"Hey, what time is it?" Zach asked again to a lady in front of us.

"Nine," she said, annoyed, not even turning around to face us.

"Our plane is leaving *now*. I'm getting us on it."

Zach pulled out his scepter and yelled for everyone to move, casting out spells to those who didn't. He dragged me to the front of the line and as we approached the security check he cast a spell that knocked the metal detector in front of us to the ground. People were screaming and dispersing every which way to get away from him. The security guards all froze, staring at what had just happened.

We were finally into the main airport, past the check-in, and Zach frantically searched the tickets for a gate number. "Stop it!" I yelled.

"We're going to make it. It's right up ahead," he said, running. He was only focused on getting to the plane in the midst of his uninterruptible rage.

The waiting area was quiet and everyone looked up from their seats as they heard us running.

The intercom went on and a lady from the front desk area by the plane's entrance began to speak. "Flight nine twenty-seven to Greece has been delayed, please stand by for more updates," she said, looking at us and pointing to the flight schedule on the wall above her head.

Zach and I took seats next to each other in the waiting area in the corner of the room, where we would be less conspicuous to everyone else. I sat looking out the window at the planes coming in and out from the airport. I could see Zach looking at me out of the corner of my eye.

"I'm sorry."

I turned to face him with crossed arms.

"Sable, please, I'm sorry." He let out a sigh of irritation. "I just, I felt smothered back there."

He waited for me to talk. "Those security guards are going to come after us."

"I masked the spells to the humans; I mean, we'll still be caught on camera, but we'll be gone by the time they see that."

"You've got to be more careful."

"I will." He had been nervously rolling his scepter back and forth in his hands and put it back in his pocket when he spoke.

"Okay, we're good then." I was finding it hard to concentrate on our conversation. Two men on the opposite side of the room, with their backs facing toward us periodically turned around and glanced over. "Zach, do you see that?" I wasn't sure if I was just being paranoid after the cab ride.

He was leaning back in his seat with his eyes closed. "See what?" he said, looking around the room.

"Those guys over there, they keep turning around and looking at us."

"There?" He discreetly pointed in the direction with a head nod.

"Yeah."

As the boys looked over in our direction again, we all four made eye contact before they quickly turned away.

"I'll be right back," he said, pulling himself out of his chair, pretending to stretch before walking over to where the boys were sitting.

I watched intently as he walked past them, throwing out a bottle of water before returning back to his seat.

"Who were they?" I asked.

"No idea." He seemed uncomfortable. He gripped the sides of his seat until his knuckles turned a ghostly white.

"Flight nine twenty-seven, destination to Greece is now boarding. We are now boarding all first class passengers," a heavily-accented voice said over a microphone. Zach jumped up and without looking back he walked to the plane doors.

The plane was cold and I turned the nozzle on the air conditioner off. The flight attendant brought out blankets and when everyone had finally boarded, we made our way to the take-off runway. I looked around for the two boys and I didn't see them anywhere on the plane.

"Do you see them?" I asked Zach.

He shook his head. As soon as we could get up and move around, Zach left his seat. He came back only a few minutes later and sat down without saying a word.

"That was fast."

"What?"

"You weren't gone long," I said, confused.

"Oh, yeah."

"Zach what was with those guys back there?" I said as he sat back down.

"Nothing," he said, shrugging.

I raised my eyebrows at him disconcertingly and then turned to my side to look out the window.

A few minutes later I heard him stirring in his seat.

"So, once we start getting the rest of the scriptures," he started, I turned back to face him, "are you going to be ready to face Duchura?"

"What do you mean?"

"I don't know; I'm just assuming that somewhere along the way we'll end up seeing her."

"Yeah, I guess I will. You'll be there, so..."

"You're right, never mind."

We sat quietly for the next few hours. I was still trying to make sense of the conversation we'd had. The plane started to get turbulent and I held onto the seat waiting for it to stop. Zach reached down and put his hand over mine, squeezing it tighter and tighter. I grimaced.

"It's fine," he said. I wasn't sure if he was referring to his grip on my hand or the turbulence.

The plane started to smooth out and Zach released his grip on me. I looked at the red marks on my hand from where he had grabbed me.

"I'm going to go get something to drink. The flight attendants haven't come around in a while," I said.

"Ma'am you need to sit back down, the seatbelt light is on," a flight attendant told me. Another turbulent bump knocked me into Zach's lap. As I went to get up and move back into my seat, Zach was knocked forward by another jolt and I was able to see a string, connected to a pendant, with a green eye, hanging from his neck.

I quickly looked away. I could feel my face getting warmer.

"Sorry," I said to him.

"You're fine," he said, smiling back.

I kept my eyes fixed on the illuminated seatbelt sign, tapping my foot against the ground, waiting for it to turn off. The intercom to the plane crackled as it turned on.

"The pilot has now turned off the seatbelt sign, you are free to move about the cabin; however we advise you to stay seated unless in the case of an emergency."

"Be right back," I said, tripping over Zach as I moved past him. I slid the lock to the bathroom door and stood inside, breathing heavily, wetting my face with water to cool down.

That was not Zach. The person I had been sitting next to for the past five hours was *not* him. It was those boys we had seen earlier. I knew it; they did something to him. But they weren't on the plane. I didn't see them anywhere. I didn't know where Zach was, or who was sitting next to me.

I calmed down enough that I was able to go back to my seat. As I walked back I noticed one of the passengers up ahead turn around and glare at me, just as the boys back in the airport had. He looked forward when I saw him, then back at me again right before I got to my seat. Then Zach or whoever I was sitting next to looked up at him.

"I'm back," I smiled. Zach, or the boy, let me past him and into my seat. He had headphones on now and read a newspaper. I could hear the music from my seat. I looked over at him and he looked back. I realized his eyes were a faded, ash black, just as the cab driver's were. They weren't Zach's brilliant blue. I couldn't believe that I hadn't noticed until just now. I turned away and he went back to reading.

I had to get up to the man in the aisle ahead, the one who had been watching me as I walked back to my seat earlier. That is where Zach was. I was sure. I went to get up one last time and Zach pulled out his headphones.

"What do you need?"

"Just going to walk around."

He breathed heavily and let me by.

This time I walked to the front of the plane. I looked back to see if I was being watched by 'Zach.' I was, and he stared with watchful eyes.

I kept moving forward until a flight attendant blocked my way. "You need to get back to your seat, miss." She had grey eyes just like the two boys. My attention was drawn back to the two seats ahead where the man was sitting by someone I assumed was Zach. He was coughing hard and quickly got up, rushing past us for the bathroom. I didn't know what was going on. I stepped to the side to get around the flight attendant and she blocked me again.

I looked up ahead and I was sure I could see Zach's hair just barely peeking above the seat. I pushed the flight attendant to the side and ran to the aisle ahead. There was Zach. Passed out, leaning against the side of the plane wall.

"Zach," I said, shaking him. I saw him move slightly. "Zach!" I shook him harder. He slowly winced with pain and looked up. His eyes were a deep, clear blue.

He straightened up in his seat. "Sable," he said, hugging my head to his chest.

"What's going on?" I asked.

"There're Boggeles on the plane. They used a morph spell; they can form into anyone around them."

"What are we going to do?"

"We've got to get off the plane. Now."

"What, Zach, we're over the ocean right now."

"They could be anyone on this plane, Sable, what else are we going to do?"

"We can't just get off the plane."

Zach looked out the window. "We've got to find them then."

We both looked around the plane, seeing if we could spot the two boys.

"Please, everyone get to your seats!" the flight attendant yelled, shooing us away from the aisle. Her eyes were no longer a diluted grey.

Zach and I sat back down, looking around for anything suspicious.

"Their eyes are black," I said.

"They can move from one form to the next so quickly though, we aren't going to be able to keep track."

"Sir," Zach and I both turned around, "sir, you dropped this," the man behind us said, holding out Zach's scepter.

I looked up and saw another man further back in the plane, with his eyes fixed on the scepter.

"Zach," I said, getting him to look.

He cast a spell towards the man and knocked him to the ground. We ran over and saw that his eyes were a dark black. Some of the passengers on the plane started to scream, but Zach paid them no attention.

"Where's the other?" Zach yelled at the man. The man started coughing and blood trickled out from his mouth.

"No," Zach said, panicked, shaking the man, trying to fix what he had done. Nearly all of the passengers were out of their seats now, headed to either end of the plane, away from where we were standing.

"Zach, mask this to everyone!"

He cast another spell and people all of the sudden seemed unaware of why they were all out of their seats.

Zach shook the man again and dropped his scepter to the ground, letting it roll away from him.

"What did I do?"

He looked back at me in concern. Right as he turned away the man on the ground grabbed his scepter and held it up to Zach's head, smirking.

"Sable, get to the cockpit," Zach said, without moving.

I started to back away, but the man moved the scepter and pointed it at me now. I looked around at the other passengers and they seemed completely oblivious to what was happening.

"Where are the scriptures?"

"We don't have any," Zach lied.

Before the man could say anything else another passenger came up behind Zach and knocked him onto the ground. Zach was able to grab his scepter back and shoot out two more spells at the men, leaving them unconscious on the ground.

The passengers started to morph back into their true forms, the boys we had seen at the airport. They lay still, and I was able to see their black eyes up close now. They seemed almost hollow, lifeless.

There was only an hour left until our arrival time. Zach picked up one of the boys and went to stash him in one of the plane's lavatories.

"No one can see what we are doing, right?" I confirmed.

"Yeah. I just want to get them out of here though," he said as he threw the second boy onto the bathroom floor, ripping their eye pendants from their necks and dropping them down the sink drain.

Finally, we started our descent and as soon as we landed, Zach got up from his seat and headed for the emergency exit. I followed behind him, not knowing if he was aware we had to wait for the plane to stop moving before we could leave. He pulled out his scepter and cast a spell that undid the door's lock.

"What are you doing?"

"I'm getting us out of here," he said, "There could be more Boggeles waiting for us in the airport."

A plastic yellow slide had inflated when he opened the door and it was dragging against the rubble on the landing as we taxied forward.

"Come on!" he yelled over the noise.

I looked back and saw the entire crew on the plane rushing towards the back emergency exit where we stood. Zach hadn't bothered to mask this spell. Without looking back I jumped onto the slide and followed Zach, away from the runway.

CHAPTER IV

We made it to the edge of the mainland where a boat could take us to Santorini. I waited on a bench outside of a boating tour kiosk while Zach got us tickets.

I saw him walk back a moment later.

"There are no more boats leaving for Santorini until tomorrow."

He sat down on the bench next to me and sighed in frustration. It was getting darker outside and the abundance of people out on the docks began to dwindle.

"How far is Santorini from here?" he asked.

"I have no idea."

A lady had been lingering near us and finally she walked over to the bench where we were sitting.

"I couldn't help but overhear, you need a lift to Santorini?" she asked.

I looked at Zach, waiting for him to say something.

"Umm," he looked back at me, reading my facial expression, "yes. That's where we're going, trying to go at least."

"There's our sailboat, we're headed there ourselves, my children and I." she said, pointing to a small boat in the harbor. I saw two figures moving back and forth on the boat, dragging rope this way and that and moving supplies across the deck.

Zach looked at me again, not sure what to say. "Thank you."

"Oh of course, dearies -- the more the merrier with this lot of mine."

She led us to her boat and called out for her children to come on deck.

"This is Jake and that is Velvet," she said, gesturing to the two people in front of us.

"I'm Thonet," she said, straddling the dock and the boat, reaching out for her son, Jake, to help her aboard.

"Think you two could man the starboard side?" Thonet asked as we jumped on board. Zach and I both looked at her, having no idea how to answer, not even sure what the starboard side of the boat was.

Thonet chuckled at us. "How about you two just start untying those ropes?"

"Sure," I said, smiling back with rosy cheeks.

We were finally out of the harbor and on the open ocean. Thonet had given us another job of pulling the ropes to the sails as we headed east and I started to get hot, only to be cooled by the sea breeze as we gained speed.

Thonet walked over to us once Jake took control of the steering.

"What are you dearies doing in Santorini?" she asked in her usual chipper voice.

"Just visiting," Zach said, "and you?"

"Just had to get away from home for a bit." She looked at us inquisitively, as if she recognized us from somewhere. Zach and I looked to each other with uncertainty.

"Sorry, it's just, you look so familiar," she said to us. "What did you say your names are?"

"Sable," I said, "and that's Zach."

She shook her head, still staring at us with a look of peculiarity.

"And you are here just for a visit?" she asked again.

"Yes," Zach said back.

"I'm sorry, but may I ask, is it Sable Writhm?"

My heart started to beat quickly now, and I could feel heat inching up my body, turning my cheeks red again.

"How did you know that?"

"And you're Zach, Zach Etan, I believe; you are a Charmer?"

Zach drew his scepter from the air, revealing himself to the woman.

"We are too." She drew out her own scepter and held it up for Zach to see. He walked over to inspect it and looked up at the lady.

"So what are you really doing here?" she asked us again.

Zach still seemed wary to answer. "How did you know we were Charmers?"

"Your wanted posters, that's how I recognized you."

Zach all of the sudden took a step back from the lady and held his scepter up to her again. "Look, you don't understand, those are a mistake," Zach said.

"Slow down, my boy," she said. "We know. We have fled for the same reasons you have."

Jake and Velvet had been listening to our conversation from afar and they now used their scepters to steer the boat, now able to leave their posts and come over to where we were standing.

"The council back home, they started to audit us. They claimed there was evidence we were helping the Boggeles. I'm just a potion maker. I don't know how I could help them even if I wanted to."

"Happened to me, too." Zach had a serious expression on his face. The waves started to get bigger as the night drew onward and the little sailboat was proving to be less functional than before.

"What did the council want from you?" he asked, holding onto the railing of the boat for balance.

"As soon as we took up interest in finding the scriptures, and suggested that perhaps Duchura had returned, the government started to threaten us. They seem to want that situation to stay concealed; but I think everyone secretly knows the truth. Duchura is back. There are so many signs that we are just ignoring."

Velvet looked scared. "At first we got letters in the mail from the government, warning us to stop bringing up the conspiracies about Duchura and the Boggeles. Then in the night, someone came to our house. They cast a spell lighting it on fire and…" She couldn't seem to finish her sentence without choking on her words.

"So now we're here," Jake said. "There are magical ties everywhere here, to the Boggeles. We thought it might be a good place to get some more information."

"What do you mean?" Zach asked.

"You haven't heard of the Matiasma?" Velvet snapped.

"No."

"The Greek eye?"

Zach shook his head.

Velvet fished around in her pocket and pulled out a string with an eye pendant dangling from the end of it. Zach jerked his head back in surprise. It looked just like the pendants the Boggeles wore, except blue.

"What are you doing with that?"

"It's the Greek eye, looks familiar doesn't it?"

"Looks like a Boggele worship pendant," Jake said, snatching it from her hand. "That's why we're here. This is the place wizards were first sent after they were changed to humans by the Charmers."

"Yeah, the *Charmers*," Zach said, still looking alarmed.

"I know, but somehow this sort of Boggele talisman became one of their legends, which means the Boggeles were here, too."

"The Greeks believe this charm deflects evil, the evil of the Boggeles is what we suspect."

"So you think the Boggeles have some link to here?" Zach asked.

"We know they have some sort of influence here, and we think that they are maybe drawing their power from here as well, from Greece."

I was confused. I didn't know what they were talking about: the Charmers changing the wizards. I could now see the island of Santorini in the distance. It was a dark mass in the mist of the night. Thonet, Jake, and Velvet went to the front of the boat to get ready to dock before the conversation was able to get any further.

"Do you think that's why Winters came here, too?" I asked Zach after the others had left.

"I don't know. It makes sense though."

Zach and I looked around to see if there was anything we could do to help, but Thonet had been using magic to steer the boat into the harbor and Jake and Velvet had gone below deck.

"Do you think the council is with the Charmers?" I asked Zach.

He looked over to me, "Of course. My family has known the council for years."

"And they betrayed you, Zach."

He looked out at the island in front of us. I could now start to see white stucco buildings lining the hillside.

"I don't know," he said, sounding upset. "I mean they are involved, there's no doubt; but they are with the Charmers, they've got to be."

"Scepters away, everyone!" Thonet said to Velvet who was still using hers to guide the boat into the marina. She huffed and the scepter disappeared from her hand.

"Mom, no one is going to see us, it's dark out," she whined.

"We can never be too sure of things. Now keep it away."

There were men at the marina there to guide us into one of the boat slips. Once we had all gotten onto the dock, Thonet went to tip them and then we headed for the hillside.

"Where are you two staying?" she asked.

"We haven't really planned that far," Zach admitted.

"Well, can't stay out in the cold all night. I happen to know just the place that magic folk find inviting."

"Thank you." Thonet was kind and gracious. She seemed to be the only one who showed real sympathy for what had happened to Zach and his father. No one else seemed to understand how hard it was for him to be shunned by his own home. As much as I tried to, I couldn't seem to comprehend it either.

"Now, what street was it on again, my dear?" Thonet said to Jake, and she flipped a map of the island every which way to get it right side up. Jake pointed to somewhere on the map.

"Ahh, yes, here we go, everyone."

"Can we please get a car to take us up? We're going to have to walk forever," Velvet said, holding up the rear of the line.

"If you see a car this time of night, feel free to flag it down."

The walk to the hostel was far and eventually Velvet insisted on using magic to get us there. She pulled out her scepter as Jake and Thonet blocked her from the street while she used it to get us a car to the top of the hill.

Even the car ride felt long. I was secretly glad Velvet had pushed to use magic for the ride up. We all sat in silence as Jake drove through the winding roads.

I was the first to break the silence. "So, why do you

think the council went after you for bringing up the conspiracy of Duchura? I mean, why would it matter to them?"

"We don't know. We just had to leave before it got too late," Thonet said.

"I just don't understand why they would be so against the fact the Boggeles have gained so much strength."

"There's no doubt the government is involved in this. The question is which side they are really on," Thonet added. "It is thought that they are trying to keep the problem contained. The last time the conspiracy was brought up there were riots and disappearances, but I suppose no one can know for sure what their motives are."

"The government isn't planning on overthrowing the Charmers, that's impossible. Honestly, what are you thinking?" Velvet was starting to annoy me.

"Darling, we never said that, but you never know who you can trust these days."

The hostel was simple and quaint. There was no room on the side of the road so Velvet got rid of the car with her scepter.

"So, the people here, they know about magic?" Zach asked.

"The man who runs it is one hundred and four. He believes all the Greek myths still, unlike most around here. We stayed here one other time, years ago, but I still remember him. He seemed to sense something about us, but he seemed so comfortable around us. Most at home I've ever felt out of the wizard world."

Inside the hostel was dark, with only a few dimly lit lights in a tiny sitting area by a desk. The windows were all open and the breeze from the water rustled the curtains. I couldn't help but notice that in each one of the window panes was one of the Matasimas, the Greek eyes.

"Hello?" We all turned around and saw that a tanned, Greek man was now sitting at the desk.

"We're here to stay for the night," Thonet said.

The man pushed his glasses up his nose and flipped through stacks of paperwork on his desk.

"You have been here before, haven't you?" he asked. I could barely see his face; the shadows on the walls covered him from plain view.

"Many years ago; yes."

"I remember you," he said, standing from his chair. He was old and seemed unstable as he got up. "Few come in the midst of the night to my hostel as you do."

I looked to Zach, I was nervous. I could tell he suspected something of us.

"Come, I will take you to your rooms."

"Thank you."

Zach and I shared a room together and Thonet and her family shared one down the hall.

Before the man left he gave us a set of keys.

"Now, there are only a few rules I must ask you to obey," he said. We nodded and he continued. "Please, do not venture into any of the other vacant rooms," he said, then looked towards Zach and me, "and for you two, the armoire in your room, please do not mess with it. It is locked for a reason."

He slowly hobbled down the hall without another word. Zach and I walked inside and found a bunk bed, a dresser, and the armoire he had talked about, all cramped into the tiny room.

I saw Zach yawning as he crawled on top of the bed.

"What do you think is in the armoire?" I asked.

"I don't know. Just personal stuff I'd guess."

I climbed up to the top bunk and Zach went to blow out the candles that were lighting up the room.

"So, we'll look for Winters tomorrow?" I asked as I lay awake, still fixated on the armoire.

"Yeah, I guess we'll just show up at his house," he said. I could hear the sheets moving around as he rolled to his side. "I still have the address from James."

I barely slept all night. I couldn't stop thinking about what was behind the armoire doors. When Zach went to wake me up in the morning I could feel that my eyes were heavy with tiredness and I squinted as he opened the blinds to the room.

"Morning," he said, peering over the side of the bunk.

I sat up and rubbed my eyes. I could barely keep them open. Zach went to get a map from the desk in the front room of the hostel. I waited behind, thinking of getting the armoire open while he was gone.

I jumped when Zach walked back in the room.

"Sable, what are you doing?"

"Aren't you a little curious about what's behind here?"

"No, not really; I'm sure he just keeps his own stuff in there," he said, pulling out the envelope with Winters' address on it.

"You ready to go?"

I nodded.

We walked down the same street we had taken on the way up, except this time we ventured onto the side streets, attempting to follow the map's guidance to Winters' house. My stomach was growling loud enough that Zach was able to hear, and when we walked past a bakery on the corner of the street, Zach stopped to sit at one of the tables outside.

A lady brought us over menus and cups of water and Zach thanked her.

"What did Jake mean when he said wizards were sent here after they were changed by the Charmers?"

Zach smiled slightly, "That is a long explanation."

The waitress came back over to our table with a plate of baklava.

"Thank you," Zach said as she set the plate down.

He took a bite out of the pastery before talking again. "Well, you knew there was a war, between the Boggeles and Charmers, but I guess I never did tell you why."

"No," I said.

"There was a period of time when humans and wizards were able to interact, to live together; but as the two started to fall in love, their children were sometimes bred out of magic abilities. The Boggeles wouldn't have it. They thought it was weakening wizards. They wanted the human race killed off. The Charmers, on the other hand, believed there was a way the two could both survive: the creation of a separate world, where humans could be at peace. Another world was made and humans were sent to live here, with no memories of magic left."

Our food was brought to the table and Zach stopped talking for a moment. I sat, not touching my plate, waiting for him to continue.

"The Charmers and the Boggeles were originally the same, able to do the same spells, looked exactly the same; but as the tension over the humans grew, the two started to grow apart from one another."

The check came and Zach continued to talk as we walked further down the street to Winters' house.

"The two could no longer get along, and the war broke out. That is when the scripture was created. Seven powerful men each created a scripture and whoever was in possession of them would hold the power over the wizard world. The Charmers have always controlled the power; have had all the scriptures, at least until now."

We had trouble navigating through the streets. There were no street signs and one would road would turn into another without notice. Finally, we asked a little Greek boy if he knew of a Mr. Winters. Without saying a word he nodded and we followed him past a crowd of people further up the street. He stopped in front of a house on the corner of a quiet street.

"Thank you." The little boy only nodded again and walked off.

Zach knocked on the door and a man, still in his

slippers, came to the door.

"Zach! Is that really you?"

"Winters, it's good to see you! It's been a long time."

"It sure has. Things haven't been so good back home. I had to get away while I could."

"We need to talk to you about something, Winters. Have you been keeping up with the Charmers lately?"

He all of a sudden looked sad. "I have, I have. Please, come inside." He led us to a sitting room in the front of the house. "I'm going to go make some tea. Be right back."

There was a slot machine sitting in the corner of the room. It was odd, especially in Santorini. I went over and started looking at it. It had more levers than a normal slot machine and I pulled on one to see what would happen.

"Zach, what kind of slot machine is this?"

"I don't know. Winters has all sorts of weird stuff. He's a collector."

"Of what?"

"Everything I suppose," he said, looking around the room himself. There were odd collectables all around the house, stacked on shelves and crammed onto tables.

I could hear Winters coming and I sat back down on the couch.

"Here's your tea." He set the tray on the table. "I forgot the cream! I'll be right back." He drew in a deep breath. "Auck's in trouble, isn't he?" He was turned away from us, but I could tell in his voice that he was upset.

"Yes."

"What did he send you here for?"

"He didn't send us actually. The Maples did."

"What did they say?"

"My father is missing, and the council is looking for me now. The scripture was taken and they are blaming our family. It was separated back into seven scriptures like it had been originally."

"Things must be bad back home. That has never happened before, not since the war. Where are the scriptures?"

"We think that the Boggeles have them all except for two. We found them back in the wizard world."

"Thank goodness they don't have them all. May I see the scriptures you do have?"

Zach took out his scepter and flicked it in the air. Then the scriptures appeared on the table. Winters picked them up and looked them over.

He held the pages of the scriptures up to one another and they seemed to glue themselves together into one larger scripture. "Ahh, yes. This is definitely the real thing. Good."

"We need to figure out where the Boggeles would have decided to hide the rest of them. James said you may know."

"So the Boggeles had them all? They had the entire scripture!" Winters all of a sudden yelled.

"Not anymore. They haven't been able to open them yet, either. They need my dad and me. Auck is in Duchura's castle. He's being held there and we need to know how to get to him."

Winters brushed his hands through his hair and looked as if he was concentrating hard on something.

"Zach, if I were to tell you where to go looking for the rest of the scriptures and Duchara's castle I could put you in so much danger."

"I know, but if you don't tell us my father could be killed, Winters."

"Zach, I don't even fully remember how to get to the castle anymore."

"Winters!" Zach yelled. I could tell that he wasn't planning on telling us anything and Zach couldn't stand it. "If you don't tell us where to go then we will find some other way." He was lunging over the coffee table, inches from Winters' face.

"I just want you to stay safe, Zach, and you, Sable," he said, looking towards me. "You need to keep her protected, Zach."

"Always."

Winters looked as though he was thinking hard for a moment.

"If you really plan on doing this then you will need to take something of mine with you." He walked over to the slot machine in the corner of the room and pulled down on the levers. A reel spun and landed on three of the same pictures in a row; I suppose it was a jackpot. Then a compartment opened up at the bottom of the machine and he reached his arm in. He pulled something out and walked back over to us. He put his hand over Zach's and closed his palm around the object.

"Bring it back safely," he said. "As for where the

rest of the scriptures would have been hidden I really am unsure; however, the man who runs the Greek inn, at the top of the hill, he may be able to help. He knows about our kind, he believes in the Matiasma. He's bound to know something. Ask him if he know of the Boggele lairs. That is my best guess to where they would be hiding them."

"That's where we're staying," Zach said.

"Many magic folk find it to be hospitable. It's where I stayed when I first came here."

"Winters, why did you come here, out of all the places, why here?" Zach asked. I knew he was curious if Winters believed the story that this was where humans were first sent, that the Boggeles may have some secret tie here.

"The Greek eye, my boy, why else?"

"So you believe that this is the place where humans first resided then?"

He nodded his head. "Many wizards come, for all sorts of reasons. Some believe that magic is still secretly prevalent here and that when they are exiled they can still live as they would back in the wizard world. Others, like me, believe that the Boggeles have had some sort of influence here, that they have been able to draw power from here. We are looking for ways to stop that, if it even is true."

"So you think that's how the Boggeles have been gaining their strength back all these years?"

"I do, and if we are able to find whatever it is they are funneling their energy from, we can stop them."

Winters poured himself his third cup of tea and

drained the pot. He seemed anxious.

"Do you know how to get to Duchura's castle?" Zach asked.

Winters sighed, sliding down further into his seat. "Zach, I don't think you understand the gravity of this situation."

"We do, Winters, trust me, if there was another way…"

"You have to realize that if they catch you there, if you are seen by a single Boggele while you are there, you will be killed, Zach."

"They can't kill us, they need us to remove the spells from the scriptures, and they know that."

"Zach, do you really think they are going to have you remove the spells and then let you go? No, they will torture you until the scriptures have all Charmer spells removed, and once they have no more use for you, you will be killed."

"Winters, there is no other way to get my father back. You have to tell us how to get there."

"The ruins of the war, that's the only way in and out of the Boggele banishment grounds. It's sealed to Boggeles, or so we thought."

"How have they managed to get through it then?"

"That's where Santorini comes in. They've got to be drawing power from something here, that's the only way they could possibly manage to get through."

Zach stood up from his seat; he seemed ready to go the second Winters told us how to get to his father.

"Zach, there is one other thing you should know."

"What is it?"

"Recently some Boggeles have found a way to use Duchura's lairs as portals to sneak into the Charmer world, bypassing the war ruins altogether. You need to make sure that when you enter them that no one sees you. Most of the Boggeles aren't experienced enough to sneak out on their own, but when a Charmer goes in or out of one, the Boggeles have a much easier time passing through with you. Boggeles tend to congregate in them, so you must stay alert."

"We will be careful."

"Good luck."

We started walking back down the road when Winters all of a sudden came running back towards us.

"Wait!" he yelled. Zach and I stopped. "I forgot to tell you what to use the rock for."

"The rock?" I questioned.

"What I gave to you, Zach, from the slot machine. It will transform into any key you need to get through a barrier. It will come in handy, I'm sure of it."

The streets were nearly empty and the day was quiet. I wondered if the hostel keeper would be of any help. Everyone seemed to think he knew about magic, and that he *liked* magic, but I didn't get the same feeling from him.

"What should we do now?"

"We'll have to see if the man at the hostel knows anything."

When we got back to the hostel there was no sign of people. It seemed as though everyone had left for the day. We couldn't even find the hostel keeper. Zach and I sat in the tiny lobby area and waited for the man to eventually show up. Still nothing, twenty minutes later. We had tried calling for him, but he didn't come.

Zach got up from his seat and peeked around a hallway behind the man's desk. Then he motioned for me to come over.

"Do you hear that?"

"No."

"Come on," he said, walking further down the hall. There were a few rooms, doors wide open, as we walked down the hall, but none had anyone in them. I started to hear what Zach must have been talking about, the sound of rustling paperwork behind a closed door, the last one in the hall.

Zach knocked and stood back, waiting for someone to come. Then he knocked once more before opening up the door and walking inside.

The hostel keeper was sitting, with his back to the door, shuffling through papers and intently looking at a map of the island.

"Hello?" Zach said.

Zach looked back at me puzzled when the man still said nothing. He walked over to the man's chair and put his hand on the man's shoulder. The man jumped and turned around to face us.

"Sorry," Zach said.

"What are you doing back here?" the man said, quickly turning over the map he had been looking at.

"We were just looking for you. We thought you could maybe help us with something."

"I'm busy, can you not see that?"

He got up from his chair and cornered us back towards the entrance.

"Hold on," Zach said before he shut the door on us. "We heard you might possibly know about the Boggeles."

He started to open the door back up for us. "Who did you hear that from?"

"Mr. Winters, he said he's stayed here before, do you remember him?"

"What did Winters say to you?"

"He said you could help us."

"With what?"

Zach knew he was taking a chance completely revealing to the man that he was magic, but he continued anyway, "He said you know about wizards."

"That's enough, I have things to do. You tell Winters he was wrong to send you two to me."

"Please!" Zach said, stopping the door from being closed all the way. "You know about Duchura, don't you? And the lairs?"

He looked at us through the crack in the door, pausing for a moment before he let us back inside the room.

"Thank you," I said, as he closed the door behind us.

"What business do you have with all of this?" the man asked us.

"We need to know if you know where the lairs are located. The scripture of spells -- the Boggeles have the scriptures and we need to get them back."

"Look, I have nothing against harboring an

occasional wizard here at the hostel, but this! I can't help you."

"You don't understand what this scripture means to us," Zach urged.

"Oh, but I do. It, it's just, it's too dangerous for me to help you."

"We won't say a word to anyone that you helped us."

The man thought for a moment before he flipped the map he had been looking at over on the table. All over the island he had marked dots and drawn circles and connecting lines.

"These are all of the places Boggeles have been sighted on the island. I don't know what they are doing here, or how they even got here, but when I discover them, I track them and their every movement."

"These couldn't *all* be lairs," Zach said, looking over the map.

"Oh, goodness, no. I only have found one of their lairs in all my years searching. It is in this very hostel."

"Where?"

"Your room, of all places."

I immediately reminded myself of the armoire. I knew there was something about it, something that made me uneasy.

"As soon as I discovered there was an entrance to a Boggele lair in this building I bought the place, securing it from the public," he explained.

"Where in the room is it?" I asked.

"Remember what I told you not to mess with when I

first showed you to the room?"

I nodded, and he nodded back in an unspoken understanding.

"What are all the rest of these circles for then?" Zach asked, still examining the map.

"I assume you know the story behind the Matiasma?" the man asked. We nodded. "My father, he was one of the first to be sent here from your world. Before he was sent here he had his wife, a possessor of magic, who cast a spell on him so that he would never forget her. He not only remembered his love, but also the magical world, even after being sent here. He longed for a way back to her, he became obsessed. Every time he heard of magic on the island, he would mark the spot, hoping that one day he would be able to get back to her again."

"He tracked every single place magic had occurred for his entire life?" Zach asked in astonishment.

"He did. And when he died, he passed the map on to me, in the hope that one day I would be able to get to the magical world and find his wife, to tell her what he had done all those years, that he had never stopped searching for a way back.

"You took on his search just so that one day you might possibly be able to find his wife and tell her all of this?"

"Eighty-eight years I've been searching."

"If you knew people from the magic world stayed here, why didn't you just ask one of them to find her?"

"None of them knew her. You really think that they would waste their time looking for some lady they had never heard of, helping a Greek innkeeper?"

Zach seemed to understand where the man was coming from.

"So you only know where one lair entrance is?" Zach asked.

"Just the one."

"Have you ever been inside it before?" I knew that Zach was hoping for some reassurance before the two of us made our way inside.

"Could never get past the seal. It's blocked by magic."

"Thank you for helping us."

"You're welcome, just please do not tell anyone what I have told you. If the Boggeles ever found out that I helped you..."

"We won't."

We started walking back down the hall, but then Zach stopped and turned back. "I never did catch your name," he said.

The man looked up from the map again, "Leo. Leo Earnst."

I was leery to get back to our room. I knew that Zach would want to get into the lair as soon as possible, and I wasn't sure what to expect when we opened the armoire.

I sat on the top bunk of the bed as Zach worked on opening the doors. He tried pulling them open with sheer strength and when that didn't work he pulled out his scepter and started shooting spells at the handles.

"Sable," he said, "look."

The doors to the armoire were open and I jumped off the bunk to get a closer look. A set of stairs led down into a dark, dirt tunnel.

Zach walked into the opening and I followed behind him. We were both careful to not make a sound after what Winters had told us. The passage finally came to a dead end where there was a small, square, green door, just as the one back in Scarlette's house had been. Zach reached out to touch the knob, and it glowed a soft yellow. He cautiously put his hand over it and then quickly jerked it back.

"What!" I said, panicky.

"It shocked me." He took out his scepter and blew the knob straight off the door. It made a crackling noise and skidded across the ground. Then Zach tapped the door open with his foot. We both peered through the jarred door and I was sure that we were in someone's basement. I crawled out after Zach and looked around the room.

"Are we under the street right now?" I asked.

"I don't know."

I whipped my head around, sure that I had seen someone. I didn't like the feeling of this place. Zach was standing next to me and put his finger up to his lips. A girl, plump and short with curly, dirty blonde hair came out of nowhere. Then I heard other footsteps briskly walking closer. Zach and I hid behind a couch and waited for the people to leave. They didn't.

"There's someone there, uncle," the girl whined. I had no idea she had seen us. "There!" the girl shouted as the man ran towards us.

Zach pulled me up a staircase and into another level

of the house. I could hear the man running after us. We found a door that led outside and before the man was able to catch up to us, we were back outside on the street.

"Was that the lair?" I asked, out of breath.

"I have no idea what that was back there, but it definitely wasn't one of the lairs."

"Do we ask Leo about it?"

"He wouldn't know, he said he's never been able to get through the passage."

"The lair has got to be somewhere in that house. That man was magic, he must know something."

"We're going to have to go back."

"Yeah, but how? We can't be seen back there again."

Zach thought for a moment. "Maybe Thonet can help us with a potion."

When we got back to the hostel, Jake and Velvet were on their way out.

"Do you know where your mom is?" Zach asked them.

"Said she was going down to the beach, by the docks," Velvet said as they walked past us.

She was sitting by a bushy shrub at the edge of the sand, studying a blackberry. It seemed to intrigue her. "Peculiar," I heard her say to herself. She had a little textscripture and she was comparing different plants and jotting down notes in a journal.

"Thonet?"

"Oh my!" she squealed, "sorry, darling you frightened me there."

"Sorry."

"What are you two doing down here?"

"Well, we were actually looking for you," Zach said. "We need your help with something."

"What might that be?"

"Do you know how to make a vanishing potion?" Zach asked.

Thonet looked up at us with a disapproving look. "I don't know what in the world you would possibly need something like that for."

"We just need to get somewhere without being seen," Zach stuttered.

"A vanishing potion is very strong; very serious stuff is done when that gets involved. Where do you need to go?"

"We think we might have found a Boggele lair where one of the scriptures might be."

There was a long, silent pause. I could tell she was thinking intently.

"Darlings, I couldn't possibly bring myself to assist you with something that dangerous."

"If we don't get a potion then we'll just have to go back without it," Zach insisted.

"A vanishing potion is much too dangerous, but perhaps, perhaps I could make you a different one."

"What do you mean?" I asked.

"I can make you something to turn your blood silver, you will be nearly transparent. It's no vanishing potion, but it should do the trick. A chameleon potion is the nickname.

"Anything you can do, we'll take it," Zach said thankfully.

"When do you need it by?"

Zach looked at me for an answer.

"Tonight, if you could," I said.

"Meet me behind the inn tonight, eight o'clock."

CHAPTER V

Zach and I were ready to go and waiting anxiously for Thonet to meet us. She was wearing a large trench coat buttoned all the way up to the top. She quickly started unsnapping it and pulled out two vials of liquid. She looked over her shoulder before handing one to each of us.

"This will keep you transparent for about an hour. That was all I was able to make on such short notice," she informed us.

"This is perfect," Zach said, holding up the bottle to her.

It was dark outside and only a tiny sliver of the moon was visible. Zach and I drank the potion right before we opened the armoire doors. The smell of the potion made me gag.

"You ready?"

"Yeah." Zach opened the door and ventured further into the house than we were able to the night before.

We split up and I started wandering through different parts of the house, looking for anything that seemed like it could possibly lead into a lair. I couldn't help but wonder about the owners of the house, if they knew there was a Boggele lair entrance in their home. Something creaked behind me and I wished Zach was with me.

Originally, I had thought the first room Zach and I were in was the basement, but as I walked further back in the room I saw yet another staircase. The stairs led into a room filled with dusty old furniture, all covered with sheets, as if they had never finished unpacking everything.

In the back of the room was one last door. I looked behind myself before walking over to it. The wood had rotted into the floorboards and I had to yank it to get it opened. There was the lair.

It was just as Winters had described. Boggeles were ever where. I also noticed it was another library, just as the lair in Scarlette's house had been. Dozens of people were bustling around looking for scriptures. Tall ladders were shifting back and forth without anyone touching them, and there was even a section of scrolls being used as a card catalog.

All of a sudden I couldn't suppress the dreams I had about Duchura. Every time I walked into a lair, the same nightmares returned to my consciousness.

I looked around at all of the people in the lair, at all of their eye necklaces. I couldn't keep the dream from surfacing in my thoughts. I remembered Zach, bloodied and in chains. Screaming, fighting. Something about the lairs triggered those dreams, and I couldn't handle it alone. They consumed me, made me lose focus and blurred my vision.

I couldn't stay in here alone. I needed to come back with Zach. I slammed the door to the lair and sat up against the other side of it, collecting my thoughts. I could tell that the potion was wearing off; tiny spots of color were reappearing on my skin.

I was fully visible by the time I found Zach. No one seemed to know we were in the house and we were able to use the passage from the armoire to get back to our room.

"I found the lair, Zach," I said, once we were safely back in our room. Both of us had been too afraid to talk while still in the house.

"Were you seen?"

"I don't think so."

"Good. We'll need to have Thonet make more next time. We can get back in tomorrow and look for the scripture."

I fell asleep still thinking about the dream I had remembered in the lair. I couldn't bring myself to tell Zach about it, I didn't want to worry him; but I felt as if it was a warning, that we shouldn't risk going back there.

CHAPTER VI

As soon as Thonet was able to make us more potion I led Zach to the lair. Right before we opened the armoire doors we touched our vials of potion together and choked them down. Thonet had made bigger portions this time and I was barely able to finish off my glass. The taste was worse this time.

"We'll be looking for something that looks a lot like the other two we've already found. It will probably be guarded or hidden, but I really am not sure," Zach whispered.

"What if we don't find it here?"

"It's here, I'm sure of it," Zach said as he opened the door and looked inside the library.

"Ready?" I asked, moving ahead of him and slipping inside the library.

"I guess so," he said, following behind me. "We probably have about an hour or so to get the scripture and get out of here. If we get separated don't wait up, I'll meet you back in the hostel."

We quickly walked into the library and I lost sight of Zach almost instantly. His silver blood made him hard to see even when I was consciously looking for him.

People were everywhere, a lot more than last time.

They were all in a small corner of the library, shouting. One person darted out of the group and ran right by me; I made sure to stay out of the way so that she wouldn't hit me. I was completely overwhelmed and I had lost Zach. I wondered if he could see me.

Someone came up behind me and put his hand on my shoulder. I screamed without even meaning to and spun around to see who it was. I could faintly make out Zach's image.

I heard the noise from the corner of the room abruptly stop and I turned back around. The people were trying figure out where the scream had come from. A lady with dreadlocks with green twine braided into them pointed straight at me and the others twisted their heads over to see.

"Oh no," I whispered.

Zach and I ran to the back of the library trying to stay hidden, waiting to see what would happen.

"I think now is as good a time as any to leave," Zach whispered.

"This might be our last chance to get this scripture, Zach. They know we're here now. If we try to come back again they'll be ready for us."

Zach seemed uneasy, but he agreed to stay. We continued our search in the back of the library where there were more places to hide if we needed to.

I wove further back behind the shelves until I hit a dead end of scripturecases. I stopped and looked at my hands to make sure that the potion was still working, they were still clear.

I heard a faint voice that reminded me of Scarlette's

and I stood motionless. I didn't know where it was coming from.

"Duchura will not be happy about this." It was definitely Scarlette talking. "We were supposed to have all the scriptures secured weeks ago!"

"And we will, we just need a little more time."

"Henry, we don't have more time." This was not Scarlette's usual callous voice, I could sense fear in it this time.

I stayed crouched down behind a scriptureshelf, waiting to see where they would emerge from. Their voices grew louder and when I looked behind me, to the farthest corner against the wall, I saw Henry sliding one of the scripturecases back into place. There was something behind it -- something of importance that needed to be hidden.

Before Henry was able to pull the shelf entirely back into place I ran for the room, barely able to make it inside before the shelf was cemented in place again.

I wasn't sure what I had done, someone must have seen me. The shelf moved aside again and Scarlette ran in the room.

"I could sense her. She's here, Henry."

"Scarlette, you're being paranoid, no one is in here. I would have seen them."

"Henry! This is not a time to take any chances, now seal the wall and look around!"

I was stuck in the room with Henry and Scarlette, and they were looking for me. There weren't many places to hide. I found a cupboard and gently opened it when they weren't looking.

"Are you even looking for her, Henry?" Scarlette shouted as I heard her throwing things aside and overturning every corner of the room. Something hit the cupboard hard and I gently pushed against the door to see what it was, but the door wouldn't budge.

"Thank God we still have this one," I heard her say.

"We've looked everywhere, Scarlette, there is no one here!" Henry yelled, leaving the room.

Scarlette ran after him, screaming and crying, and when I knew that they had both left for sure, I kicked at the cupboard trying to get myself out.

I knew I couldn't yell for help because there were too many Boggeles who could hear. I pushed my feet against the door and kicked over and over, but I was stuck.

I heard someone else walk into the room, "Sable?"

I thought it must be Zach, but I wasn't sure. I stayed silent. "Sable, I know you're in here, it's Zach. We have to get out of here fast."

"Zach!" I knew my voice would sound muffled.

"Where are you?"

"Over here!" I heard Zach walking over to open the door. I crawled out and realized I hadn't had a chance to see where I was before I had to hide. The room looked nearly identical to Duchura's first lair we had found. Zach grabbed my hand and pulled me to the door.

"Hold on," I stopped him, "this has got to be where the scripture is, I heard Scarlette saying something about it.

"We can't stay any longer."

"Zach, we're so close, we have to look!"

"The Boggeles know that we're here. I saw

Scarlette and Henry running through the library. They are going to bring Duchura, no doubt. They are going to catch us if we don't get out now!"

"How much time do we have?"

"Ten minutes, maybe."

"Then we'll look for just a minute then. What if we aren't able to come back here again or the scripture has been moved?"

"It doesn't matter right now; if they find us, we're dead."

"No, they need us."

"They will use us and then kill us, Sable, you know that! Come on!"

I ignored him and quickly scanned the room. "Where could it be?"

"Sable, I have no idea, this might not even be the right spot."

"I know this is the right spot. I heard Scarlette talking about it just a minute ago!"

Zach looked to the door impatiently. It was quieter outside the room now.

Then the crowd of people outside the room suddenly erupted with noise. Zach and I both stopped what we were doing and listened.

"Silence!" one voice bellowed over the rest.

"Oh, my God," Zach said, with a ghostly look on his face. "She's here already."

I was too scared to move. The only exit to get out of the lair was through the library. We were stuck.

"Zach, I'm sorry. This is my fault," I said

hysterically.

"Sable, I don't know what to do."

I looked at him, distressed.

Zach frantically looked around the room and pulled his scepter out. "I have one idea. It might not even work though."

"Do it."

"They might be able to sense my magic when I do this."

"It's our only choice, just do it." I didn't know what he was planning on doing, but I would rather risk trying than do nothing at all.

Zach shouted out a spell. It sent a bright ball of light through the air and then drifted to the side of the room, evaporating as it hit one of the floorboards. Zach rushed to where the light had gone out and stooped down on the floor, attempting to pull up the floorboards.

He was loud. I didn't think our whereabouts would be kept a secret much longer. "What are you doing?"

"The scripture is here. Now I just have to get to it. There might be enough room for us to hide down with it."

"We can't hide with the scripture! Duchura is probably coming to get it right now!"

The potion had totally worn off and all I could think of was that I should have listened to Zach when he said we needed to leave.

I watched Zach, hoping that he would find something, be able to do something -- *anything* that would help us stay hidden. I could hear the Boggeles outside the room, traipsing around. Then I heard someone approaching the door to the room, or more so, I could seem to sense someone approaching the door.

Zach had found a latch, revealing a small hatch door, and the scripture beneath it. "Come here," he whispered. I could tell there was just enough room under the hatch for us both to fit. I ran over, but then something stopped me. I clasped my hands over my ears and sank to my knees.

"What is it Sable?" Zach said, trying to get me to my feet.

"That sound, it's horrible."

"I don't hear anything."

"That ringing noise," I gritted through my teeth.

The Boggeles seemed to be hearing the same noise I was. I could hear agitation in their shouting. Zach picked me up and helped me to the hatch door. Once inside I crouched on the ground, still with my hands over my ears. I couldn't help but to cry out.

Then the noise stopped and Duchura spoke again. "Now that I have everyone's attention, I have come to find the girl. She is here! And that Charmer, he'll be with her."

Zach and I were squeezed tight together. I could feel something wet inside my ears now and reached my hand up to touch it. When I brought my fingers back to my face I saw drops of blood on them. I looked to Zach in alarm.

He looked startled, too. He wiped the blood from my fingers and then motioned for me to stay silent. Someone had just walked into the room.

"Scarlette!" I was sure it was Duchura.

Scarlette was sobbing. "Please, please! She is here, I promise you!"

"You have wasted my time."

"Please!" she screamed.

"Your time as a Boggele is finished."

I stayed motionless as I listened. I could feel droplets of blood pooling in my ears, but I didn't move.

"I will find her, both of them; I will find them and bring them to you!" she pleaded.

There was a long pause and then Duchura spoke again: "I will give you one last chance, Scarlette."

"You have my word. I will bring everything to you."

"Good." Then it was silent again. Something lit up the entire room, even the hatch space down below. Then Scarlette screamed again, this time in pain.

"I want the scriptures and I want Sable Writhm," I heard Duchura say.

The door to the room closed again. Zach and I waited a moment until we were sure no one was there.

"Enough! They are not here," Duchura announced from the library.

We slid out of the hatch door space. Zach brought the scripture up with us. "You okay?" he asked, seeing the blood dried on the side of my neck where it had dripped from my ear.

"Yeah."

Zach looked confused.

"What is it?" I asked.

"That noise, it was a Boggele torture tactic."

"Makes sense."

"No, it doesn't," he said, "only a Boggele should be able to hear it, that's why I couldn't."

Now I was the one confused. Zach shook the thought away from his head before I could say anything.

"Everyone is going to be able to see us now. We have to make a run for the exit," Zach said.

"Okay."

"You have to go fast. I will protect you from their spells while you get to the door."

"What? Zach, we have to go together. We only have one shot to get out of here."

"Here, take the scripture with you. You have to promise me that you won't come back for me."

"Zach, I can't."

"You have to, I've got to stay back and block you from their spells. There's no doubt they are going to see us, and try to stop us in any way possible."

Zach came over to the door behind me and opened it without warning. "Go!" He pushed me out into the library. I didn't have any choice but to run. The Boggeles saw me right away.

I was only hit once by someone's spell, and it stung, like I had been scorched by fire. I got to the exit and slammed the door, waiting back in the house for Zach to come. I waited for what felt like forever. I had been waiting for too long. He should have been here by now. He had no one back there to protect him from the spells. I could barely handle being hit once, if he was hit, if he was slowed down, there would be no one there to help.

CHAPTER VII

I needed to go back in there. I had waited too long, he should have been here.

"Please, please be okay," I whispered to myself as I opened the door to the lair back up. I didn't see him. All I saw were Boggeles, everywhere. They must have known he was with me and they were searching every corner of the library for him.

I slipped inside sure that no one had seen me. I concealed myself behind a scriptureshelf by the door and looked for Zach. I didn't see him anywhere.

"Sable, move!" I heard someone yell. Zach dove out from behind me and knocked me to the ground, blocking me from a spell. He was hit. He winced in pain. "Go. Get back to the house!"

"I'm not leaving you back here." I helped him to his feet and he put his arm over my shoulder for support as we ran. He was hit again. The Boggeles had all seen us now. We just needed to get to the door. We were right there.

Zach yelled in pain again, this time refusing to move forwards.

"Zach, please."

"Sable, go without me. I can't make it."

He was hit a third time and fell completely to the

ground, grasping at his side.

"We're going to make it!" I pulled Zach to his feet and got him through the door just in time. I was hit in the back on the way out, but we were safe now.

I struggled with shaking hands to make sure the door was locked. Then I turned around and saw Zach, nearly unconscious, lying on his back.

"You should have left me," he whispered. He tried to look me in the eyes, but he couldn't seem to keep his focus. His eyes wandered the room, looking at nothing in particular.

"Zach." I had to keep him conscious until we were back in the hostel. "I'm going to get us back to the room," I said, pushing his hair away from his blood-stained forehead.

He had come in and out of consciousness on the way back to the room. "Get Thonet," he whispered, falling to the ground when I opened the door to our room.

"Zach, you're going to be fine," I said, attempting to calm him down, "you have to be fine," I said, running from the room to find Thonet.

"Dear, what is the matter?" Thonet said, rushing over to me as I burst into her room.

"Zach needs help."

It seemed as though she already knew what for. She grabbed her scepter off the bed and a few jars of what looked like leaves before heading for our room.

When Thonet opened the door she gasped. She crouched beside Zach and took out the jars, mixing the contents together.

"These are from Boggele spells, aren't they?"

I nodded, I couldn't speak. I was too upset.

She looked at me with an expression filled with dread and I began to cry again.

"He, he will be fine, dear, I will do everything I can." She poured a few drops of the potion over Zach's forehead and he yelled out. "Get Velvet and Jake," she urged nervously.

I fled the room again and yelled down the halls for the two of them. Jake was the first to come.

"Sable," he said, out of breath, "What is it?"

"It's Zach," I sobbed. "He's in our room."

Jake ran past me and Velvet soon followed.

I went to open up the door to the room after them, but Velvet held me back.

"Velvet, move!" I demanded.

"Sable, you need to wait here," she said, holding me back. I could hear Zach screaming in pain all night long as I sat outside the door waiting. Morning finally came and Velvet came to open the door again. I pushed past her and ran to Zach. He was sleeping, but seemed to wake right when I got to him. He opened his eyes and smiled. I sighed in relief and sank to the ground beside him.

"Thank you," I said to Thonet.

"Wait till the morning and he should be up and ready to go."

"By tomorrow?"

"You're lucky I know how to treat things like this, you two," she said. I knew Zach didn't know what she was saying, he was barely conscious. "If you hadn't come and gotten me when you did, this would have been a whole other story."

"Thank you," I said again.

"You're welcome," Thonet said, as she and her children left the room.

Zach woke up the next morning violently coughing, but he was still much better than the day before. I quickly crawled down the ladder to my bed to see how he was.

"Are you okay?"

"You have the scripture, right?"

I sighed with relief. "Yeah," I said, handing it to him. He quickly flipped through it and seemed satisfied. Then he took out his scepter and the scripture disappeared.

"I'm sorry I came back."

"It's not your fault; I shouldn't have made you wait all alone for me."

I nodded, still upset.

I could tell Zach was still in pain. He got up slowly and winced when he stood up to get dressed.

"So, I've been thinking," he said, trying to change the subject.

"About what?"

"I think we should maybe change our focus now that we have more of the scripture. We need to get my dad."

I knew his dad would know more about everything, he would be able to help; but I also knew what finding him meant we had to do, and I was scared. I didn't want to go anywhere near Duchura again, but there was no other way to get him. He was in her dungeon.

"We should get out of here as soon as possible, tonight if we can," Zach said, after waiting for me to agree.

"Tonight?"

"We have nothing left to complete here, and Scarlette is looking for us. We can't risk her finding that passage while we are still here."

"You're right, we should leave tonight."

"We'll be okay in the castle," Zach said. "We'll get in and we'll get out and we'll find the rest of the scriptures after that."

I was still scared, but I knew we didn't have another choice. We had to get Zach's dad back before it was too late.

"I'm ready when you are," I said wearily.

Zach smiled at me with longing eyes. I knew he had heard Duchura talking when we were back in the library. I was her target, I was what she wanted and neither of us knew why.

"We'll wait for the flash tonight, like we did to get here. That's going to be the easiest way to get back." Zach informed me.

We were both quiet the rest of the afternoon. It was a melancholy feeling, knowing that we would soon free Auck. It was going to be dangerous.

Neither of us had anything left to pack. We spent the rest of the day walking the island; enjoying the little calm we had left before the storm.

"What is Auck, your father, like?" I asked. We sat with our legs hanging over the edge of a rock wall, overlooking the ocean, watching the sun slowly set over the ocean.

"You'll like him."

As the sky grew darker a pit in my stomach started to form. We would be leaving soon, with nothing left to do but hope for the best.

"Ready?" I hadn't even noticed Zach had already stood up.

"Yeah," I breathed.

I saw the green flash this time. The light had switched worlds and we were traveling with it.

"The war ruins," Zach said, looking around, "this is it."

The land was barren, with all life scorched by heat. Old remains of trees and bushes were charcoaled over and the ground had no fertile soil. Zach reached out to touch a scar on one of the trees.

"This was from the war, got hit by a spell."

"Nothing ever grew back?"

"This land was drained of all resources. It couldn't ever be restored after something of that intensity."

In the distance, beyond the desolate landscape, one single tree stood out among the others. It had life.

"The Orion tree," Zach explained, "that's how we get through to the Boggeles." He started walking towards it. "The wood used to make the seven scripture scriptures is from this tree," he said.

"Orion, like the constellation?" I asked.

He pulled down the collar of his shirt to reveal a mark on his neck, the three starred constellation created out of freckles. "The scripture protectors were all born with these marks. The war that raged through here was so powerful, had so many spells being cast at once, that they exploded upwards and into the sky, creating the constellation of Orion."

We stood at the base of the tree, under the foliage of leaves. They cooled me immediately, and a light mist of water rained down off of them.

"Did you know Orion is a hunter, in Greek mythology?" I asked, thinking of the ties the Boggeles had back in Greece.

Zach shook his head. He was thinking the same thing I was. It was ironic, the Greek ties to the magical world. The Greek humans seemed to know too much for having their memories taken away.

"How do we get through?" I asked. "To the other side."

"I've never done it before, I've only ever heard of this tree."

I walked around the base of the tree; there was no entrance. "Are you sure this is how we get through?"

"It's got to be. Everyone's heard of the story about this tree." He took out his scepter and pointed it at the tree. Then he whispered something to it. We waited for a moment, wondering if anything was going to happen. I walked closer to Zach and watched where he had cast the spell. Nothing changed.

A moment later I looked down to my feet. Then I glanced back again, I wasn't sure if what I thought I saw had really happened. The tip of my shoe appeared to be inside the tree. I reached my hand out to touch the tree.

Right as I thought I would make contact with the bark, my hand moved forwards. I pulled my hand away from the tree and looked up to Zach in surprise.

Zach slowly moved towards the tree, walking into its trunk. He looked back at me warily then stepped back out.

"Should we go together?"

I grabbed his hand and walked through the tree with him. Everything looked the exact same as before when we made it out on the other side.

"Is this it?" I asked.

Zach pointed to something in the distance. Above the charcoaled trees I saw a black weathervane.

"That's the castle." He took a step forward and snapped a branch in half. We both jumped.

The closer we got the more I swore I could sense Duchura's presence, a sensation gripping at my heart, a coldness penetrating through the forest.

"Did you hear that?" I whispered.

Zach put his finger to his mouth. Then he shook his head no. I heard the noise again, this time in front of me. I turned to Zach and looked at him fearfully. No matter which direction we went, the noise followed us. It sounded more like a horse gallop now, steady beats clamoring against the dry ground. Zach started to hear the noise now, too. We were both on edge. Zach motioned me over to a tree in the distance. We were able to hide under the tangle of branches and wait to see if the noise would pass.

I breathed in deeply to calm myself down. Zach put his arm around me as we crouched below the tree. The noise was louder now, much louder than just a moment ago. It was definitely the sound of an animal, running. I saw a dark mass in the distance, slowly getting larger as it grew nearer. I kept my eyes locked on the darkness. I squinted and leaned forwards as far as I could to make out the blur.

It was a lady all in black, with a cape waving behind her as she rode a black horse through the forest. The horse clamored past us; I could feel a wind as it ran by: a bitter, cold wind. As soon as the lady passed us I rose to my feet.

"You don't think she saw us, do you?"

"No, she was riding too fast to notice anything."

I looked forward, at the path the woman had ridden. There was a thin layer of frost permeating the ground where the horse's tracks had been.

"What is this from?"

"That was a storm rider." Zach squatted down, touching the frost, watching it melt from the heat of his fingertips. "They bring on extreme weather conditions. It's a Boggele trait."

"A trait?"

"They have an intrinsic magic inside of them creating an uneven balance to nature, a curse, laden with black magic."

"Do we keep going?" I asked nervously.

Zach looked around. We had walked a long distance from the Orion tree already. The castle up beyond the trees was starting to come into view.

"We don't have a choice."

We traipsed through the forest as quietly as we could. The lingering feeling I had that Duchura was near only became more prevalent. The castle became more substantial as we got closer. The walls rose tall, teeming with ivy. The weathervane appeared taller, the sheer vastness became daunting, and we didn't even have a full view of it yet because of the trees.

I was paranoid that we were being followed. The ground was so dry that every movement could be detected under the decaying leaves. I heard a crunch from somewhere around us and looked in all directions, making sure we were still alone. Zach and I walked closer together now, attached at the side, on high alert.

The trees started to thin and the full extent of the castle came into view. We neared the edge of the forest line, where the trees gave way to the castle grounds. I saw no way of entry besides the front door.

"How do we get inside?"

Zach scanned the front lawn area. He pointed to a rock well on the other edge of the property.

I crinkled my forehead, confused.

"I don't think that's actually a well. Charmers use them as fire escapes."

"Let's try it then. We can't go through the front door."

He nodded and checked the surrounding area before making his way across the grounds. I followed unwillingly; he was being too risky, walking across the front lawn like that. Someone would be able to see us through a window.

Before Zach could make it any further onto the

grounds I pulled him back to the tree's edge by the collar of his shirt.

"Look." A short, grungy man in a trench coat and black boots walked out the front door, slowly trudging across the lawn.

We watched him intently. He walked back and forth, to the door then to the side of the lawn, and back again.

"When he turns to walk back over that way, run to the well," Zach said.

"What if he looks back and sees us?"

The man had already turned away, and Zach had gotten to the well. He looked back at me to see what the problem was, why I hadn't run. The man turned back in our direction and Zach ducked behind the well; I slunk further into the trees. He turned away again, and still I couldn't get myself to move. I went to run this time, but I felt like I was too slow and I couldn't make it over by the time he turned back. He was about to turn. I was halfway there. I froze -- dead center in the middle of the lawn.

"Sable, come on," Zach whispered.

I still stood frozen, I was too scared. I couldn't get myself to run either way, back to the forest or over to the well. Zach ran back out from behind the well and grabbed my hand, forcing me over to the well. Once we were both hidden again I peeked around the side. The man had turned back. He didn't appear to see us.

"Thank you," I said to Zach.

He nodded back silently.

I looked around the side of the well wall again and

saw the man walking closer to the well than he had the previous times.

"Zach," I whispered.

He looked around the corner of the well. He pulled me farther around the well, as far away from the man as we could get.

"We've got to go down there now," he said, pulling his scepter out.

The man was still walking closer to us. I prayed that he would turn back in the other direction. He didn't.

"Zach, if you try to go now he's going to see you."

Zach slowly inched his head around the corner. He was going to see us; he must have been right in front of us by now.

"Zach," I breathed.

"He turned back."

I sighed with relief. Zach cast a spell with his scepter. He opened up his hand to reveal some sort of marble.

"I'll go down there first. If I don't say to come down get back to the carpet and get somewhere safe." Then he handed me the marble. "If this turns red that means there's danger, just listen for the okay to come down otherwise."

"Wait." He was already lowering himself into the well.

"You have to promise me you won't go down if you don't hear the okay from me."

I clenched the marble in my hand and he descended further into the well. He must have been right about it being an escape exit from the castle. There were iron bars fitted to the inside walls to use for a ladder to get in and out quickly.

I had no idea how deep the well was or when Zach would call for me to come down behind him. I wasn't even sure I would be able to hear him if he did call for me.

I realized I hadn't looked at the marble to see if it had turned red. It was sweaty in my hand. I closed my eyes before looking to see the color: red. All red.

Not even a cloud of smoky red, just a solid, dark red. I jerked my head behind me to see if someone was there. I was alone as far as I was aware. I looked to see if the man was still outside the castle doors. I saw him, still walking the same path back and forth. He seemed to notice nothing unusual. Then I realized, Zach never told me if the red was danger for him, or danger for me.

When the man turned back to walk the other way I peered into the well. There was no sign of Zach anymore. I listened for his movements, but all was silent.

There was no place I could think that was safer than with Zach. I called for him inside the well, but heard no response. I called again, louder. Nothing. The man had turned back again. I ducked behind the well waiting for him to go back, so that I could climb inside the well. I had to. I was too exposed out here, and Zach had been down there too long without saying anything back.

I thought of the Boggele library, where he had told me to stay back. I bit my lip, thinking if I really should go down or not. I should. I should go, I had to.

I climbed down the first rung and listened for Zach again. I climbed down the second and third. Everything was still silent. Water droplets sliding down the sides of the walls were the only faint noises I could hear.

I lost track of how far down I had climbed. Fifteen rungs? Twenty? I could no longer see light from the top; it shouldn't have been so dark. The silence was finally broken: a loud crack further down the well echoed off the walls.

"Hello?" I whispered.

A bright light shined up towards me. "Who are you?"

"Zach? Zach, it's me."

The light was waving across the walls, then directly on my face.

"Sable," he said, lowering the light away from me. "Why did you come down here?"

"The marble, it turned red."

He let the light from his scepter go out. "Charmer magic is hard to use here," he said.

"Was the red for me?" I asked. "Was I the one in danger?"

"Yes. What shade did it turn?"

"Dark red; solid, dark red."

"I don't know what's up there, but we need to keep climbing down."

"We're safe in here, aren't we?"

"Sable, I don't know. We have to get to the bottom."

I looked at the marble to see the color. It was too dark; I couldn't see any color at all. I reached down for the next rung and my hand grabbed at nothing. My other hand then slipped and I frantically reached out at the wall for anything to grab onto. My chin hit the next rung down and I caught it.

"Sable! Are you okay?"

"I slipped," I said, dabbing at my chin. "There was no rung."

"Oh, my gosh! That was from me. I'm sorry." I could hear him climbing towards me. "It pulled away from the wall when I grabbed for it."

"I'm okay." I was startled, I hadn't expected that. "Let's just get keep going."

I didn't tell Zach, but I had dropped the marble when I slipped, and could have sworn I still saw red.

CHAPTER VIII

My feet finally hit solid ground. We landed on a grate, and I could finally see the smallest amount of light shining through the slats.

"What do you think is down there?" I asked. The holes were too tiny to see anything, but I could hear faint, muffled noises from below.

"I don't know." Zach bent down to the ground and tried looking through the slats.

"What do you see?"

"It's dark, but I see a common room or something down there. More of those men are in there."

I knew that if we got down there and the men tried to fight us that Zach would have a hard time casting spells back.

"Should we still go?"

Zach stood back up to face me. "I don't see any other way we can get inside."

He stamped his foot on the grate. Nothing happened and whoever was down below didn't seem to notice.

"What do you think the people down there are going to do when we get through?"

"I have no idea, but I have my scepter. As long as there aren't a lot of them we should be okay."

"What if there are more? We can't get caught, not here."

"We'll be okay. Promise, I'll keep you safe."

He took out his scepter and cast a spell at the grate. The bolts that held it together unscrewed themselves and floated upwards.

"Do you still have enough magic to keep going?" I asked, concerned. I knew he would have to save his energy for whoever was down below.

"Yeah," he whispered. "Step up a few rungs for a second."

He kicked again at the grate and it turned sideways. We both looked down into the room below. The men still didn't seem to notice us.

The room was dimly lit by candles and the ragged men sat around a small fireplace to keep warm. Their clothes were in shreds and most looked like they had been beaten to some degree. Bloodstains were prevalent on their trench coats and as one stood up I could see he had a severe limp.

There were more rungs that led further down into the room. I looked to Zach, wondering if he was going to venture down. He stayed perched on the final rung that was still concealed by the well, staring into the room, looking at the men.

"Who are they?" I asked.

"Servants of Duchura is my guess." I realized that they were locked in the room by a heavy steel door.

"Is this the dungeon?"

Zach shook his head.

"Too nice to be a dungeon."

The man that had stood up looked over to where we had twisted the grate sideways. I saw him point and yell something to the others.

I looked down to see what was happening and made eye contact with one of the men.

"Someone's up there!"

I leaned my head back, pressing my body against the side of the well.

"Don't worry," Zach breathed. He took out his scepter and cast another spell.

I didn't notice anything different. "Do we need to get out of here?" I said, already starting to climb back up the rungs.

"Hold on."

I now heard the sound of rushing water. It was getting louder. I felt the well get colder, the rocky inside of it damp. I could see the men take a step back from the well's opening.

"What did you do?" I asked Zach.

He looked up into the well. "I'm getting them out of here."

I was still confused. I felt something wet run over my hand. Water was streaming down the sides of the well walls, pooling up in the room below. Zach moved down further into the room, now visible to the men.

The fireplace they had been using was drowned with water and went out; it was past the men's knees, with nowhere to drain. The room was completely sealed off by rock walls and a locked door.

The men scrambled to the rungs to escape the room, pushing and shoving to be the first ones out.

"Ready?" Zach asked me.

"What?" I couldn't concentrate; the men were scaling the wall, getting closer to us. I looked over to Zach and he let go of the rung he had been holding onto, jumping over the men and down into the room.

"Sable!" he yelled, treading water now, "jump!"

The first of the men had nearly reached the rung I was clinging to. "Sable!" Zach yelled.

I let go of the rung, landing in the room, almost completely submerged in water. The men clawed at one another to get to the exit. The last one was headed for the exit and Zach cast a spell to stop him.

"Wait!" Zach yelled to him as he climbed back up the rungs yet again.

"Wha' yew want?"

"Do you know of a man named Auck?" The man grunted and kept climbing, slowly trudging forwards with his hurt leg. Zach cast another spell towards him and he yelled in pain, falling yet another time back into the water below.

"Dungeon room, ye' will find 'um there!"

"Where is that?"

The man was already up into the safety of the well, paying us no more attention.

"Okay, Zach, stop the water." It now rose to our necks and I tilted my heard towards the ceiling for air.

"I don't have enough energy," he said between breaths.

I looked back over to the room's exit and saw the last man who Zach had shot a spell at pull out his scepter and lock the grate back in place. He looked at us one last time with a menacing expression before fleeing.

"You've got to try!"

Zach cast a spell, but nothing happened. I took in one last breath of air before the water filled the room to the ceiling. I opened my eyes under the water to search for Zach. I swam for the grate at the exit and kicked at it, threw myself against it, but it didn't budge.

I was feeling lightheaded, my lungs were giving out. I could see Zach on the other side of the room, with something in his hands, hurtling the object against the door. I could hear the sharp blows echoing through the water.

Blackness started to give way to my vision. I could feel hands around my waist, I was moving, somewhere. Then the water was gone. I coughed it up from my lungs, replaced it with air, heaving for enough breath.

"Sable," Zach whispered, hugging me to his chest.

I breathed hard, still replenishing my breath. I looked around and noticed the handle to the door in the room had been axed off, the door had been opened, and the water had stopped running.

I realized Zach was bleeding. He took off his shirt and wrapped it tightly around his forearm where he had nicked himself with the axe.

"Are you okay?"

"I'm fine," he said, pushing my wet hair away from my face, "are you?"

I nodded, finally aware that we were in a tiny

hallway.

"Do you know how to get through to the rest of the castle?"

"No, but this is the only other exit to the room back there, so this has got to be the way in."

The hall took a sharp left turn. Before we went to turn the corner Zach stopped and pulled a bag out of the air with his scepter. He pulled out two clear tubes of watery liquid.

"I had Thonet make some extra for us just in case."

He handed me one of the vials and I took a few sips before handing it back to Zach. I held my hands out in front of me, watching as they slowly became transparent.

As we turned the corner we saw a rock staircase, twisting around yet another corner. Zach went first, walking silently as we continued upwards. I knew the only reason I was still able to make out his image was because I was consciously looking for him, but it still scared me that he appeared visable.

As we neared the top of the staircase I could see sunlight. Zach was the first to make it to the top and he motioned me to come up with him. The room before us was filled with massive tables, hundreds of scriptures scattered over the tops of them and bow and arrows covering the walls.

"Do you think some of the scriptures might be here?" I whispered.

"It would be too risky to keep them out in the open like this."

"Do you have any idea how to find the dungeon?"

"I have one idea, but I would need help. Charmer magic is nearly entirely masked here."

"What is it?"

"I need to channel some of your energy to cast the spell." Zach held out his scepter towards me. "Grab on to it."

I reached out for it, unsure of what he was planning on doing next. When I touched the tip of the scepter I immediately drew away.

"What is it?" Zach asked, surprised.

"It shocked me." I could feel blood pulsating through my hand where the spark of electricity had been sent through my body.

Zach looked confused. "I don't understand." He mumbled something to himself and then held out the scepter towards me again. "Okay, it shouldn't do that this time."

Zach watched as I reached for the scepter again, I grabbed hold of it this time, then pulled back yet again and grimaced. I could feel the shock move through my entire body and I stumbled backwards.

"Zach, I can't to do that again."

"I know," he said, leaning over me, keeping me from falling. The jolt from this shock was strong. "We won't do that again."

"What are we going to do then?"

"If I wait long enough I might be able to do the spell by myself."

"Why did it do that, your scepter, why did it shock me?"

I could tell Zach was thinking of the right words to explain.

"You weren't compatible with it," he said, not making eye contact with me, looking down at the scepter, "it would do something like that to a Boggele."

"We better keep searching while you get your strength back," I said.

Before we were able to exit the room we heard shouting from somewhere around us. Zach pulled me under one of the tables that we were standing next to and we stayed completely silent, listening as the conversation grew closer to us. "Ethrum! Get it to me *now*."

"I don't know whe' it is, I've looked all morning," a quivering voice answered back

"Find it!"

"Master, we don't have a clue whe' else it could be."

A bright light shot out of the room nearest us. I could hear glass shatter. Then there was a scream, followed by a long silence.

The potion was slowly wearing off and Zach and I crouched further under the table as heavy footsteps entered the room.

"Affle! Lenthil!"

I could hear soft footsteps pad down a staircase and make their way into the room Zach and I were hiding in.

"Where is it? Where is it!" The footsteps walked closer to us.

I could sense Duchura's presence, my blood felt cold, hair on my head prickled, and my heart beat a different pattern.

"Whe' is wha'?" a voice squeaked.

"The scripture!" The voice yelled in rage.

I could hear the little man wailing in pain now, begging for the noise to cease. The noise -- the sound that nearly burst my eardrums when I heard it last -- I could hear it now, too. I hunched over, holding my hands tightly over my ears, trying not to scream. I couldn't make a sound, whoever else was in the room was right next us. I had to stay silent. Zach grabbed my hand; I squeezed his hard, focusing all my attention on keeping my pain silent.

The other two men in the room screamed, I was able to notice one sink to his knees, writhing in pain, holding his hand up in defeat.

Zach looked at me, silently pleading for me to keep quiet, trying to comfort me, trying to distract me from the noise; but I couldn't hold off much longer. I felt a tear seep out through my eyes, clenched tight. Zach was trying to help me up, to get me away from the noise, but I couldn't pull myself off the ground.

The noise stopped in one sudden moment. The men got back to their feet, panting hard, still distraught over the pain.

"I need the entire scripture *today*, do you understand?" Without a word the men went for the exit.

I reached up to my ear, I knew there was blood; I wiped it away and felt more rush down the side of my face. I looked to see if it really was blood, it felt cold, viscous. When I looked, I saw that it was silver; the potion was still inside me.

I heard the men stop in their tracks. "Wha' is tha'?"

The other man sniffed the air, "Smells u' blood."

"The scripture!" The last voice yelled.

I could see one last pair of feet still in the room. Shoes slowly clicked towards our hiding place. I slunk further under the table. There was no time to run; we would be heard.

Footsteps walked straight over to our table. I peered up and saw a glimpse of the figure's face, Duchura's face. I recognized her from my dreams. I had never seen her in person before; she had merely been an image in my mind, until now. Her deathly thin stature loomed over us, her eyes black and piercing, her clothes carrying a bitter odor.

She inhaled a deep breath. I held my hand over the blood on my ears, trying to hide the apparent smell.

"Peculiar," she said, walking away.

Zach and I left the room, going the opposite way of Duchura.

"She had to have seen us, Zach."

"I don't think she did."

"She looked right at us, she smelled my blood. She must have known someone was there!"

"She would have done something if she saw us."

Zach and I walked into another room, trying to figure out the extent of the castle.

I pulled Zach back and let out a slight scream before we ventured any further into the room. There was a man, one of the trench coat servant men, lying on the floor. Dead. Shattered glass was strewn around him; that was where the scream had come from earlier.

Zach stared at the man, blinking away the water from his eyes. I knew what he was thinking about, how easy it was for Duchura to kill, how easily she could get rid of his father.

"Let's keep going," he said, walking past the man.

"Do you have a plan?"

"No," Zach said, holding his fingers to his head as if he was thinking hard. "I can't think of any other way besides using my scepter, and Charmer magic is blocked."

I stood quietly, thinking. The house seemed too quiet. I heard no more footsteps, no other sounds or signs of life. It was just too strange. There should have been more movement and there should be people.

"Zach, I feel like people know we are here."

"If anyone knew we were here we would be with Duchura right now."

"Maybe we should take the last of the potion, just to be safe."

"Sable, we're fine. I have no idea how long we're going to be here; we have to save it."

I trusted that Zach was right, but I still had an uneasy feeling, suppressed deep in my mind, that we were being watched.

"I have one other idea."

"What is it?"

Zach grabbed my hand.

"Maybe I can channel your energy," he said, as he pulled his scepter out. "Don't worry; it can't shock you this way."

He looked at me, trying to figure out if I was okay

with doing this.

"Okay," I agreed.

"This spell is only going to be able to help us find the scripture though."

"Not your dad?" I asked.

"No, but finding the scripture first may be better. Duchura doesn't know where it is either, so if we get it, she won't have a clue; but if we get my dad we won't have time to stay and look for the scripture. They'll figure out who took him right away."

I nodded. I tightened my grip on Zach's hand, bracing myself for the spell. Zach looked back at me, seeming unsure of harnessing my energy himself.

"Illumination seeker!" A light shot out of the scepter and lingered in front of our faces for a moment before drifting away. Zach looked surprised.

"I didn't even have to use any energy for that. Did I drain too much from you?"

"No," I said, "I feel fine."

"It still shouldn't have been that easy," Zach said, noticing the light had already drifted out of the room. "We've got to follow it."

I wasn't even thinking about trying to stay quiet anymore. As the light floated up to the second floor we thudded up the stairs behind it. It took us around a bend and wove through hallways. Finally it stopped at a dead end wall and floated to the ceiling before dimming into darkness.

"It should have taken us straight to the scripture. Something must have gone wrong when I cast the spell,"

Zach said, looking at the ceiling where the light had gone out.

"It did work," I said. Zach looked at me, confused. "The light didn't go out until it hit the ceiling." Zach opened his mouth as if he was going to say something, but he just looked up and stared.

"We just have to find a way to get up there."

CHAPTER IX

"I don't think I can harness the energy I'd need from you to get up there," Zach said. "It would be too much on you."

"You have to try it."

"I could hurt you, Sable."

"I didn't even feel anything last time. This is the only thing left we have to try!"

"It's going to take a lot of magic, Sable, especially with the Charmer block."

"It's okay," I said, reaching for his arm. I held onto him, waiting for him to do something. "Zach."

Finally he cast the spell. I felt lightheaded, but still stable, still okay. The ceiling boards started to detach; I could see an opening start to form.

"Okay, now just one last spell," Zach said.

Now I was starting to feel the exhaustion hit, but I didn't say anything. I didn't know there was going to be a second spell. I gripped his arm which now took much more effort than before. Zach cast the second spell. I was drowsy; I blinked long, slow blinks and stared motionless at nothing.

I didn't know how we had gotten up to the opening.

"Sable, you okay?" Zach asked.

I was just now aware he was talking to me.

"Yeah."

"I can't believe I was able to harness that much energy from you. I can't believe I was even able to use that much Charmer magic in the first place with the blockage." He looked at me funny. "You sure you're okay?"

I felt less drowsy already; my energy was being quickly revived.

"Really, I'm good. Let's get inside." We had been floating by the entry and I could feel my weight starting to fight the spell, pulling me downwards.

Zach turned the knob to the door, it wasn't locked. We walked inside and I was overwhelmed by shelves and jars and books and furniture, chairs, couches, trinkets, all cramped into the room.

"You think this is really it?"

Zach shrugged. It looked more like a place to carelessly toss unwanted junk.

"Could have ended up here I suppose."

I lost track of where Zach had gone behind all of the clutter. My shoe snagged a box lying on the ground and I tripped, falling into a shelf of pewter statues.

"Sable? You alright?"

"Yeah," I said, picking myself up off the ground, avoiding shards of the broken figurines.

I could have sworn I saw a bird fly past me a moment later. I looked around, but nothing was there. I kept up my search for the scripture, scanning the shelves, the ground, looking through piles of objects. The bird flew past me again. I was sure of it.

I searched the quiet room for it. I felt something tangle in my hair; squawks gave way to the silence. I batted at my hair, swinging my head around.

"Zach!"

The bird flew out of my hair, violently flapping its wings, getting ready to strike down at me again.

Zach ran across the room towards me. "Duck!"

He cast a spell at the bird. I watched as it turned lifeless, back into pewter and shattered as it hit the ground.

"There's some sort of enchantment in here," he said, cupping the shards into his hand. "Everything we come in contact with is going to come to life, and contain Boggele magic."

I stood still, thinking about *everything* I had touched since we had gotten inside.

"Zach. I knocked over an entire shelf of those statues."

"Where?" Pieces of the rest of the statues vibrated along the floor. "It's okay, they can't do anything; they're broken."

I made sure not to touch anything as we continued searching for the scripture. I thought about what Zach had said, how he was able to harness so much of my energy. It was like the Charmer block didn't even exist. I couldn't see Zach in the room, but I could hear him walking around.

"Why do you think it was so easy for you to use Charmer magic when you had my energy?" I asked.

I saw Zach step out from behind a wall of boxes. He shrugged.

"I don't know." I knew the same thought had

crossed both our minds, but neither of us said anything. Somehow the Boggele blocks to the Charmers didn't affect me. I could hear the Boggele threat noise that Zach couldn't. Zach's scepter read me as a Boggele. Somehow I had a link to them, and we both knew it.

I heard another sound of shattering glass.

"Was that you?" I asked.

"Don't move," Zach gritted through his teeth.

I saw a black mass swarming over everything around us. Bugs covered the room. I felt a light tickle on my arm and flicked one of the bugs away. I felt a burning sensation on my leg. The bug had let out a spurt of fire.

"Fireflies," Zach said.

I heard the door to the room open up and looked to Zach. He had slid behind furniture and motioned me towards him. I stepped on some of the bugs as I made my way towards him. Fire singed my skin.

I could see a group of the trench coat men enter the room.

"Huffle! What happened!" one of them yelled, looking around at the fireflies.

"I have ner idea!"

"We got to get em' back! Master ell' be furious," another yelled as he extinguished a set of drapes that had caught fire.

Zach and I were forced to search the back of the room for the scripture while we waited for the men to leave.

Finally the men had jarred all of the bugs. They threw them onto a shelf and tore out of the room.

I saw one last puff of fire ahead of us. Zach went over and stepped on the last of the fireflies.

"Do you think they came to get the scripture?" I asked.

"I don't know. They didn't take anything with them when they left though."

We had gone through every shelf and cupboard imaginable and still, no scripture. Hundreds of objects had come to life and the room got out of control. Zach was determined that it was here somewhere.

"Zach, we've looked everywhere."

"Not everywhere. We must have missed it."

"We couldn't have missed it. Look at this place." We had bulldozed through everything.

"The spell, it led us here. It's *got* to be here."

"Maybe something went wrong."

I could tell Zach was discouraged, his face sank, lips turned downwards, with only his eyes looking up at me with a crystal glazing. He shook his head.

"You're right, let's get out of here. Finding my dad is more important."

I sighed, staring back at him. There was nothing left we could do; if the seeker spell wasn't working, we would have to search the entire castle. It had to work this time.

We went for the door to exit, Zach pulled out his scepter to float us back down. Right as I was about to grab for the knob I saw it turning on its own. Zach pulled me aside. Someone walked in. If they turned in our direction they would see us, there was no time to move; they would hear us if we did.

A man walked further into the room, another followed behind. I squeezed Zach's hand, squeezed my eyes shut, buried my face beneath my hair.

I heard someone take something off a shelf, the footsteps walked back towards us. Then there was silence. I looked up to see if they had left. A pair of dark eyes stared back at me through the dim lighting of the room; then quickly looked away.

"That man saw me, Zach," I breathed right as the door closed.

CHAPTER X

"We should have taken more of Thonet's potion," I said, replaying the scene of the man's eyes staring into mine over and over.

Zach paced in the room, walking to the door then back in the other direction. I listened for even the faintest sounds. Nothing; complete and utter silence bore down on us.

"Here," Zach said, handing me the potion. "Let's just take the rest now."

I handed Zach back the empty vial.

"He had to have seen us, there's no way he couldn't have."

"We've just need to get away from here; this will be the first place they come back to."

"Let's try the spell again."

"You sure you want to?" Zach asked.

"Yeah. Use it to find the scripture again."

I held onto Zach's scepter. I felt a shock of energy pulse through my body again.

"Illumination seeker!"

I let go of the scepter right as the spell was cast. My hands shook from the pulse of energy and I tried to hide it from Zach. I couldn't help but to reach out for him and balance myself against him. He looked at me concerned, lightly holding onto my shaking hands.

"Come on," I said, moving away from his grip, "the light is moving."

"Sable, we should wait a minute, I drained too much energy from you."

I watched as the light slowly drifted across the room.

"Really I'm fine." I didn't even feel that Zach had taken any of my energy. "It's just the shock," I said.

"I don't know why it does that. It makes no sense."

I followed the light as it moved across the room. It hung above a stack of boxes before dimming back into nothing.

I looked to Zach. I was sure we had already checked there. He walked over and peered over the stack, looking down inside the box on top.

"What's in there?"

"I can't really tell." He took out his scepter and used it to cast more light on the room. He peered in deeper, making sure not to touch anything. As soon as the room got brighter he jolted back, slamming into me.

"What!" I said in surprise.

It took Zach a moment to compose himself again.

"Zach, what is in there?"

"A Boggele," he said, taking another step back, "and the scripture."

"Are you sure it's the scripture?"

Zach nodded. "Something must have happened to him before he was able to get it to Duchura. That's why she thinks it's missing."

I peered into the box and saw the Boggele, mid-scream, hands wrapped tightly around the scripture, looking upwards as if something was above him, and the eye necklace, choking at his neck.

"Don't touch him," Zach warned, "that enchantment spell will work on him, too."

"How are we going to get it then?"

"We don't."

"What do you mean we don't get it?" I asked.

"If he comes alive again I won't have enough power to fight him. We'll be caught."

"Siphon my energy."

"No."

"Zach, do it. The scripture is *right* there."

"Your body can't handle another shock from my scepter."

We didn't have time to find another way to get the scripture, the potion wasn't going to last much longer and we both knew it. Zach's scepter was in his pocket and before he was able to stop me I grabbed it. The surge of energy vibrated through my body as soon as I touched it.

"Do it. Quickly!"

In one swift motion Zach grabbed the scripture and cast a spell at the man as he started to stir.

My arms shook this time, too. I held on for too long. I sank to my knees, holding them to my chest, waiting for the voltage to pass through me.

"You have the scripture?"

"Yes," he said, handing it to me.

"Sable, you shouldn't have done that, that shock is too hard on you."

"And the man?" I asked, ignoring his concern.

"Still dead."

Zach lifted me back to my feet when I attempted to stand on my own.

I looked at the scripture, puzzled. As I flipped through I saw nothing but empty pages.

"This is wrong."

"What do you mean?"

"There's nothing in here."

Zach took the scripture back from me.

"What?" he asked, confused.

"The pages, they are all blank."

"Sable, no they're not." He held out the scripture and I saw ink, seeping back into the pages. We both watched as the letters disappeared and the pages became blank again.

"It must have something to do with the protection spells, they're blocking you from reading it," he said, crinkling his forehead, flipping to another page and watching as the same thing happened again.

"Did that happen with the others?"

"I never tried to read them."

I still found it hard to walk after the last shock, but slowly we made our way to the exit. We had stayed in the attic for much too long. Zach took out his scepter and used it to hide the scripture with the others we had found before opening the door to leave.

I was happy to be out of there, I hadn't realized how

dark and confined the room had been.

"We'll have to keep looking for my dad without magic until I get enough energy back to cast the spell on my own," Zach said as we turned the corner, making our way back to the center of the castle.

We moved further into the castle. A faint ringing, deep in my eardrums kept me from focusing.

"There's got to be an entrance to the dungeon or *something* around here," Zach said as we tried yet another staircase, leading down into a wine cellar.

The ringing was growing louder. The Boggele threat -- I knew that's what it was -- I just didn't want to believe it. I held onto a rack on the wall for balance, it was as if instant vertigo set in when the noise became more prevalent. Zach didn't seem to notice that I wasn't following behind him. He headed for the staircase. He walked further up the staircase, winding upwards until he was no longer in sight.

The noise was louder now, as loud as it had been when Duchura was standing right next to us earlier. I was no longer aware of what was going on. I relied on the rack more now for support. I grabbed at it, trying to stay upright. I couldn't hold on any longer, the shelving came loose, bottles of wine crashed down, staining the ground and cutting through my skin at impact.

Zach screamed. That was the last noise I heard before the piercing ring blocked out all other sound.

I looked around me at the pool of red, from the wine, or my blood, I didn't know any longer.

I saw Zach's leg slip out from underneath him and

he fell to the ground, not getting back up. There was red there, too, now -- wine, blood, it all looked the same.

The noise stopped abruptly. The muscles in my body relaxed. I looked at the palms of my hands, glass shards penetrated my skin. Still in a bout of confusion I wiped my hand against the ground in an attempt to remove the glass. It only punctured my skin deeper. I saw more red: red, drenching my clothes, staining my skin, filling my open wounds. Then I saw Zach's body, first his head was dragged out of sight, then his torso and finally his feet were pulled out of sight.

Someone else walked into the room. Shoes crunched over the glass. I could feel the figure's presence; blood turning cold, heart beating to a stranger beat. I could smell a distinctive odor on her clothes. She bent down, grabbing my wrist, examining the blood on my hands.

"With the boy," I heard her say, "until she's more lucid."

CHAPTER XI

I lay on a cold, wet floor, disoriented for a moment. I awoke to chains rattling, rage, screaming, all in the dark, unable to see anything.

"Where is it?" someone yelled.

There was no reply.

A bright light lit up the wall behind me. I was able to see Zach, blood dripping off his body and pooling below him as he stood chained against the wall. Another man, thin, barely being held by the grip of the chains was beside him.

The man that stood in front of Zach screamed, casting another spell at him.

"Zach," I whispered to myself, trying to pick myself up off the floor, to get over to him. The man seemed to notice me. He lowered his scepter from Zach and looked in my direction, curling his lips as he grinned down at me.

"Duchura!" he wildly yelled, "Duchura!"

I kept crawling to Zach. He writhed in pain under the chains.

"Zach," I said, pulling at his pant leg, too weak to get his attention any other way.

"Get out of here," he panted. I saw his bare stomach, clothes shredded from his chest, skin ripped away from his body.

The man approached the two of us closer now. He held his scepter to Zach once more.

"No!" I yelled, using all my strength to get to my feet, to pull the scepter from his hands. I had it; no shock pulsated through me this time.

Energy flowed from me, into the scepter, and back out towards the man. He now was the one to fall to the ground. I didn't know what was happening. I kept my focus as long as I could. It hurt to stand, it hurt to hold onto the scepter, but I didn't move until finally I couldn't take it any longer. I dropped the scepter, falling back to the floor.

"Duchura!" the man yelled again, snatching back his scepter. He held it towards me with shaking hands and a sweaty brow.

I could suddenly sense a presence, same as earlier. It was Duchura's presence.

The man's scepter was knocked from his hand by an outside force; Duchura came into view, holding out his scepter in front of her by the tips of two fingers.

"The scripture?" she snipped.

"Not yet, master."

Duchura exhaled with contempt and motioned the man over to her. His arrogance withered and he cowered as he neared her.

"My scepter, master?" he said looking at her arm still outstretched with it.

He reached out for it and right before he was able to grab it Duchura pulled her arm back, aiming the scepter at his head and casting a spell. The man stumbled back, taken by surprise, and tripped. He held his head where blood gushed. Duchura dropped the scepter into his lap.

"I need that scripture, Henry."

Henry. I had been too disconcerted to realize who the man was.

Henry crawled further away from Duchura.

"Yes, yes I know."

"You don't know, Henry!" she yelled, "and that it why, when you figure out the whereabouts of Scarlette, the two of you will *both* be killed," she scoffed, stepping over him and moving towards where Zach and I stood.

"Isabella," she sighed, "it's been a long time."

She spoke slowly, her worlds slithery and unhurried. She looked at Zach and the man beside him, with almost a slight smile on her wrinkled face.

"You know my full name," I pressed.

"But of course I do," she said, circling me.

I looked at her, confused.

"I'm sure this man could explain," she said, looking to the figure next to Zach. "Do you recognize him, Zach?" she smirked.

Zach stared at Duchura with an expressionless, exhausted face then slowly turned his head to the man next to him.

"Dad," he whispered in shock. "Let him go!" he yelled, lashing out in an attempt to free himself from the chains.

"You do not command me!" Duchura yelled back, casting a spell at Zach. It sent him hard against the wall.

"Stop!" I pleaded, watching Zach hang limp from

his chains.

She looked over to me. I was unsure what she was about to do, but then she lowered the scepter. "For you, daughter."

Duchura cast a spell at both Zach and his father, the chains holding them against the wall came loose and they fell to the ground.

"No," Zach's dad whispered softly as he pulled the chains off of his chest.

"No?" she said to the man. He looked up. "You cannot keep the truth from her any longer."

She stroked my face and I turned away. She moved my hair to the side and I could feel her breathing on my bare neck.

"It's still there," she remarked.

"Don't touch her!" Zach stumbled forward, dragging the chains still connected to his arms and legs behind him.

Duchura stared, a brazen expression threatening Zach.

I pulled at my shirt, trying to see what Duchura had been looking for. Trying to see what exactly was 'still there.'

"Your mark," Duchura said, turning back to face me, "the mark that shows who you really are." She paused for a moment, "A Boggele. My *daughter,* Sable."

"No!" Auck said again, weakly, trying to sit upright. "Sable, she cannot be trusted."

"Why is that, Auck?" Duchura yelled. "All the signs are clear. She can't seem to touch your scepter without it attacking; she can hear what only the Boggele can. She can even break past the Charmer spell blocks!" she said, looking directly at Zach. "The scripture, it knows she is one of us, too; it seals up when she touches it. I have been watching her, everything makes sense."

"She knows how powerful you are, Sable, she wants your support." Auck lifted himself up, propped himself against the wall.

I looked over my shoulder, examining my back the best I could. Something was there. I could feel it engrained on my skin: the Greek eye image. I was taken aback, no idea what was going on.

Zach came closer, intrigued at the image that had appeared on my skin. He reached out to touch it.

"She's what you're drawing from, isn't she?"

Duchura looked unnerved. The room was silent.

"Isn't she!" Zach yelled.

"She is my daughter!" Duchura yelled back, grabbing me by the shoulder.

I just then picked up on what was going on. The Greek talisman etched into my back, it was there because I was able to help the Boggeles, I was one of them. I was the piece of this unspoken legend that had been missing, and needed for the Boggeles to come back into power. That's why Zach wouldn't tell me the legend. He knew this entire time. He didn't want me to choose to side with them.

"Sable is *not* a part of that legend! It isn't possible," Zach said, shaking his head with confusion.

I didn't know who to trust. I didn't even know what the legend was. All I knew was that both sides needed me for something that I wasn't even sure I could provide to them.

"Of course it is possible!"

"Sable, this isn't true. She *needs* your support; she needs you to keep the Boggeles strong."

"No, Isabella, you are my daughter and I only need your love, I need to be with you. It has been too long."

Zach shook his head, staring at me with brilliant eyes.

"You'll both be dead by morning. It shouldn't matter to you anymore," Duchura said to Zach and his father, dragging me towards the staircase.

I knew that Zach was already dying. Dying from the pain of torture, the pain of thinking he had lost my trust.

I stayed silent. I felt as my eyelashes were doused by tears, I felt the image on my back, I felt Duchura's fingernails digging further into my shoulder.

"Zach!" I screamed as we turned the corner, now out of view of the dungeon. I refused to move forward, fighting Duchura's unrelenting grip.

I made up my mind in that one moment. It would always be the Charmers, I would always side with them. I didn't need to know what the legend was to decide. I had already learned enough of the cruelty of the Boggeles and that was enough for me.

They are liars, Isabella! Everything they have told you, a lie."

"No!" I cried. "You are not my mother!"

Duchura lessened her grip at hearing my altercation.

"You do not believe me!" She pushed me back

down the stairs into the dungeon room. I tripped, crying, screaming as she approached me. "You cannot see that I am your *mother*!"

"How could you be?"

She dragged me back into the room. Zach and his father both lay motionless on the floor.

"Auck!" Duchura yelled.

He stirred.

"Explain our history," she demanded.

I crawled to Zach's side, frantically searching for a heartbeat. Ignoring all else.

"Zach!"

Duchura drew out her scepter. A persistent beating noise grew stronger, echoing off the stone walls.

"This is his heartbeat," Duchura said, "he is alive. Now listen." She demanded.

The noise of the beat grew softer and Auck began to speak. "Sable, there are many explanations to your birth. This is just one."

"Auck," Duchura warned.

"Your birth dates back to the war," he began. "Magical beings and humans had lived together for thousands of years, in peace. Tension started to build between some of the wizards and the humans. Some wizards wanted the humans gone; they thought it weakened their magic. There was talk of creating another world for the humans, and eventually the humans were slowly wiped of their memories of the magic world and sent to live on their own. That wasn't enough for some wizards. They wanted the human race dead." Auck began to cough and struggle for air. He was too weak to even expend the energy to talk.

Duchura waited for a moment, but the coughing fit ceased to stop. She pulled me away from Zach and to the exit. "I will finish telling her myself."

"Wait," Auck breathed heavily. "That's when the war broke out, when wizards started going to the human world and killing off their race."

"It was for the best. It was the only way, and you know that!" Duchura cut in. "Magic would have been destroyed!"

Auck ignored what she was saying and continued, "Wizards started to divide; they themselves started to form two distinct races. Different magic abilities started to develop between the two. Finally, the magic between them became so different that wizards began to call themselves by separate names, Charmers and Boggeles.

Auck stopped again, deeply inhaling air.

"Finish it," Duchura demanded.

"The legend is…"

"It is no legend! It is the *truth*!"

"In the midst of the war the leaders of the two races disappeared. It is said that they had a child, a daughter who possessed magic from both the Charmers and the Boggeles."

"You were the Boggele leader?" I asked Duchura.

"I still am the Boggele leader, and you can lead with me, Isabella."

"It is said that your magic was taken from you when you were discovered. You were sent to live with the humans, where you would be safe, and where wizards would be safe from you," Auck explained.

"I would have never left you so vulnerable," Duchura said. "That is why you have that mark. Your father and I both gave you a mark, through which we could restore your magic."

"That mark could be explained in so many ways, Sable," Auck said.

"I don't believe you," I said. Neither Duchura nor Auck knew who I was talking to. Then I turned, facing Duchura, daring her to make a move towards me.

"What other explanation is there?"

"You hated humans, yet you allowed me to be sent to live in their world with them! And then planned to destroy them? No mother would make that choice."

"You were taken from me! I would never have made that choice."

"Either way I don't believe the legend. A Charmer could never have loved you!"

"That's enough!" Duchura yelled. She pointed her scepter at Auck and a flash of light hit him. She almost laughed, and the cacophonous noise echoed throughout the room.

Auck no longer twitched in pain; his muscles went limp and his body slid from against the wall and onto the floor. Duchura held her scepter out to Zach now.

"Auck," I whispered in shock. "What did you do!"

Duchura said nothing. She grabbed my shoulder and pushed me up the staircase one last time.

CHAPTER XII

Duchura's scepter dug into my back as she forced me up the stairs.

"You *will* help us," she warned.

We made it into a room with nothing but a table and chair on either side: an interrogation room. I was forced down into the seat. I went to get up and someone pushed me back into it; four of Duchura's men were standing around me.

Duchura slapped Zach's scepter on the table.

"Get the scriptures," she demanded.

The servants and Duchura stood back to watch. I felt my face get hot, my hands cold and sweaty. I couldn't do it, even if I wanted to. I stared at the scepter, both my hands in my lap.

"Well get on with e'!" one of the servant men snorted.

I looked up at the people around me; their heads leaned forwards as they intently watched. They couldn't know the scepter would shock me, they would think I was no use to them. I grabbed the scepter, showing no expression of pain, keeping my body from shaking.

I knew the spell to get the scriptures, I had seen Zach do it; but I couldn't bring myself to do the same.

There was a small chance, a tiny bit of hope that I clung to, that if I didn't retrieve the scripture then they would believe Zach was still needed. He would be kept alive.

"Do it." Duchura leaned over the back of my chair, her hair brushing against mine.

I held the scepter in my hand, I couldn't control the shaking anymore; it was noticeable now.

"Do it!" A scepter jabbed into my throat.

I sat still. Zach had to be kept alive, and this was the only way to ensure that.

I saw Duchura draw her scepter out. She looked to the men and they nodded. My heart beat faster. I braced myself for the spell about to hit me. Duchura slid the scepter down my neck and to my back, to my Boggele mark.

All my muscles tensed. I held Zach's scepter tighter. Another heatwave rushed over my body. I felt something moving through me, inside of me.

The men smirked, watching as Duchura finally lowered her scepter. I felt as though something was different.

"What did you do?" An intolerable anger, something I had never felt before became insuppressible.

"Get the scriptures," she demanded yet again.

This time I obeyed. Rage flooded through me. I cast the spell with an unexplainable, newfound strength. The scriptures appeared on the table. I dropped the scepter on the floor. I didn't understand what had just happened, why I had just done that.

I frantically reached for the scepter again. I had to

get rid of the scriptures. Duchura had already picked one of them up. She opened it, looking dissatisfied. Then she looked to me. She saw I had gotten the scepter again -- ready to cast a spell at the scriptures. One of her men grabbed me. Another pulled the scepter from my hand.

"E' those them, master?" one of the men asked.

Duchura nodded. "There's a block."

"Wha' you mean?"

"It's sealed!" she yelled, pushing the man to the ground. "There are Charmer spells on it!"

"Get the girl to open e.'"

Duchura turned to face me upon the man's remark. She walked back to the table where I sat and forced the scripture into my hands.

"Remove the blocks."

I looked at her with unwavering eyes.

She breathed in heavily, her entire chest rising, nostrils flaring as she waited. I set the scripture on the table, all attention focused on me.

Something had changed. I had been unable to open the scripture myself earlier, but now I had Zach's scepter: a Charmer's scepter. I knew I would be able to us his magic do it now.

"Open the scripture!" Duchura's scepter was under my chin, the sharp tip pushing harder and harder against my skin.

"I can't," I cried sheepishly.

Duchura lowered her scepter. I sighed with relief. She believed it.

Then I felt the mark on my back; I could feel it

reappearing on my skin. I looked up to meet Duchura's gaze. The intense rage again flooded through me. Emotion took control over my senses. I took the scripture in my hands and picked up Zach's wand.

First spell removed, I felt it; second spell, destroyed. I couldn't stop myself. I felt as though I had to, Duchura had done something to me. I forced an image of Zach into my head; for Zach. I would stop for Zach. Another spell, gone. Auck had been imprisoned for months over this. Auck sacrificed his *life* to keep these spells in place. I had to find the will to stop.

The rage within me smoldered. Energy streamed from all around me, I harnessed it from every living thing around me. The image of Zach was still there, clearer now. He would *die* if I didn't stop. Duchura would *kill* him.

I concentrated hard, on Zach's face, his eyes, his deep blue eyes, vivacious, filled with life. I dropped the scepter from my hand. I stopped.

Duchura reached for the scripture. She flipped through the pages, finally looking up at the men around her, smiling with vengeance. I had stopped too late. The protection spells were gone -- all of them.

I jumped from my seat, lashing at Duchura, trying to get the scripture back. She took out her scepter, dropping the scripture, and casting a spell at me. I was knocked from my feet, scrambling for the scripture along with Duchura and the men. They got to it first.

Duchura opened it, this time not just flipping through the pages. She held her scepter to it and green rays of light pulsated through the pages. I got to my feet again, only to be stopped by a spell from one of the men. I coughed, a light red liquid coating my hand.

Duchura concentrated on the spell, closing her eyes as she cast it. The men looked to each other and smiled. I didn't know what any of it meant.

The knob to the door started to turn. I was the only one to notice. It opened slightly, left ajar for a moment before opening further. Duchura was still concentrating on the spell; the other men didn't seem to notice. There was no noise except for the sound of Duchura's incantation.

A face appeared in the crack of the door, a scepter poked through and was aimed at Duchura. She lost her concentration on the spell, dropped the scripture to the floor, and the door to the room was swung open wide, hitting the back wall. Thonet stepped inside, Jake and Velvet following behind her.

Thonet cast a spell at the men, Velvet went for the scripture.

"Drink this," Jake was standing over me, his arm outstretched with a vial of potion. I reached for it, drinking it without contemplation. I felt a recharge in energy; my red-stained skin began to clear itself of blood.

"Where's Zach?" I asked, ignoring my newfound rejuvenation. "Is he alive?"

Jake blocked me from being hit by a spell as he pulled me to my feet.

"We don't know. We haven't found them yet."

"Velvet!" I screamed as two of the men came up behind her. Jake cast a spell at them before they were able to advance on her any further. When she turned around I saw that she was clinging to the scripture.

Jake looked over to see that Thonet was outnumbered, circled by the men and Duchura. He tore the scripture from Velvet's hands and shoved it into mine.

"Go, find Zach and Auck. We'll come to get you guys."

"Auck's dead," I cried. I hadn't said it out loud to anyone else yet. It didn't seem real.

Jake looked at me with disbelief, then he turned his attention back to the room.

"Then find Zach, go!" Duchura looked in our direction right as I slipped out of the room.

I had forgotten how to get back to the dungeon. I ran through the halls, looking over my shoulder to see if anyone was following me. My feet moved faster than I could keep up with; I let them fall out from under me. I tripped, the scripture sliding further down the hall. I got to my feet, grabbing the scripture again. I had to keep going. Nothing looked familiar. Then, finally, I recognized where I was. I ran through hallway after hallway, turning corners, wandering through corridors. There was the stairwell, blood still on the steps.

"Zach!" My voice echoed down the winding rock walls.

The door was locked. I slammed against it, kicked violently at the lock. Then I realized I was still clenching Zach's scepter. I cast a spell at the lock, a spell of sheer rage. The latch holding the door to the wall snapped and the lock was blown to the ground in pieces. I stepped over the pieces of the door that remained intact and rushed into the room.

"Zach," I sighed with relief. He was there. He was alive. He was stooped over his father's side, holding his wrist, checking for a pulse. He heard me come in and jumped, startled by the sound of the door.

"Zach." I looked to him, his eyes watering, his face and chest bloody. "I'm sorry." I dropped the scripture down next to him and sat on the other side of Auck.

"He's suffering, Sable."

I looked up from Auck's body, unsure what Zach was talking about.

"He still has a pulse." Zach reached for the scripture. It was still glowing green, but the color was fading, becoming softer and softer. "We got it," he whispered to Auck. "We got it back."

I grabbed Zach's free hand. I felt a tear drip onto my arm. I relaxed my muscles, letting the scepter roll out of my hand and onto the floor.

Zach looked at the sound of the noise as the scepter hit the floor. Then, only with his eyes, he looked back up to me.

"You have my scepter?" he whispered, his eyes looking less grim. I nodded, handed it to him. "It might not be too late." He pointed it at Auck, casting the same spell over and over. I saw Auck's eyes start to flutter, his fingers weakly reached out towards us. Zach clenched his eyes shut, concentrating hard, refusing to cease casting the spell. He started to breathe heavier and his forehead grew damp from sweat.

"Zach, he's going to be okay. You should stop

now." His hand shook in mine as he gripped it more tightly.

A glowing light floated into the room. It slowly made its way over to where we sat.

"Zach." He still cast the spell time after time. The light hovered over us and dimmed into nothing. "Someone just found us." I heard footsteps echoing on the staircase. Auck was just now regaining consciousness; we didn't have time to move him and hide. Zach finally stopped the spell. He now held his scepter to the stairs. I looked at him, but his attention was focused on the other side of the room. He couldn't use any more magic, he had drained himself; I knew it, but he wouldn't accept it. I could hear the footsteps getting closer. Thonet rounded the corner. I had been holding my breath; I let it all out in one loud breath.

She hurried over to us, pulling something out of the air with her scepter.

"Here, drink." She offered Zach a vial of the potion and forced one into Auck's mouth. Jake and Velvet came into the room a moment later.

"We don't have much time," Velvet urged.

"Are you two strong enough for a Hermitian spell?" Thonet asked her children. They looked at each other warily nodding. "Quickly now, everyone link together."

Velvet reached for my hand; we were all linked in a square.

"Dad, you can't let go," Zach said to Auck. He was still weak; the potion had only made him more lucid, but he nodded understandingly. I held onto Zach and Velvet's hands, unsure of what was about to happen.

I didn't see anything around us anymore, a blur of

colors and vaguely recognizable figures consumed the emptiness. The colors started to focus, the figures I now recognized as trees. We were back in the forest, outside of Duchura's castle.

Velvet and Jake were panting hard; everyone had used too much magic. We still all stood in a circle, all looking back and forth at one another. Zach and I made eye contact, he smiled, the first genuine smile I had seen on his face in a long time. Then he laughed slightly. Thonet was smiling now, too, Jake and Auck, even Velvet. We did it. We had the scripture and we were safe.

Thonet offered Auck another vial of potion. He drank it without hesitation now. His muscle mass grew quickly, and his wounds shrank into nothing. The thin, tired man looked younger now. He looked up at me, his eyes blue, exactly like Zach's, an almost eerie resemblance.

He smiled, hugging his son, but still looking at me from over Zach's shoulder. Then he walked towards me.

"Sable," this time as he spoke he did not cough or struggle for air, "It is good to meet you. I am Auck." He stuck out his hand.

I went to shake hands and the same surge of energy flowed through me and into him that I had felt the first time Zach and I touched. Auck looked startled; he felt it too, but he didn't say anything.

Zach looked to Auck and me; he was the one to break the silence. "Thonet, thank you."

Thonet nodded.

"How did you know where we were? How did you know we would be in trouble?" Zach asked befuddled.

"Winters came to our hostel. He asked if we had seen either of you. He said he had made a mistake. He was beside himself. It took almost the entire afternoon to get him to tell us what was going on."

"He told us he shouldn't have told you where Duchura's castle was. We knew you went for your father."

Zach shook his head, I knew he was upset. "If you hadn't come for us…"

"But we did," Thonet interrupted.

Velvet looked around the forest.

"We should leave," she snipped. "There's going to be Boggeles everywhere looking for us."

"She's right," Thonet said.

"You use the Orion tree to get through to here?" Jake asked Zach. He nodded. "Do you remember how to get back to it?"

"No," Zach sighed.

"Auck, do you know?" Jake asked.

Auck was faced with his back turned towards us. He didn't answer.

"Dad?" Zach asked. Auck still didn't reply. "Dad, what is it?"

Auck turned around with the scripture in hands and watched the green rays of light seep out into the atmosphere. "What was done with the scripture?" he asked gravely.

My heart leaped. I was the one who had done that. I took the scripture from Auck and stared wide-eyed at it as I frantically flipped through the pages. It was the first time I was actually able to see what was inside of them. All the spells, all the pictures, everything was visible.

"What did I do?" I said to myself. "Auck, I, I couldn't stop myself. I didn't even know what I was doing back there!" I felt as though I was hyperventilating and Zach put his hand on my shoulder. I looked around at everyone and they all had the same worried expressions. "What did I do?" I yelled. I could feel the unexplained energy surging throughout my body again. It was making me crazy.

"Sable," Zach said with both hands on my shoulders. I couldn't even focus on him. All I could think about, all I could feel, was the energy entering and exiting my body in a frenzied manner. "Sable!" he yelled a little louder.

I could process what he was saying, but I was too overwhelmed to answer him back. I could feel my hands start to shake and I looked up at Zach for help. He quickly jumped back from me as our eyes met.

"Dad!" he yelled.

Auck came closer and looked into my eyes. "Oh, my God."

I was finally able to concentrate enough to speak, "What is happening?" I asked them.

"She's somehow channeling Boggele energy through the scripture," Auck said to the others.

"Auck, help me!" I begged. I didn't know what to do. I could feel something foreign inside of me fighting to get out. I couldn't explain it.

"It's okay Sable, we'll fix this," he said to me. "Hand me the scripture." I couldn't get myself to let go.

That's why her eyes are green. She tapped into Boggele magic, a lot of it."

"What do we do?" Zach said. "How did this happen?" he said, worried.

"Duchura did this," Auck said. "She restored her Boggele magic."

"Thonet, hand me my scepter," Auck said.

Thonet picked it up, but didn't throw it over to him. "Auck, what are you going to do?"

"I need to take away the Boggele energy from her."

"You can't do that. She has too much, and you couldn't harness that energy anyway, you don't have the Boggele power to do that."

"There is no other way! Duchura gave Sable her Boggele magic back. I have no idea how that is even possible, but she did it! And if we don't get rid of that energy I don't know what's going to happen. No one could possibly control that amount of magic all at once!"

"Dad, you can't do that. It's not possible," Zach said.

"Hand me the scepter!" he yelled to Thonet.

"You are too weak, Dad, and it wouldn't work anyway!"

I screamed out in frustration, I couldn't think.

"Hand me the scepter! I can do it myself."

Auck and Thonet exchanged looks. I reached out for the scepter with a shaking arm, but they didn't give it to me.

"Please," I begged, "I can do it."

"Sable, you don't even know the spell to do that.

I'm not sure I even know how to do that," Thonet said.

"I can do it."

"Look at her! She's going mad; she needs to get this magic out of her!" Velvet yelled to the others as she gave me her scepter.

I took the scepter and held it up to myself. I wasn't even sure what I was saying, but it was some sort of spell. I felt myself relaxing. I could feel my energy draining, but that was good. The magic was leaving me.

"Sable, stop!" Zach yelled.

I ignored him and kept the spell going.

"Sable! You're killing yourself! You've drained the magic!"

I could feel that all the Boggele magic had left my body, but I couldn't get myself to stop the spell.

"Sable!" Jake and Zach both lunged towards me at the same time. Someone grabbed the scepter from me and the other pushed me out of the spell's range. Zach kept me from falling. He lowered me to the ground.

"It's gone," I whispered, closing my eyes.

CHAPTER XIII

I could hear the others talking, Zach in particular.

"Why isn't she awake yet?" he asked again.

"She's okay. Just give it a little longer."

"Is the magic gone for good?"

"No," it was Auck who was talking now. "Duchura has restored it. Every time there is Boggele magic she will be able to tap into it."

"Does that mean..." Zach grew silent again, wondering if he should even ask, "she's really Duchura's daughter?"

I already knew what the answer was going to be.

"No. Not for certain. Duchura is powerful, there could be many ways she could give someone Boggele magic. She wants us to believe that the legend is true."

"How else could it be explained?"

I rubbed at my eyes now, getting back to my feet. Auck looked to me.

"It's just a legend," I heard him whisper to Zach.

Zach noticed I was awake.

"Sable." He looked into my eyes. I presumed they were no longer green. "Are you okay?"

I nodded. Then I looked over to the others again, huddled around in a circle.

"What are they doing?" I asked.

Zach looked over to the group then back to me. "They're fixing Velvet's scepter."

"What happened to it?" I asked.

"When you were doing that spell, it caught fire."

"What?" I asked confused. I had no memories of that. "I did that?"

"We don't know what happened. You were harnessing too much energy I guess, and for a Charmer wand, it just couldn't take all the magic."

"All the Boggele magic."

"Yeah."

We were both thinking the same thing; there was no other explanation other than my Boggle magic was restored, by Duchura, by my mother.

"Can they fix it?" I saw Velvet glance over to me before turning her attention back to the circle.

"They'll figure something out. Don't worry."

"What about the scripture?" I asked. "What did I do to it?"

"We're going to figure all of this out, I promise."

"Zach. What happened with the scripture?"

"The Charmer blocks are gone."

"No," I looked up to Zach. "They can't be. All of them?"

He nodded.

"What does this mean?"

"They are able to get into the Charmer world now."

"They are going to come for the scripture again, aren't they? In the Charmer world this time."

"We can restore the spells, it will fix everything."

"Okay, well they need to do it now," I said walking towards the others.

"They can't until we are back in the Charmer world, but we will. It will be okay."

"The Boggeles will kill, won't they? They'll kill the Charmers until they get what they're looking for, or until we restore the spells."

"You can't think like that. It's not your fault this happened."

"Yes, it is."

Thonet walked over to the two of us before we were able to say anything more.

"Is Velvet's scepter fixed?" I asked.

"Nearly good as new, don't you worry; it'll just need a day or two longer to strengthen up a bit more."

"I'm sorry. For everything."

"Everything is going to be alright. You can't blame yourself for what happened. It was Duchura."

"No. It was me. And everyone who dies from this point on will have died because of what I did."

"We'll fix this before anyone has to die."

"Well then," Thonet quickly changed the subject. "We best get out of here soon, I wouldn't quite like to spend the night here."

"Thonet is right. We need to get back to the Charmers," Auck said as he started walking deeper into the woods. "Boggeles are going to start flooding the portals as soon as they realize the spells have been broken, but if we act fast we still will have time to stop them."

"No one knows where the Orion tree is?" Velvet asked irritated, still inspecting her scepter from top to bottom.

"We'll have to split up to be able to find it before dark," Auck said. "When someone finds it send a spell into the air for the others to see.

"Do you really think it is a good idea to split up right now?" Velvet interrupted. "There are going to be Boggeles everywhere, they'll see any spell we send out also. We'll be safer together."

Everyone looked to one another for an answer.

"Let's go then," Velvet demanded, "We can't just stay here all night thinking of a better plan."

We all walked further into the forest. No one recognized anything that looked familiar. "What if we try a seeker spell?" Jake asked.

"Charmer magic is blocked, it wouldn't work," Velvet snapped.

"Well, like you said, we can't just stay here all night."

"Fine, try it."

"Illumination seeker!"

We all waited in anticipation to see what would happen. Nothing did.

"I can do it. The Charmer block won't affect me."

"You can't, Sable, it could trigger the Boggele magic in you."

"Try it again Jake," Thonet said. "I'll merge my magic with yours. That might be enough to break through the block."

"Illumination Seeker!"

A faint light lingered in the air this time. We all watched as it drifted through the trees. It moved faster now. We ran to keep up. Thonet couldn't keep up with the rest of us and Jake stayed back to help her maneuver through the branches.

We stood at the tree's base, waiting for Jake and Thonet. It looked different now: the dead spindles of branches seemed more prominent. They penetrated through the green on the far side of the tree. The leaves looked dryer, less vibrant.

"The magic is merging," Auck said, looking up at the branches. "Boggeles will be able to enter through here."

I could hear the sound of dried leaves crunch as Thonet and Jake grew nearer.

"Okay," Thonet said, breathing hard, "we're ready."

Auck looked up wearily at the tree. "As soon as you get through get to our village. Don't wait up for the others. It's safer to get out of sight as soon as possible."

"Where do we go once we're at the village?" Jake asked.

Auck drew out a piece of paper with his scepter, then tore it in three and wrote something on each.

"Our shop, this is the address." He handed Velvet and Thonet the other two corners.

"Sable, you stay with Zach; he'll travel with you."

Auck was the first to go through the portal. Finally, just Zach and I remained.

"Ready?" he said, grabbing my hand.

We walked through, back out into the Charmer

world, to the war ruins. It was dark; we must have just missed the sunset. I couldn't see much through the forest, but I knew there were Boggeles around. There had to be -- they had to know the entrance was no longer sealed by now.

I saw Zach looking around, too, we were both silent, listening for any noises, looking for any movement in the dark.

"I've got to do a Hermitian spell to get us back to the village."

"By yourself?" I asked, remembering how much magic it took to do that spell the last time.

"Our magic was blocked the last time we tried, that's why Thonet needed help. I can do it alone now." I could hear in his voice that he himself was not convinced.

It was too dark this time to see what was going on; I only saw blackness, no shapes morphing in the dark. Then Zach let go of my hands. He squinted, trying to make out anything familiar. I waited for him to say something. He only motioned me forwards.

Blurred lights came into focus in the distance. Zach's village was down below. We walked at first, both unsure of what might be out ahead of us. A steady thumping noise broke through the silence. Zach listened intently to see where it was coming from.

"Thonet?" He whispered.

There was no reply. The noise grew closer, the beat became faster. Zach and I quickened our pace; we jogged, sprinted as the noise became louder. I looked over my shoulder. The noise was still there, but no figure, no explanation for the noise revealed itself.

A dim light appeared in front of us. Zach stuck his arm out in front of me and we stopped, waiting to see what would happen. The light went out. Zach walked in front of me, guarding me from what might lay in front of us. There were Boggeles here already, we both knew it; they just hadn't made their move yet.

From the corner of my eye I saw the light again, this time moving towards us.

"Zach." He saw it too now. We ran forwards, whoever else was out here was behind us, following us.

Something hit the back of my leg, I stopped running. Zach must not have noticed; I could hear him still moving.

"Zach," I whispered. I saw the light again, moving closer to me, it was a spell, about to hit me again. I cringed as it hit me. "Zach!"

I could hear movement from all directions. I got to my feet but when my foot touched the ground pain seared through it. I looked for the light again, but it was gone. I stumbled forward loudly; I couldn't seem to keep any quieter. Footsteps were moving towards me -- I didn't know whose, I didn't know if Zach had realized I was no longer behind him. I felt a shove and I was knocked to the ground. Someone was on top of me. I screamed.

"Sable," I kicked at the body on top of me, "Sable, it's me."

Another light came towards us; Zach had pushed me out of the way. He got to his feet and ran towards the soft glow that was out ahead. Light streamed through the air; Zach must have hit someone. I got to my feet, running towards him, trying to see where he had gone. I saw him standing, looking over a figure I was unable to make out. Then I got closer.

"Oh, my God," I said with relief, "Velvet."

Zach helped her to her feet, she too stumbled forward. She shook with fear.

"I thought you were Boggeles. I was all alone; I didn't know how to get down to the village," she cried.

Zach led the way down into the back alleys.

"The others are probably worried about us," he said, unlocking the back door to the shop.

It was empty inside. Zach walked to the opposite side of the store and motioned us over. I could hear faint voices now, coming from above. He led the way up a staircase and lifted up a hatch door to the attic. The others were all there.

"You're here, thank goodness!" Thonet hugged each of us as we entered the room. "We were going to go back out to look for you."

"We're fine," Velvet said, squirming out of her mother's grasp.

Six hammocks had been hung from the ceiling.

"We'll stay here for the night," Auck said. "The wanted posters of the three of us are still up, so we must stay out of sight."

"The three of us?"

Auck nodded, "Sable has been discovered."

"How are we going to go out in public?"

Auck shrugged, "We keep our heads low and move

quickly, it's the only way."

"Do we have any sort of plan yet?" Velvet said. She was in a bad mood, not surprisingly.

"We've got to get the scriptures somewhere safe," Zach said, "The vanishing spell I've been using isn't secure enough anymore."

"Zach is right, I'm surprised Duchura hasn't figured that out yet as it is."

"I know a place where we can hide them temporarily," Zach said.

"Good. As soon as we find a way to get into the Prism Building we can move them there and I can work on restoring the spells," Auck said.

"The Prism Building?" I asked confused.

"Where the scriptures are stored. It's the only place the spells can be restored. It's a government building though. We'll have a tough time getting past everyone without being seen," Auck said.

"We only have four of the sections though, don't we need them all?" Zach had pulled the scripture sections into the room with his scepter, they had all been merged back into one scripture so far, but there were still three parts missing.

"There have been others in search of the scriptures as well. I have lost contact with them since Duchura found me, but I will find a way to reach them. Let's hope they have the last three by now."

I crawled into the hammock closest to the hatch door. Zach took the one beside me. Everyone else seemed to be asleep. I couldn't close by eyes; they were fixated on the hatch door. Duchura was here somewhere, looking for the scriptures, looking for me.

The darkness in the attic gave way to dim light. I jumped when I saw it. Jake and Zach were awake, too. They had their scepters out and cast streams of light at the walls. I watched as they collided against the ceiling and dimmed into nothing. After a while Velvet thrust a flaming red light out of her scepter towards the other two lights. I saw Jake and Zach exchange smirks and then the lights went out.

The hammocks creaked as everyone in the room tossed and turned. My eyes fluttered as I continued to stay awake, looking at the hatch, sure that it was being slightly lifted then closed again; but I was tired, and the hatch had blurred into two as I stared. Everything blurred until my eyes were too dry to keep open.

A banging sound jarred me awake. It was coming from downstairs. I looked to the others but they were still asleep. I heard the noise again. I slid out of my hammock, wincing as my foot touched the ground. I looked back to the other hammocks: Thonet's was empty.

I shook Jake lightly. I thought he might know where his mom went. It startled him so much that he rolled out of his hammock onto the floor. He got to his feet, rubbing his eyes.

"Jake, where's your mom?" I whispered.

He looked to her hammock then back to me. We both heard the banging noise from downstairs and woke up the others.

Auck was the first to go over to the hatch. We stood

back in the room and watched as he lifted it. Someone was standing down below. Auck climbed down the stairs and into the store front. I looked to Zach. I saw his forehead crinkle. The rest of us ventured down the stairs.

Thonet was standing at the bottom, hitting her scepter against the side of the stairwell.

"Mom, what are you doing?" Velvet asked, irritated.

"You're finally here," she sighed. "I've been trying to get your attention all morning."

"What are you doing down here?" Zach asked, looking around the room.

"I cooked breakfast, but the door to the attic had locked when I went to get everyone."

In the middle of the store there was a wooden table propped up by a broom hovering vertically above the floor, and six seats were placed around it. I looked around confused.

"Well, come on now, sit," Thonet said, gesturing to the table.

The only sign of food was the lingering smell of something terribly burned. Thonet finally sat down and took out her scepter, pointing it at the tablecloth. Plates appeared, filling the entire surface, covered with pancakes.

"Thank you, Thonet," Auck said as he finished the last of what was on his plate. I couldn't remember the last time Zach and I had eaten; and when I looked over at him I saw as he reached for yet another pancake.

"What's our plan?" Velvet said, interrupting the rest of the table.

Everyone grew quiet. We all turned to one another, but no one spoke.

"I have an idea, I guess," Zach said, "but it's," he paused, "it's crazy."

"What is it?" Thonet asked.

"If we can get Elchyard to believe us, that we are trying to protect the scriptures, he'll be able to inform the council. We'd be free again."

"Elchyard?" Jake asked.

"Our mayor."

"Why wouldn't it work?"

"Well, the three of us can't be seen in public, which means that you guys would have to be the ones to find him and get him somewhere quiet where the rest of us can meet with him to explain. He's not just going to follow strangers out into some back alleyway though."

"What do you mean?"

"You'll have to force him."

Jake nodded, raising his eyebrows.

"The rest of us can hide the scriptures until we gain entry to the Prism."

"I would make more potions for us but I am afraid I am out of supplies," Thonet added.

"We can do it," Jake said. "We just need some time. Where will we find Elchyard?"

Auck held his finger in the air, indicating for us to wait. Then he walked into a back section of the store. He came back in the room with what looked like a large telephone book.

"This is him," he said, flipping through the pages,

stopping on an ad with a picture of a tall, thin man in a suit and tie. "Ask anyone for directions to the Prism."

Velvet pushed past the rest of us for a closer look at the picture.

"Where do we meet once we have found him?"

"The alleyway behind the Prism; we'll wait there."

"Okay," Jake sighed; I could tell he was nervous.

"Think there will be a lot of Boggeles by now?" Velvet asked to no one in particular.

We all knew the answer to that already. Velvet looked back and nodded without anyone saying a thing.

"We'll be careful."

"Mom, I want you to stay back with the others," Jake said, "If you're with them it might not be as noticeable that they are fugitives."

"You can't go out there alone, Jake. I'm coming with you."

"I have Velvet. Promise, we will be safe, we won't get caught."

"He's right," Auck said. "It would make more sense if you stayed back with the rest of us."

Thonet looked to Auck with longing eyes. Then she turned back to Jake and Velvet.

"By now the Boggeles will have found out the blockade spells have been lifted. They will be flooding through, all looking for the scripture. Be careful."

Jake walked towards the back door, Velvet reluctantly following behind.

The three of us stood back in the store, peering through the back windows as the two of them walked further down the alleyway.

"Zach, where is the hiding place you have for the scripture?" Auck asked.

"By the Prism. I can't get us there through the alleyways though. It's not far from where Jake and Velvet are headed."

"May as well leave now," Auck said, peering down both sides of the street before stepping outside.

We had nothing to hide us or disguise us when we emerged onto the streets. Zach and I wore hoods over our heads and Auck stood between us, keeping his head low and his face towards the ground. It was raining and we each held umbrellas close to our heads to help stay concealed from the public.

There were no signs of Boggeles yet. It made me uneasy.

As we walked I noticed a few people were starting to stare. One man walked along side of us and looked intently at Zach. Zach looked forward, only glancing at the man through the corner of his eyes. Finally he walked away and we quickened our pace.

Our wanted signs were plastered on a building ahead. I looked to Zach and he looked back with an expression of uncertainty. Guards stood in a village square that lay ahead. It was too obvious who we were; we weren't going to make it through without being caught, but Zach continued to lead us forward through the crowds of people.

Without warning Zach grabbed my hand and we ran through the remainder of the square. An outlet to an alley was nearby and he ran towards it, Auck and Thonet following behind.

"I shouldn't have taken us through there, there were too many guards," he said, checking to make sure we weren't followed. Auck and Thonet emerged around the corner a moment later and Thonet rested her hands on her knees trying to catch her breath.

"The guards didn't see you two?" Auck asked, confirming we were okay to keep moving forward.

"We got out of there just in time," Zach said. The rain was picking up and I hope that people assumed we were running to get out of the storm.

The alleys were much different than the streets. They weren't filled with people and vendors on every corner. They were dirty and became darker as the heavy cloud cover moved closer to the village.

"You think this could mean the first of the Boggeles are moving in?" Zach said, looking up at the grey sky.

"Storm riders, no doubt," Auck said back. "It won't take long before the rest of the Boggeles start to follow."

"There!" someone shouted and we all turned back, squinting through the heavy rain to see who had caught up with us. There were three guards with a short lady standing between them, pointing her plump finger out towards us.

They ran towards us and Auck, Thonet, and Zach pulled out their scepters. Zach shouted out a spell and four of the dumpsters that had been sitting by one of the shop walls were knocked over, blocking the men's path. Garbage blew out of them and littered the ground behind us. The lady ran away without hesitation, but the guards pulled out their scepters in response and continued in our direction, hurling the dumpsters out of the way.

The ground became slick from rain and loose gravel. I ran without contemplation, trying to keep up with Zach. I heard someone skid across the ground moments later -- Thonet had slipped. The guards advanced on her.

"Zach!" He looked back to see the guards nearly caught up with Thonet and pulled out his scepter. He pointed it at a set of streetlights suspended above the first guard's head. The light bulbs shattered and the man stepped back in alarm. Thonet had just enough time to scramble away.

"Oh, thank you, dearie!" she said as she caught up to us.

The alley opened up into a large square area of concrete with four separate openings to choose from.

"Which one?" I asked, panicking.

Zach looked around, "This way!" he yelled, choosing a path at random. "Go back!" he shouted. Two more guards had appeared further down the walkway. The other guards had caught back up with us and closed in on us from the opposite side of the narrow alleyway. Zach cast a spell out at one of them and they quickly cast a counter spell, thrusting Zach's magic back in our direction. It hit Zach and a deep gash bled on his arm. He grunted with frustration and then cast yet another, only to be stopped again.

Auck shook the doorknob to one of the back entrances to the stores, pulling on it, casting spells at it, nothing made it open. The guards drew in closer. Zach ran to one of the doors, blew off the doorknob with a spell, but it still would not open. Blood trickled down his arm and dripped from his fingertips as he banged against the door.

"Here! Get in!" Auck had opened one of the doors.

The guards ran towards us now. Thonet cast one last spell at them before the door was slammed behind her. Zach stood with his back pressed against the door. He wiped his forehead, leaving a stain of red on his face. We all stood quietly, waiting to see what the guards would do. I could only hear the sound of rain battering the other side of the door. Water droplets splattered the side of my face, and I turned to see an open window facing the alleyway. Zach tried to get the door locked, but his hands were stiff and wet from the cold of outside.

I could hear the guards talking as I approached the window. I watched as they looked around confused, all pulling at the same umbrella for coverage.

"What did you do to them?" I asked looking back at Thonet.

As I spoke the guards turned their heads in our direction. Thonet pushed me away from the window and we stood pressed against the wall. I could hear them walking towards us. They breathed loudly as they peered through the opening in the window. They seemed to have forgotten what they were doing.

"Hello," one of the guards said, "someone in there?"

"No one is in there! The store's locked." The other guard grunted. He pulled the two men away from the window and they slowly walked back down the alley and into the streets. Thonet and I both peered out to see where they were going. The largest of the guards at the back of the line couldn't seem to walk in a straight line. He swayed back and forth and ran into a garbage can.

"Sorry, ma'am," he said, leaning against it for support.

"Somewhat minor confusion spell," Thonet said, as the guard in the front of the line halted, the other men piled up behind him and started chuckling.

It was dark inside whatever place we had just entered and Zach sent a spark of light through the room. As my eyes adjusted I watched as thousands of different objects filled the shelves. Carts of food rolled past us and up a ramp to the second floor.

"What is this place?" I asked, craning my head back as far is it would go to see the upper level of the store.

"It's Mr. Lu's Everything Store," Zach said in astonishment. "When a person walks in they will find whatever it is they desire occupying the room." We wandered further into the room, looking at the constant new appearances of items that filled the store.

"What are you children doing?" Thonet exclaimed, "Stop, come back!" she shouted.

"What?"

"We can't stay here. We have to find Jake and Velvet."

I wasn't sure if Zach hadn't noticed Thonet talking or if he was just ignoring her, but he continued to wander through the building.

"We have to go!" Auck yelled.

"Hold on," Zach said. He had grabbed something

off one of the shelves and walked back over to us. It was dark. I couldn't see what it was until he got closer. He set a radio on the table for everyone to listen. He adjusted the wiring at the top until the crackling noise faded away. "They're talking about the disappearances."

I looked to Zach, worried.

"What do you mean the disappearances?"

"All the spells that were broken from the scriptures, the people who cast them are starting to disappear."

"Why?" My heart was beating faster now. I caused this.

"Charmers become more vulnerable to outsiders when their spells are overtaken. Boggeles have moved in on the village, no doubt. They've begun the killings."

"Seek shelter in numbers," I heard the radio crackle. Zach moved the antennas, but the signal was gone.

"We need to find my children, now," Thonet's voice shook.

CHAPTER XIV

We were all less at ease now. The few people who remained outside were scattering, running every which way, searching for their family members in the alleyway in a chaotic frenzy to seek shelter. Zach led the way through the back streets, constantly checking to make sure we were all following close behind.

A lady in a rain jacket ran by us screaming out someone's name. Then she ran back towards us and stopped Zach from going any further.

"My daughter, Analyse, have you seen her?" she begged for help, pulling on Zach's arm, trying to drag him back the opposite direction. "Please!"

A blaring siren began to drown out the lady's screams. She let go of Zach's arm at the start of the noise, looking around as mascara drenched her face in black ink. She ran again, screaming the girl's name, turning the corner of a building, gone.

"They've spotted one," Zach yelled over the alarm, squinting back at us through the thickening rains.

We turned corner after corner, weaving aimlessly through the streets, trying to keep up with Zach's sudden path changes, swerving out of people's way as they ran into stores, slamming doors behind them, locking their windows, fighting over cutouts in the alleyways for even the slightest bit of coverage from the storm, from the Boggeles. Abruptly, we halted. The alleyway we were about to enter had been sealed by a locked gate.

"Come on!" Zach yelled, slamming at the gates, yanking on their metal bars. "Come on! Someone!" he yelled, pressing his face through the gate's metal slats. No one came. "We're going to have to go out onto the main streets."

We headed back in the other direction, frantically scanning the alleys for an outlet back onto the main street. The alarm sounded stronger now; we were getting closer to the sight of the spotting. I passed Zach; he started to slow to an almost complete stop.

"Sable!" Zach's voice sounded faint now. It took me a moment to even notice he was calling out my name.

I looked back. He was still at the edge of the alleyway I had already entered. Goose bumps brandished my skin as I realized I was alone in the alley. I ran back, my feet nearly falling out from under me.

"Why didn't you come?" I panted as I made it back to where they stood.

"We can't go down that way. It's too dangerous, especially right now." Zach looked to a wooden sign that had been staked in the ground by the opening. The letters carved into it read 'Rancorous Cauldron.'

"What's Rancorous Cauldron?"

Thonet had already started walking away from the entrance and Zach ran to catch up with her.

"Boggele followers are known to congregate in

those areas. Bad place to be spotted, especially now," Auck said.

We came to an opening to the main street after trying countless walkways. There were more people in the streets than in the alleys, all seeking somewhere to conceal themselves from the public.

"We just need to get to the alleyway across the street, that's the place for the scriptures," Zach said as he ran out into the square. The rest of us followed, not trying to hide our faces, or keep discreet, no one would be watching us; no one had a care for what we were doing. Everyone scrambled for shelter. We were the only ones still venturing through the streets, not looking for a hideout.

"We're close now," Zach said, walking into yet another alleyway. The sirens became quieter as we walked, and my heart began to beat slower. I felt safer, more secure in the narrow back streets.

Zach stopped at a dead end. We all circled around him. He whispered a spell to the ground. We stood watching in anticipation. Auck pushed us back slightly as if the ground would give way. Nothing happened.

Zach pulled the scriptures out of the air with his scepter and held them above the ground, letting them drop. As they hit the concrete they disappeared.

We looked at him with amusement. Thonet stuck out her foot and tapped at the ground. Solid

"They're soft spots," he explained, "I've only found a few, but the ground is hollow underneath."

"They're secure then?" Auck confirmed.

Zach nodded. "The alleys behind the Prism are just

up ahead. It's faster to go through the main streets though."

"We need to get there as fast as we can. I'm surprised that the Boggles haven't made their presence more noticeable by now. The faster we can secure the scriptures the better. We'll go through the main streets," Auck said.

I was confused as we entered the main streets again. Even more people than before were out.

"I thought the streets would be empty by now," I said, feeling more paranoid about being seen. More sirens were going off and people pushed past one another, all moving in different directions, children being led into buildings, adults standing guard, all with their scepters in hand. A cluster in the center of the square attracted more and more people. We were forced deeper into the midst of the crowd. Everyone was shouting. Some people moved closer to the middle, others pushed their way out, expressions of terror on their faces.

"What's going on?" I looked around for Zach and the others; we were all being pushed in separate directions. I reached for Thonet's hand and we managed to reconnect.

We were in the heart of the crowd. Everyone had been circling around a man, dead, lying on the ground. I looked away at the sight, but something made me glance back one more time. The man was a Boggele, around his neck was a Matiasma, the worship pendant.

"Hurry, this way." Thonet pulled me away from the crowd, my eyes fixated on the pendant until it was out of sight. I controlled the energy that pulsated through me. It wasn't as strong this time. Thonet didn't even seem to realize I had tapped into the Boggele magic.

"You okay?" She asked.

"Yeah." I turned my head away from her as I spoke refusing to meet her eyes for fear that mine were green, that I had accidentally drawn too much energy from the Boggele's pendant.

I felt a hand grab my shoulder. I turned around and Zach was being engulfed in the crowd again. He pushed his way out and we stood in a close huddle.

"Do any of you see Auck?"

"There!" Zach pointed over the crowd.

"Auck!" Thonet yelled, trying to make her way over to him.

A stranger's head turned in our direction as Thonet screamed Auck's name. He recognized us. Zach pulled me through another group of people and out of sight of the man.

"Thonet!"

Thonet thrust her arm in the air, she had grabbed hold of Auck and we had all managed to get away from what now appeared to be the start of a riot.

"Thonet, a man back there recognized us when you called Auck's name. We need to keep quiet."

"Oh, yes; sorry, dearie."

"Did any of you see what the crowd was all about?" Auck asked.

Thonet and I exchanged glances.

"There was a Boggele, dead," Thonet said.

"First of many I presume," Auck said, looking back at the crowd, now starting to disband.

"Across the street," Zach said, "there's the Prism." I saw the tip of the old building rising high in the distance. "It'll be guarded even more heavily than usual by now."

The street was packed with cars; horns honked and they all swerved around one another. Thonet and I were the last to cross. Zach and Auck had already made it to the other side and disappeared behind a stone wall. Cars changed their shapes to avoid hitting us as we ran across; sometimes ten at a time passing us on the same narrow road, expanding after they went around us.

A network of buildings lay on the other side of the street behind the rock wall. Thonet spotted an opening between two of the buildings to an alleyway. It was quieter there.

"Zach?" I whispered.

"What took you so long, I was ready to come back to get you," he said, emerging from a small cutout in the wall.

"Velvet and Jake should be right around here," Auck interrupted. "Are you all ready?"

We nodded and Auck explained what to do once we were with Elchyard.

"We won't have much time before people come looking for him, and remember, no one says where the scriptures are hidden until we know he believes us. This is our one chance to clear our names and get into the Prism."

"It's here, right around the corner," Zach whispered, motioning us forwards. "I hear them." He was the first one to step into the alley where Mayor Elchyard stood waiting. Jake and Velvet stood on both sides of him with their scepters at the ready.

"Thieves! Thieves!" he shouted as he saw us. He attempted to run past Velvet to get to us but she cast a spell knocking him back. Jake cast another spell and the exits sealed themselves off. Elchyard stood frozen. "Where are the scriptures?"

Zach stepped past Velvet and approached him. Elchyard slowly stuck his hand in his pocket, wrapping his fingers around something.

"Now, let us explain," Zach said calmly, watching as Elchyard tightened his grip on the object.

"Give me the scriptures and you can leave with no punishments," Elchyard said as he discreetly slid his scepter out of his pocket.

Jake and Velvet both shouted out a spell when they saw him pull out the scepter. The exits to the alley shimmered and then went back to normal. I wasn't sure what they had done, but it put Elchyard on edge. He fiddled in his pocket and tightened his grip on his scepter.

Zach yelled another spell and Elchyard's scepter was flung to the ground. Elchyard lunged for it and Zach cast another spell, leaving a light ring of fire burning around the scepter.

"Listen to us," Zach demanded. "We never took the scripture, we never separated it back out into its seven sections. My father was taken by Duchura. She was the one who has been stealing the scriptures, not my dad. She knew she couldn't open the scripture herself, that's why she took him in the first place. She thought that if she framed my dad…"

Auck took over the conversation, "We have almost all of the scriptures back now. If you can get us into the Prism Building and clear our names we can restore the spells. The Boggeles will be gone."

"You lie, Auck!" Elchyard yelled, leaning in towards Auck's face.

"And why would you think that!" Zach yelled. He was angry, every time he yelled the flames around Elchyard's scepter rose.

"Because, the night the first scripture section went missing you were the only one in the building. No one else went in or out that night besides you!" Elchyard abruptly stopped speaking and watched the flames creep closer to his scepter.

Auck looked as though he was thinking hard for a moment.

"How did you know I was the only one there that night?"

Elchyard paused for a minute before talking, "I watched you with the orbs."

"An orb wouldn't work around the Prism, you of all people would know that," Zach said, somewhat bewildered. "Why would you lie?"

"Enough!" Elchyard's yell echoed off the alley walls. I will give you two options. Get me the scripture, the full scripture, and you can leave like none of this ever happened, or I will have you all imprisoned."

"The scriptures would be no use to you, Elchyard. Just listen to me!"

Elchyard was silent. He glanced from Auck to the

ring of fire as he listened, watching the flames creep in towards his scepter.

"The scripture keepers are the only ones who can restore the spells. I *have* to be the one to do it, but I can only do it if you can get us into the Prism, if you state our innocence. Do you understand that?" Auck begged.

"You cannot be trusted!"

"I have to be trusted! It is the *only* way."

"Just give me the scripture. I will deal with all of this myself. Where is it?" Elchyard pressed.

"It's hidden, protected for the time being."

"Isabella Writhm," Elchyard turned to speak to me now, "Tell me, where is the scripture, where are all of the sections?"

Isabella. No one knew my full name, no one except Duchura had known. His voice all of a sudden sounded familiar. He worked for Scarlette. He was the man I wasn't able to see in the orb back on Scarlette's street because of the missing piece of glass. He was the one that 'they could trust.' He was a Boggele.

"We can trust you, that's what Scarlette said isn't it?" I yelled. Zach and the others looked confused.

Elchyard took a step towards me as I moved back.

"Give me the scripture." He stared at me, squinting, scowling as he approached me further.

"Who are you siding with?"

He looked to his scepter again, approached it so closely that the flames nearly singed his skin. The fire rose up higher, hotter. I shielded my face as a wave of smoke blew in my direction and embers poured down on my bare skin. Even with the storm the fire grew, the rain was not enough to stop it.

"Zach!" I yelled. "Stop!"

Elchyard lunged into the fire, flames erupting around him. I became separated from the others by a growing wall of ash and fire. I could see Elchyard's outline through the cloud of smoke. His narrow shoulders, slightly hunched back, hands clenched with a small, elongated object. He had gotten his scepter back.

"Now," I heard a voice say from behind me. "Where is it?" Elchyard lunged over me, whispering hot breath into my ear.

"Get away from me!" He grabbed my wrist, unrelenting in his grip, dragging me away from the fire, from the others.

"Zach!"

"They won't come," Elchyard said. "They are trapped." He grinned as he pulled me into the distance. He cast a spell at the exits and the invisible shield Velvet and Jake had put up crumbled down. I could hear the sound of glass shattering, but nothing was visible.

"I won't help you!" I yelled, jerking my arm from his grasp.

Elchyard looked at me, his nostrils flared, his face turned a deep red. I stared back with an expressionless face, refusing to look at anything but the black centers of his eyes. He was the first to turn away, letting go of my wrist as he turned to look up at the exit. I ran forward in my one chance to get away. I could feel glass cutting into me, falling from above. Blood from unseen shards of glass puncturing my skin forced me to stammer back into Elchyard's grasp.

He shook his head disapprovingly, lips pursed and eyes yet again piercing through mine. He grabbed for my other hand now. He had begun a Hermetian spell. I could sense it; shapes blurring, colors morphing.

Blackness took over my vision and a damp coldness set in. Someone approached me and I stepped back in alarm. It took a moment for my eyes to adjust, to realize where I was. Zach was there, standing in front of me, and the dewy quarters where we were confined became more familiar -- it was Duchura's dungeon.

"Zach." I reached out, letting his strong embrace caress me, looking around the room for Elchyard and the others. We both knew what being back here meant.

"We were ambushed. The seals to the exits in the alley were broken and Boggeles flooded in. We couldn't stop them, or come to find you," Zach said, looking back to everyone else, sitting against the far wall in the room.

"Do you think the scripture will be safe?"

"I don't know."

"Elchyard must have known it was nearby. He tried to force me to take him to it, but I refused."

The gates that held us inside the dungeon room swung open and we looked up at the sound of them slamming against the wall behind them. Duchura walked inside. I could hear the sound of another set of feet making their way down the staircase. Duchura said nothing; she stood, waiting for the other person to emerge. Elchyard came into view, his skin brandished with heavy bruising and one of his eyes swollen and dark. He clung to the bars of the gate, not venturing any further towards Duchura.

Zach and I looked to each other, only moving our eyes, staying still as we watched to see what Duchura was going to do.

"Edgar, come!" We watched as Edgar released his grip on the bars of the gate and came cowering to her side

Elchyard stood facing us, terror in his eyes. Everyone was silent; Duchura was the only one at ease.

"How could you." We all turned our heads to Auck. He stood up from his space against the wall and walked past Zach and me, towards Elchyard.

"Tell them, Edgar," Duchura looked to Elchyard.

"I am not Elchyard. Your mayor has been in the Boggele territory."

"Charmers, so gullible, so *trusting*. Can't even realize when their own mayor is a fraud," Duchura said, pinning Auck against the wall as she moved closer to him.

"Where is he!" Auck demanded, shoving Duchura aside.

"You are stronger now," Duchura smirked. "Give us the scripture." She turned to Thonet, a bright light shot out of her scepter, knocking her to the ground.

"Mom," Jake held Thonet by the shoulders. Thonet held her hand up to him, gesturing she was alright, too out of breath to say anything.

Duchura waited for a moment before talking once more. "Have it your way. Edgar!"

"Yes, master."

"It's time. I want you to send every last man,

woman, and child to look for the scriptures. Any Boggele who has not passed through to the Charmer's territory by the time I leave this dungeon will be dead."

"Yes," he nodded.

"Come back when it's done."

Duchura took out her scepter and cast a spell to the far corner of the room. A glass sand timer appeared and slowly, flakes floated to the bottom of the container.

"You have until the timer runs out to change your mind. We *will* find the scripture either way, but your life will not be spared if we do not hear of its whereabouts from you."

I could hear Edgar's feet running back down the stairs into the dungeon. When he got to the edge of the steps a bolt of light struck him and he fell into the room. Duchura locked the gate and walked up the stairs, stepping over Edgar as she left.

"Wait!" Edgar yelled, pressing his face in between the bars of the gate. Duchura came back down the stairs once more. "Master, why am I in here?"

"I gave you a simple task, Edgar. Find the scripture sections and bring them to me. You have had years!"

"Master, I can still get the scripture, I am so close!"

"You're a waste Edgar."

"You would leave your own daughter in here!" Edgar jabbed as Duchura turned the corner of the staircase.

"She is a disgrace."

The flakes continued to slowly fall to the bottom of the glass. No one knew what would happen when the timer ran out.

"We're going to die," Velvet said, sinking to her knees in the corner of the room.

"No, Velvet. We will make it out of here. Somehow," Thonet said.

"There is no way out of this."

"She's right," Edgar chimed in. He was sitting on the floor in the opposite corner of the room with his head on his knees. "When that timer runs out it will break apart, the magic inside of it will kill us. I've seen it before, it doesn't take long."

The timer was already half empty.

"We have to try something – anything," I said, looking around at everyone sitting in the darkness.

"The gates have been charmed. Duchura is the only one who can open them," Edgar said.

"We at least have to try," Zach said. He and Jake went over to the gate and cast spell after spell at the lock. Nothing happened.

"We'll have to think of some other way," Zach said.

"The lock's stuck. Nothing is going to open that," Jake said, shaking the bars of the gate one last time.

"Wait, Zach," I said, getting to my feet. "We have Winters' stone."

"Winters' stone," he smiled.

"We've got to hurry." I looked at the timer and the last few flakes were about to fall.

I watched Zach as he tried to pull the rock out of the air. A whisk of color would appear and quickly fade.

"I can't get it with the Charmer block." He frantically grabbed at the air trying to draw the rock into the room. Everyone else watched intently.

The last flake started to fall. Thonet was the first to notice. She yelled something aloud and the timer stayed frozen.

"Hurry, Zach! I can't keep this frozen much longer." Sweat had already dampened her forehead.

A flash of bright light appeared and everyone looked to Zach anxiously. He had the rock. He held it up to the tiny keyhole and nothing happened.

"Zach. Fix it," Thonet warned. She was trembling now, using all of her strength to keep the last flake from falling.

I could tell Thonet was about to stop the spell.

"Just another minute," I pleaded.

"I can't," she breathed. The last flake fell to the bottom of the timer. It broke apart just as Edgar said as the flake fell. A fine black mist started to fill the room. Edgar ran from his corner to the gate, breathing in the last few breaths of fresh air.

I searched the ground for the stone, holding my breath, already starting to feel lightheaded. It was gone. Zach didn't have it either. I shook the bars of the gate, breathing in my first breath of the black mist. It burned my throat, choked me, and stung my eyes.

I looked to Zach; he stared intently at the gate, watching something. The rock was molding into the keyhole. The handle of the key was the last to form. I reached out for it as soon as it was molded together and turned the lock. The gate flew back and hit the wall behind it. I ran through, Velvet and Auck right behind me.

The mist stopped as it hit the stairwell, we were free from it; but Zach, Jake, and Thonet were still in there. I went to go back in, to get them out of there, but Auck stopped me.

"We've got to get them!"

"We can't risk anyone else going back inside," he said, worried, trying to squint through the thickening mist to see if the others were on their way out.

We waited at the edge of the gate. Zach had been right next to me, I didn't know why he wasn't out yet. I was worried. Jake was the next to make it out.

"Where are Thonet and Zach?" I immediately asked.

"I thought they were out here," he coughed, rubbing at his bloodshot eyes.

Auck didn't have time to hold me back this time. The dungeon room was big and I quickly became disoriented from the thick, black air. I saw a figure on the other side of the room. It was Zach, searching for the exit, helping Thonet move through the room, too confused to know which way to go, stumbling, holding onto the side of the wall to keep from falling. I grabbed him, helping him to the exit, dragging him and Thonet forwards. Once we were close enough to the gate I pushed them through, exhausted from the lack of air and feeling the sting from the one breath I had taken while inside.

I caught my breath, feeling a wave of heat run through my body as I started to calm back down. Everyone else was coughing a black liquid from their lungs, hunched over, facing the wall, coughing up profuse amounts of black, viscous blood.

Auck and Velvet started to seem alright again.

"Are the others going to be okay?" I asked.

"Once they get the rest of that magic out of their systems they should be alright," Auck said, "They were in there a lot longer though."

"Sable, are you okay?" Zach coughed, still facing away from everyone else, refusing to let anyone see his face as blackened blood continued to rush from his lungs.

"Of course the girl is fine." I looked up. Edgar was standing on the steps above us. "Duchura wouldn't let her die," he said, stepping around the corner and out of sight. Jake looked up from where he lay on the steps, only the whites of his eyes staring up with the anger of betrayal burning inside of him. I could see sweat on his forehead and his skin turning pale.

I stood on a step above the others, watching them, and then turned my attention to where Edgar had stood, but he was gone. No one spoke. They were in pain; their eyes growing red even out of the mist, still coughing blood. My heart beat faster as I looked at them. We were alone and I was of no help to them. The Boggeles had all left for Charmer territory; they were headed for the scripture.

CHAPTER XV

A silence and uttermost emptiness had taken over the castle. There were no Boggeles here anymore. They were with the Charmers now, looking for the scripture, killing as they went.

"Wait, stop. We've been in here already," I said, looking around the room in front of us. Long dining tables lined the walls, scattered with ink jars and paper and towering stacks of books.

"Are you sure?" Zach said, taking a quill out of an ink jar, scribbling on an empty sheet of paper.

"Yes," I said, taking the pen back from him.

A tower of books crashed onto the floor, nearly hitting Zach. Then I watched as they piled themselves back up to the ceiling. Out of the corner of my eye I saw someone run to the other side of the room. I turned my head and saw Edgar squatting behind a table.

"Zach, move!" I shouted. I watched Edgar as he pushed another stack of books to the ground. When they failed to land on Zach he used his scepter to stack them up again.

Auck ran into the room after Jake to grab hold of Edgar. I watched as papers were strewn across the ground and ink jars were spilled onto the wood floors. Edgar was running, trying to get out of the room. Jake was close behind him this time. Edgar made a break for the exit and Auck cast a spell. Edgar fell to the ground and Jake jumped on top of one of the tables, casting another spell at him, refusing to stop it until he was close enough to grab him.

"Where's Elchyard?" he yelled, both hands around Edgar's skinny neck.

"I don't know." His face was turning red; Jake was cutting of his airway.

"Where is he?"

"I haven't seen him in years!"

"Jake, calm down," Auck said, approaching him and Edgar. "Right now we just need to worry about finding an exit."

Jake let go of Edgar. He crawled backwards in an attempt to get out of Jake's reach. As Jake lunged for him again Edgar took out his scepter, disappearing as quickly as we had noticed him.

"Stay next to me," Zach said as we walked across the room to Auck and Jake. He held out his scepter as he walked closer, looking around the room.

Something hit Zach from behind. Edgar ducked behind a table as I turned around. Zach and I made a run for the others. Bolts of light were shot back and forth from where Edgar was hidden and where the rest stood across the room.

"Sable!" Zach yelled. I looked up and screamed. There wasn't enough time to move before a stack of books landed on me. I braced myself, ready for the impact, but right before they hit me they seemed to levitate for a moment and Zach was able to run over. He grabbed me and pushed me out of the way. We landed on one of the tables and ink sprayed up into the air.

Edgar must have known he was too weak to fight us all. His spells were overpowered, and without attempting to fight back any further, he vanished.

Everyone stayed closer together this time as we maneuvered through the castle. All of a sudden Velvet ran ahead of the rest of us, we followed her, she had spotted an exit.

The dead forest was thick and mangled just as before. We had to get out fast, back to the Charmers and the scripture. The temporary spot couldn't keep the scripture safe for long, especially with all of the Boggeles out looking for it now.

"Are you guys strong enough to do another Hermetian spell?" Thonet asked.

"We've got to save our energy for when we're back in the village. The Boggeles will be attacking, we have to be ready," Auck said gravely.

"We need to find the Orion tree," Zach said, looking around the forest, remembering nothing familiar. "Anyone remember how to get back there?"

No one said anything. The forest was too dense to tell, especially the further in we wandered.

Dead branches lashed our legs and the thorns crawling along the ground snagged my shoes. A ringing noise became faint in the distance: the Boggele death threat. I looked around to the others, but they didn't notice; they weren't one of them, one of the Boggeles.

The ringing grew louder. We were getting closer to someone.

"Stop!" I yelled to the others. I plugged my ears, but the sounds kept creeping in.

"Sable, we have to go keep moving," Zach said, "we just need to make it to the tree."

"Sable..," Thonet started.

"Wait, I think I hear something, too," Velvet said and held her hand up to silence everyone. Without warning she vanished out of sight, pulling me away with her. "Get down," she ordered.

Everyone looked around confused, but followed what Velvet was doing and hid themselves as best as possible.

"Velvet, what..."

She hushed me and peered through the vines of an old tree that slouched over our heads and made an overhang just big enough to crouch under.

I was deathly quiet as I saw a jet black figure thundering towards us. The thudding of horse hooves grew louder along with the noise. Velvet stared as a lean woman in all black sitting on a saddle came into view with the horse. A brimmed hat that concealed her face sat on her head and she was wearing some sort of green cloak that flowed behind her as the horse ran.

All of a sudden the horse stopped in front of the tree branches that Velvet and I hid behind. It grunted and snorted and the ringing noise pierced through my entire body more than it ever had before. Velvet leaned her hand over and pushed down on my shoulder. We sank into the ground as the horse sniffed at us. The woman didn't seem to notice us. The horse started to lash out at us and rise to its hind legs. It clattered down into the bush and barely missed landing on us. Velvet rolled to the side as the horse struck the bush yet again.

"Whoa!" The woman yelled as she pulled back on the reins. The horse paid no attention and all of a sudden I had the impulse to leap out of the bushes and run, but before I had the chance to, Auck did. The horse turned to face him and right before it rose to its front legs he pulled his scepter out and cast a spell leaving the horse frozen.

Zach came out of the bushes behind Auck, "That's a storm rider isn't it?"

"Yes. We don't have much time. We've got to get to that tree," Auck said.

The horse now continued to run in our direction, clamoring through the bushes close behind us.

"Where is the damn tree?" Velvet yelled from behind.

As the horse caught up to us a heavy rain poured down. The sound of the Boggele threat grew louder and the sky grew darker. I could hear the horse's strides beating down like thunder and feel cold rain soaking through my skin. Occasionally a flash of lightning struck the ground and I could smell smoke from where it hit in the distance.

A cold gust of wind blew over everything around. I could see ice crawl over the barren ground and coat the trees in a layer of frost. The cold stung my skin, making it harder to run.

"This way!" Zach yelled, but the others had all

taken off in a different direction. Thonet and I were the only ones still with Zach. The storm rider must have been following us, not the others. Lightning hit the ground more frequently around us, closer to us.

Zach found somewhat of a shelter behind a thick redwood trunk further in the forest. The three of us rested there while we scanned the distance for the others.

I thrust my head back and leaned against the tree trunk as lightning hit the ground in front of us.

"Let's keep moving," Thonet said.

Without hesitation we started running again. All I could see was a few feet in front of me. Everything was grey; thick, foggy clouds engulfed the forest. I had no clue if Zach or Thonet were close by, but I kept running. Through the fog I could tell there was a clear patch in the distance, the storm seemed less powerful up ahead.

"Zach, Thonet!" I screamed. I was now aware that they were not with me. Through the thick smoke and dense fog nothing was visible. The haze crawled across the desolate land and covered everything, except for a small ring at the base of the Orion tree. I had made it, but I was the only one.

"Thonet!" I yelled; I just needed to find someone. I didn't want to be alone.

A yellow ball of light floated out of the fog. I heard something briskly moving my way. A figure burst through the smoke and rushed over to me. Zach was the next person to find the tree.

"I had no clue where you went, I lost track of everyone in the smoke."

"What are we going to do? We can't just leave the others behind."

"We'll wait here," he said. "I think the others are all together. They'll find the tree soon, I hope."

We waited for what felt like a long time. It was cold and we were already wet, with frost clinging to our clothes. Zach wrapped his arm around me to keep us warm and I was able to shield my face from the rain by leaning close into Zach's chest.

Four small, yellow balls of light finally floated towards the tree. Then we saw Auck and the others moving towards us through the fog.

"Are we all here?" Thonet asked as she looked around counting everyone.

Zach sighed with relief. "This is everyone."

"Well, let's leave then," Velvet said. She was the first one to approach the tree, but she seemed weary about going alone. She stopped at the base and looked back at everyone for help.

"Everyone ready?" Zach asked as he walked up next to Velvet.

We nodded. "It's going to drain your energy from the pull of both worlds, so everyone go through quickly."

Something broke through the trees and we all turned around to see what it was. There were now two storm riders, both thundering towards us.

"Go!" Auck yelled.

The ground started to frost over even faster, now inching closer and closer to the tree. The wind was strong and pulled the stems of the leaves of the tree, strewing them through the air.

Before I went through I looked back at Zach to make sure he was ready, but he stood, still a good distance from the tree, looking out at the riders, his skin frosted and cold, his hair pushed away from his face by a violent wind.

"Zach," I warned as thunder cracked loudly overhead.

"They are going to follow us back. I've got to kill them first."

"Zach, you can't do that. They have Boggele magic, a lot of it!"

"Sable, go. There is no barrier anymore to stop them. I've got to kill them."

There are already Boggeles back at the village anyway, two more won't matter. I'm not going back without you."

The noise of the Boggele threat was overbearing, and I sank to the ground, crying out in agony as I covered my ears to mute the noise. I looked into the rider's cold, hollow eyes as she raised her scepter into the air. A wave of light hit the ground and I frantically rolled to my side to keep from being in the path of lightning that tore across the forest floor. The more I struggled to get to my feet, the colder I got. My muscles stiffened in the cold and I prepared myself to feel a bolt of lightning pulsate through my body.

"Sable!" I heard someone scream out. I slowly turned my head and I could feel the cold biting into my skin. Zach, wet and stained by blood and smoke, pushed me out of the way right as the next bolt of lightning hit the ground. He was on top of me and I immediately felt the warmth of another body radiating over me.

He yelled out in pain as the lightning struck him instead of me, but quickly got back to his feet.

He looked down at me, and then back to one of the riders, casting a spell back at them.

"Okay, Sable, you've got to go through now!" Zach yelled.

"Sable! Get to the tree!" Auck ordered. I waited for a moment to see if Zach was going to come this time.

"I'll come," Zach agreed, looking back as the riders sent bolts of lightning even closer to the tree.

Auck was the first one to go through the portal. Zach took me by the hand and we stepped through together. I immediately felt warmer.

The storm riders hadn't made it through the portal yet. Auck made his way to the village with the others as soon as we were on solid ground. Zach and I were still numb, finding it hard to move quickly.

"Zach?" I said and he turned in my direction.

He hurriedly got up from where he had landed and came over to me. He reached out his hand and pulled me to my feet.

"You ready?" he said.

I nodded.

I could see sparks and hear screams coming from the village, but they all seemed so faint at that moment.

"Promise me you will do whatever it takes to keep from getting hurt down there," he said quietly, his chin brushing over my shoulder as he spoke. "Stay safe."

"You, too," I breathed deeply.

For the slightest moment I blocked out the pain and suffering that we had both endured; I refused to hear the noises below. But then it was over, the cries from below came back to my attention, the spells that penetrated the air and lit up the dark sky in the canyon below seemed brighter again.

Adrenaline flooded my body as we got closer to the base of town. The realization of what we were about to do all of a sudden became more frightening. We had no plan anymore. Everything was left to chaos.

I thought about the last war between the Boggeles and Charmers as we drew nearer. This was the start of another. My run slowed to a walk. I didn't know what it would be like once we were in the village. I didn't know if I would be able to handle it. I looked up to the stars, squeezing my eyes shut, letting tears seep through the corners of them. I pushed the hair that clung to my face away with both hands; breathing heavily, I looked into the dark night.

"It's going to be okay," Zach whispered, leaning over me, seeming to know what I was thinking. The rain soaked him, his cotton shirt offered no protection, and his clothes stuck to his skin. Droplets of rain ran down his face and over his eyelashes. The only thing still bright in the blackening storm were his eyes, blue, full of light. He knew what we had to do, and if he was scared, he didn't show it. He grabbed my hand without warning and we ran, to the heart of the village, to the scriptures.

I stopped to catch my breath in a dark corner of the

back alleys once we were on the outskirts of the village. I could sense there was someone else nearby; we were being followed, and not by Auck or Thonet or the others.

Zach jerked his head up at the next sound that came from behind us. He motioned for me to stay where I was as he started to walk back in the direction we had come from. He could sense a presence, too. I looked around the corner of the building from where I was hiding and saw Zack draw out his scepter. I couldn't judge how far we were from where the fighting was going on in the village. This could be our first Boggele encounter of the night. I was worried that he wasn't prepared to fight quite yet.

I heard what I thought was the sound of cans falling to the ground and someone yelled out in terror. As quickly as I heard the noise I ran from the hiding place and went in the direction Zach had gone. There seemed to be many more turnoffs into other small streets that I hadn't noticed before. Without thinking I turned into one of them and kept moving forward.

I paused again to see if I could hear any noises that indicated Zach was near. Nothing. Only the sound of rain splattering hard against the pavement and cracks of thunder, or maybe spells -- and screams from all around were heard.

Zach and I were separated; I knew I was lost. I tried to retrace my steps back to where he had left me. I made another wrong turn. I was at the base of Rancorous Cauldron. I abruptly stopped and went to turn back the other way.

Someone had seen me. The shadowy figure

approached me before I could get away.

"Child, come," a voice said from inside the alley. The scratchy tone made my heart jump. I started to run faster and right as I went to turn into another street someone stopped me.

An old lady walked slowly towards me and grinned as she drew out her scepter. I turned to go the other way and a man appeared out of nowhere. They cornered me until the man was able to grab my arm and force me back in the direction of Rancorous Cauldron. I screamed, but it was drowned out by the other shouts and spells and the storm.

"Help!" I screamed. I flailed my arms and tried to escape his tight grip. "Zach!" I cried out in a panic. They dragged me through the entrance of the alleyway and brought me into a little shop. I was thrown down into a chair and the old lady pulled one up across the table from me.

"Where are they?"

I didn't say anything.

"The scriptures! Are they still separated?" She lunged across the table grimacing. I saw her crooked, yellow teeth and smelled a foul odor as she leaned in closer to me. I noticed that she was wearing a green eye necklace. I looked around the room for another exit. There was only the one, up at the front of the store where I had been taken in.

"Tell me now," she warned.

I still said nothing.

"What was his name again?" she started. I looked at

her confused. "Zach, Zachary? And Auckmonrahado, we've already tortured him once. We can find him again," she cackled.

"They are still in Duchura's dungeon," I lied.

The lady pointed her scepter towards me; it shook in her old, unsteady hand.

"He's dead. So are the others." I looked to the floor as I said this; she couldn't know they were here.

"You are lying." She reached over from her chair to a shelf and pulled a glass orb down onto the table.

Smoke inside of the ball started to stir and I saw a faint image of Zach appear. "It looks like they have already found him."

"No," I breathed and grabbed at the orb. The lady pulled it away from my reach and put it back on the shelf before I could see what was going on.

"Fine, fine!" I cried, "I will take you to the scriptures, the sections are all in different places," I lied again, "just don't let them hurt him." I slowly got up from the table and stood waiting for the lady to do the same. She followed me back out into the alley. I stood under the tiny eave that hung over the building, water still splattering onto my clothes. I looked to the lady. She clutched her scepter tightly in her hand. I ripped it from her grasp and ran.

I heard her scream and fight to catch up to me. I gripped the scepter tightly with fear and kept running. I didn't know where the man who had accompanied her had gone, and I hoped that he wouldn't show up again. I heard the lady holler for someone to help her, but no one came.

I found a small cutout in one of the walls in another

alleyway and hid there for a moment to see if the lady was still following me. I heard nothing that seemed to be nearby. I thought desperately for a way to find Zach and get to the scripture. Then I had an idea. It was a crazy idea, but the only one I had. I held out the lady's scepter.

"Luminous seeker!"

A light shot out from the wand and started to drift away. I was nervous, I didn't know if the Boggele power from her scepter could overtake me. The light moved quickly and changed directions often. It stopped right before it turned another corner and then it burnt out.

CHAPTER XVI

I stood with my body pressed tightly against the wall, waiting for a sound or a movement. I tried to breathe lightly for fear that someone might hear me. I could still sense that there was someone near, but no sound gave away their hiding spot. I looked down at the scepter and clenched it as I swallowed with fear. Then I stepped out from behind the corner.

A burst of bright light caught me by surprise and I lunged back covering my eyes. I had managed to wander back into the main part of the village. Everywhere around me was fighting and streaks of light from spells. I felt blinded and deafened by the chaotic noise.

A spell brushed my shoulder, barely missing me.

"Luminous seeker!" I shouted stupidly again. It hadn't worked, but I needed it to. The light shot out again and moved only the slightest bit away from where I was standing until it faded away into nothing. I ran after it and still there was no sign of Zach.

People were everywhere. I dodged a bolt of light and looked back to see what damage it had done. It hit another man and he fell unconscious to the ground. My eyes widened and I ran from the sight, dropping my stolen scepter by mistake.

Someone rushed by me and knocked me into the street. A lady with a few other people straggling behind her came over to me and they all drew out their scepters. I noticed the same green eye necklaces around all of their necks and struggled back up to my feet. I gasped and turned to run but a steady stream of cars kept me trapped.

The Boggeles' necklaces began to glow and right as a powerful green light struck the air a car sped in front of me and blocked the impact. The driver seemed to have done a counter spell. A light came from his direction and the Boggeles stammered backwards.

"Get in!" he yelled to me. Without hesitation I ran to the man's car and slammed the door shut behind me.

"Thank you," I said, still shaken.

"What do you think you're doing out here? Are you mad?" he shouted.

The car seemed to be moving quite fast and I leaned over the seat to check the speedometer: three hundred forty miles per hour.

"Where are you taking me?" I asked.

"Out of here," he said and snorted with distaste.

"No. I have to stay!"

A car cut in front of him and he slammed on the brakes.

"We are in the middle of a war!" he shouted. "Just look! Anyone who would want to stay in this blasted place is crazy. There are too many Boggeles, it's not safe anymore."

"Stop the car!" I yelled back at him.

He leaned over the seat and stared before turning

his attention back to the road.

"I need you to take me back to where I was," I said.

"Stupid, stupid girl," he mumbled as he made a U-turn.

"Thank you," I said.

He huffed.

"You best have a plan together if you're going to stay alive," he said, as I opened the door.

I knew that if I could make it back to the Prism Building that I could possibly find Auck or Thonet. They were the only other people besides Zach and me who knew where the soft spot for the scripture was. There was a chance they could be there.

I knew the general direction of the building, but nothing was easy to make out through the storm. There were so many people filling the streets that I could barely see past them all, and finding an alleyway that wasn't inhabited by Boggeles became impossible. I moved quickly, hoping I wouldn't be noticed, praying I wouldn't be hit by a spell or stopped in one of the riots. I had nothing to protect myself. The lady's scepter I had was gone, and I was completely alone.

The top of the Prism came into view and I ran towards it. Only when I had made it into the square before the entrance did I notice Boggeles swarming the area. I saw no one without the green-eyed necklace in sight. They seemed to have no interest in me, only in getting into the building. They pushed against one another and attempted to break down the door, casting spells to blow it apart.

One lady, who was in the back of the crowd, cast a

spell and it hit the others in front of her. It seemed to start an uproar and when she was pushed away from the rest of the crowd she was followed by the Boggeles she had hit. They surrounded her, and when she was unable to escape, they each sent out their own spell towards her, killing her before they reentered the rest of the crowd again.

I ran as I saw her lifeless body left in a puddle at the edge of the mob. Even a Boggele death was painful to watch. I knew I had to be close to the soft spot. I couldn't help but wonder if it was a bad idea to get the scripture now. There were too many Boggeles, and I knew I wouldn't be able to keep the scriptures safe with them so close.

The Boggeles seemed to be concentrated at the entrance of the Prism; none lingered in the alley where the scripture was hidden. This was my chance to get it.

"Sable?" I heard a voice bleakly say from around a corner.

My heart leapt, I had thought that I was alone.

"Yes," I whispered.

Right then Jake stepped out from behind the corner.

"Jake!" I could not have been happier to see him. "Where is everyone else? Are they okay?"

"Don't worry," he said, stopping my stream of questions. "My mom and Velvet showed me where the scripture was and then they went back out to help some of the Charmers. They are outnumbered; the Boggeles will seize complete control if they get the scripture."

"What about Zach and Auck?"

"I don't know." He knelt down to start opening the

soft spot without making eye contact. I knew he was hiding his face because if I saw the look on it, the uncertainty of whether Zach and Auck were okay or even still alive would have been too much. I thought about the lady in Rancorous Cauldron and the orb with Zach.

"As soon as we get the scripture the Boggeles will be able to sense it. Auck said something about a passage to get into the Prism. We need to find it fast once we get the scripture out."

"Jake, there are thousands of Boggeles, right around the other side of the building."

"What do you mean?" he said, now with more tension in his voice.

"They are all trying to get inside."

"That doesn't make sense! They know the scripture isn't there."

"We have no choice. We need to get the scriptures inside that building."

Jake tossed the scripture to me without warning. "Alright, we've got to hurry now."

I clenched it in both hands as we ran. We wove through the alleys in no apparent direction, but Jake seemed to know the route back to the Prism by heart at this point. The scripture started to feel warmer in my hands. As we kept moving forward it became nearly unbearable to hold onto.

"Jake! The scripture is getting really hot."

"It must sense Boggele magic in you. It's trying to get rid of you."

"I can't keep carrying it."

"We're close, you've got to. I can't hold it either. The Boggeles would be able to counter my spell on the scripture; you have a better chance of keeping it safe."

"Jake!" I yelled angrily.

"It's just for a little while longer," he promised.

I could feel the scripture burning my skin. I thought that the feeling might start to numb, but it never did. Finally Jake stopped at the entrance to a tunnel from one of the alleys.

"Is this it?"

"It should be," he said, slowly walking in. "Wait here. I'll make sure it's safe to go in."

I stood at the entrance and waited for Jake to come back out. The tunnel was dark and as he walked farther in I could no longer see him.

"Sable! Come here!" he yelled a minute later.

I ran into the darkness, his yelling made my adrenaline rush.

"The entrance to the inside is closing! There must be Boggeles close by. You have to go without me; we can't let a Boggele get in there."

As the entrance into the Prism sealed itself off a sound of wind rushed through the tunnel and I had to yell back to him.

"Jake, you have to come with me. I don't know what to do when I get inside!"

"I've got to keep the Boggeles away from you while you get in there."

"Jake, just come with me," I pleaded. "The entrance will seal behind us and it will be fine!"

"Sable, you've got to go!" he said, looking at the nearly sealed entrance in front of us. The wind was blowing through my hair and strands got tangled around my face. I couldn't see where Jake was; then all of a sudden I felt a shove. He had pushed me through. I tripped; falling to the ground of what I suspected was the foyer of the Prism. I quickly got to my feet and realized that the pain in my hands from holding the scripture was gone. I had lost it. I quickly got to my feet and scanned the entry. I sighed with relief as I realized it had slid across the floor toward the front doors.

When I went over to get it I realized that I hadn't been fully aware of what was going on outside. I heard screams and pounding on the door from the Boggeles. Then I heard a sharp crack and I knew they were about to break the seal and get into the building. I ran over to the door and snatched the scripture up before running up the staircase to the second floor of the building. It was only a matter of minutes before they were going to be able to get through now.

I heard a loud thud from downstairs. The Boggeles had managed to get inside. They must have broken down the door. Sheer chaos raged through the building as people flooded the Prism foyer. I felt dizzy, the scripture grew sweaty in my hands, and as I reached out for the nearest doorknob for someplace to hide, I could feel it slip through my grip. I tried the knob again, but the door was locked, each one I tried as I made my way down the hall was closed. Fourth door, I was running into a dead end. I tried the knob just as I had the others and this one opened. I stumbled into the room, not realizing who would be standing inside.

CHAPTER XVII

"Oh, my God," I stammered back in surprise.

Zach stared back at me with confusion, quickly pulling me into the room and closing the door.

"Sable, how are you here?" I handed him the scripture. He reached for it and quickly dropped it onto the desk besides him. "It's so hot."

"It knows who I am."

Zach reached to touch the scripture again and I quickly changed the subject to keep from talking about the blocks the scripture had against me.

"There are Boggeles right outside the door, a lot of them. They know we have the scripture."

Zach turned back to face the door, listening to the Boggeles outside. He took his scepter and cast a spell at the door's frame, watching as the knob glowed softly before turning back to a brass coloring.

"This is Elchyard's office. It was charmed after everyone found out what had happened. Boggeles shouldn't be able to get in here." He still sounded concerned.

"The council knows you're innocent then?" I asked eagerly.

"Edgar was spotted outside of town with a Matiasima."

"So, they believe you now, that your father never took the scripture?"

"No, until he reinstates the spells we're guilty to the council. Edgar got away; they had no time to question him. The council is spreading rumors now that a trusted inner circle of the government is siding with Duchura."

The Boggeles had found us. We could hear them on the other side of the door, pounding against it. They were casting spells at it, an odor of firewood wafted into the room; the wooden door was smoking from the other side. They were going to get past the Charmer blocks.

"They can't get in?" I looked to Zach, breathing heavily, feeling trapped.

"We just have to wait for my dad to come. He'll reinstate the spells and the Boggeles will be gone."

"Zach, the door isn't going to hold them off for that long."

"He'll be here soon. He's getting the last three sections of the scripture. He'll come."

"How? He'll never make it through the entire Prism without being seen."

"There are other entrances the Boggeles wouldn't know about. They were built after the war."

The crowd outside the door was getting louder. We didn't have enough time to wait for Auck to come. The Boggeles were too strong; they were going to get in before he came.

"We've got to find one of those exits, Zach. They're going to get in here."

"We have to wait. I said I would be here."

I looked at him, then to the door, without saying another word. Then I reached out to touch the scripture, but quickly jerked my hand away. It was untouchable, too hot to even hover a hand over. I wasn't the only one setting off the protective spells anymore.

"If we leave now he won't know how to find us, Sable. The sections will still be split up and we can't reinstate the spells anywhere else."

"Then we'll go find him." I nodded at him, desperately trying to get him to agree with me. I breathed in another scent of smoking wood. "We have to go now!"

Zach went to lean against the side of the table, brushing his hand against the scripture and then pulling back in surprise from the heat. He looked to me silently. I looked back, then to the door where the crowd grew increasingly louder, then to the scripture, practically an inextinguishable ember.

Finally Zach spoke, "You're right."

"Do you know how to get to one of the passages, any of them?"

"There's one in my dad's office, which means there should be one in here, too. Start checking everywhere. The entrance could be anywhere. It could be set off by anything."

Zach frantically paced back and forth across the room, tearing away the drawers to the desk, pulling everything he could down from the tall scripture shelves that lined the room. I watched as he began to lose control. He was no longer searching for a way out, but an outlet to his fear and anger and pain.

"Zach," I said from across the room. He said nothing back. He had blocked out all noise, consumed only by his own destruction of what lay out in front of him. I walked to him slowly, stepping away when he turned to a shelf near me and knocked all its content to the ground, letting glass shatter, picture frames break, and book ends beat down into the floorboards.

He still didn't stop. I ran toward him this time, grabbing him around the waist and forcing his arms to his side the best I could. He closed his eyes as he looked up.

"I'm sorry."

"It's not your fault."

"The Boggeles; they are making me crazy, and my dad should have been here by now. I'm worried."

"Don't worry."

We searched the remainder of the office in silence. I looked out of one of the tiny windows that lay along the walls. Boggeles were there, too, standing outside in mobs. I didn't say anything to Zach.

I looked to the ground where a broken picture frame lay. Elchyard was in the image, standing with a group of other men. When I went to pick it up I noticed a piece of glass wedged between the book shelf and what should have been the wall, but blackness took its place. Something was back there. The passage; it had to be.

Zach pulled at the shelf and it moved to the side just enough to see that there was a dark hollow space beyond.

"This is definitely it," he said.

Zach grabbed ahold of the shelf, wrapping his arms around it as he forced it to the side. I crawled into the opening behind him. He used his scepter to throw the scripture into the tunnel without us having to touch it.

A long dirt tunnel stretched out in the darkness, winding underground, under the village. It got colder the farther in we went and steep drop-offs in the blackness caught us off guard. The scripture started to cool enough that we were able to carry it. Zach handed it to me while he took out his scepter and cast a spell for a dim light.

"Where do you think it will lead to?" I asked.

"I have no idea."

Our shoes grating against the dirt made the only noise in the entire tunnel until screams broke the silence. The sound of running feet came into earshot. The Boggeles had gotten into the office, and we hadn't closed off the passage behind us.

Zach and I ran until the tunnel branched into two separate paths. We both came to halt and looked down each.

"Which one?" I panted.

The screaming was getting louder and blurry green light started to come into focus. Zach and I looked back and saw the first of many glowing green eye necklaces moving through the darkness. He quickly chose a path at random.

A scuffling noise on the ground stopped me from running forward any further. I focused my attention on the floor of the tunnel and I could make out Zach and two other Boggeles on the ground grabbing at the scripture.

I screamed as the scripture was thrown in my direction.

"Get it!" someone from the mix of scrambling

bodies shouted.

"Run!" Zach yelled.

I felt a hand touch my shoulder and jumped. I hadn't even been aware that someone was so close behind me. I made out Zach's face and tossed him the scripture.

He grimaced when he caught it.

"It's hot again."

"It's not just from me," I said, looking over my shoulder to see if the Boggeles had caught up again.

"I sealed the tunnel off back there, but I couldn't concentrate very well; the Boggeles will be able to counter the spell pretty fast. We need to keep moving."

A dim light began to penetrate the darkness of the tunnel.

"Finally," Zach mumbled as he flicked his scepter and made the light that had previously been guiding us go out.

"I have no clue where we're going to end up," he warned. He slunk towards the opening and plastered himself against the side of the cave as he moved forward with his scepter at the ready.

I had been used to the dark for so long that the light of the day stung my eyes. When they adjusted I realized that we were nowhere near the Prism anymore. We were now at the tip of the island. There was nowhere to hide once we got out of the cave. A cliff dropped down to the ocean on one side and sloped back towards the village on the other, with a few trees and short grasses dotting the hillside.

We both looked around confused, wondering why

the exit would lead to here of all places.

Zach's scepter sent out a soft light without him doing anything.

"What was that?" I asked.

"It's my dad. He's trying to send a message to me through my scepter."

"What's the message?"

"I don't know."

He took something out of his pocket and handed it to me. It was the tiny orb he used to detect danger.

"Just in case we get split up," he said.

As he dropped the orb into my hand the inside of the ball started to fog. It turned a brilliant red. I nervously handed it back to him and he clenched it in his fist. He then motioned me away from the cliff's edge and towards the hillside where the gradual slope gave way to a thinly wooded forest.

"Do you think the Boggeles back in the cave made it out already?" I whispered.

"No, not that fast. It's something else that's setting off the orb," Zach said, looking to all sides of us, waiting for whoever else was out there to give away their hiding place.

I saw a wisp of dark hair move further down the hill, behind a tree just large enough to conceal a small person. Zach saw it, too. He handed me back the scripture and it again began to grow to an intolerable temperature to hold onto.

Zach slowed to a halt, looking for the tree, waiting for a movement, but there never was one. We waited behind our own tree further up the hill, too small to fully hide us both, hoping that the figure would emerge. Zach's scepter let out a second round of sparks. His father was still trying to tell us something.

"He's in trouble, too," Zach whispered.

Whoever was hiding behind the tree below must have seen the sparks from Zach's scepter as a threat. They countered what they thought was a spell and Zach pulled me back behind the tree just in time to miss the sparks of light that streamed towards us.

The girl appeared again, this time running behind another tree closer to where Zach and I stood. Without warning Zach left his own spot behind the tree where I still stood and moved closer to the girl. Before he had moved he dropped the scripture on the ground, still concealed behind the tree. The grass around it dried from the heat.

I looked down to the place where Zach now stood, hoping that he would look up to me and motion me to come down with him, but he didn't. His eyes were fixed on the tree ahead. A movement farther left from where Zach stood caught my attention. There was a second person hiding among the trees. It was a man, and as he turned to the side I was able to see his face for a short moment. I realized I knew him. It was Henry.

Zach was still only fixated on the girl. He had no idea there was another person just a few feet to the left of him. He was going to be ambushed, caught off guard that there were two people there. The girl had to be Scarlette. I hadn't ever seen her without the presence of Henry. I stared at Zach, desperately hoping that he would look up at me. I needed to warn him. It was too late to follow him down to the next tree, I would be seen. I had to wait where I was.

Finally Zach looked up towards me. He wanted me to follow him down the hill. I shook my head, 'Scarlette,' I mouthed, looking to where the girl stood. Zach didn't understand. I whispered it this time, "Scarlette."

He crinkled his head in confusion.

Henry made a run for a tree closer to Zach and still he didn't seem to notice, still he was concentrated on Scarlette. I looked back to where Henry had been standing just a moment ago and he was gone. He and Scarlette could take Zach down easily now, both were safely hidden, both knew Zach's exact location.

A cry of pain turned my attention back to Zach. Scarlette had made her move. Zach fought back; he was stronger than Scarlette, but she had an edge that Zach was unaware of. Henry came out from behind a tree surprisingly close to mine, but he didn't seem to notice me. He walked silently down towards Zach, pulling out his scepter when he grew closer. Zach had cornered Scarlette against a tree.

"How did you get here!" he demanded.

Scarlette cowered to Zach, but refused to answer.

"How did you find us?"

Scarlette screamed and before Zach had the chance to cast another spell, Henry did, knocking Zach to the ground. Scarlette quickly stepped away from the tree.

"Us?" Henry questioned, stepping closer to Zach, crushing his scepter with his foot.

Zach remained silent; he looked at his scepter, as Henry's foot pressed harder into it. Henry looked to where

Zach's eyes remained fixated then he took a step back, off of his scepter. Zach reached for it, but Henry was faster; he took his own scepter and used it to thrust Zach's into the air, towards the tree I hid behind.

"The girl is with him," Henry said, nodding to Scarlette.

Scarlette tilted her head to the side, intently listening for any noises. She wanted to find me. She needed to find me, and bring me to Duchura if she wanted to stay alive.

The grass around the scripture still continued to desiccate and made a soft crackling noise. The dead patch was spreading; it wouldn't stay concealed behind the tree much longer. 'Scarlette couldn't notice, she couldn't,' I thought to myself, replacing the sound of my light breath with a heartbeat.

Henry cast another spell at Zach, keeping him on the ground. Zach's scepter sent out more sparks. Henry and Scarlette both jerked their heads at the sound of the noise.

"Someone is trying to tell you something?" Henry asked, smirking, seeming to know something that Zach didn't.

Scarlette approached Zach's scepter, closing in on my hiding place. This is my one chance, I thought, running from behind the tree and grabbing Zach's scepter before Scarlette had the chance. A sharp pain shot through my body; it was from Scarlette. I cast a spell back at her. I had to distract her from the scripture. I cast one after another towards her, forcing her back towards Henry.

I didn't think using a Charmer's scepter would

allow me to channel so much Boggele magic, but it did. I fought for control. Scarlette seemed to know what was happening; she cast spells back towards me, forcing me to defend myself. Henry walked away from Zach and towards me; casting more spells in my direction. They wanted me to lose control; they could use me to get to the scripture if I did.

"Sable, drop the scepter!" Zach yelled. I couldn't bring myself to do it. "Please. Throw it to me," Zach begged.

Scarlette turned around and knocked Zach back to the ground. Rage flooded me, it was done; I lost control. I let all of my energy flow through me and into the scepter then back out towards Henry and Scarlette. They stumbled back.

"Take us to the scripture!" Scarlette yelled over the steady stream of spells being cast towards them. I ignored them, knocking them both to the ground.

I felt a shove from behind and fell down along with Scarlette and Henry. Zach had taken his scepter back. It took me a moment to calm down, the energy continued to flow through me even without the scepter.

"It's okay, Sable." Zach had three scepters in his hand now. Henry and Scarlette stood frozen, looking at the two of us, unsure if I had siphoned enough magic to turn my allegiance to the Boggeles for the time being. Zach, too, couldn't seem to tell. My eyes were shut tight, no one was able to see if they had changed to the dark green of the Boggele worship pendants or not. I breathed heavily; I needed to calm myself down.

"Sable?" Zach asked cautiously.

I breathed out now, opening my eyes.

"I'm okay," I said to him. Henry made a run for the cliffs as soon as I spoke. He knew he was defenseless. Zach stopped him and held Scarlette in her place with another spell. They both stood unmoving and I looked to Zach to see what we should do.

"I'm surprised the Boggeles from the cave haven't made it through yet. As soon as they do, they'll be able to counter the spell on Henry and Scarlette."

"Where do we go from here?" I asked.

Zach looked back up towards the cliffs.

"Back to the village is the only route we can take."

Zach went back for the scripture. It was warm, but he was able to hold onto it as we made our way down the hill.

"How did they find us?" I asked.

"Edgar must have told them about the passage while he was still in office. They must have known someone would use the tunnel at some point or another."

We walked in silence until Zach's scepter sent out another flare of light.

"I'm worried," Zach said. "Auck wouldn't be doing this unless something was really wrong."

I looked to him, concerned, but I didn't know what to say that would make things any better.

We continued to walk in silence. Then Zach's scepter sent out more light; it was happening more often now.

"I almost lost control, and with *your* scepter. A Charmer scepter," I said. "How could that happen?"

Zach looked like he was thinking hard for the right thing to say. Finally he spoke.

"If the legend of you is true, then maybe if your father restores your Charmer magic the two sides will balance out. I don't know why that happened, Sable, but you *didn't* lose control, that's all that matters."

"Do you think it's true though, the legend?"

"I don't know. Auck didn't either."

I knew he was holding back.

"Zach. Just tell me."

A path finally emerged in the forest and we followed it for a long time before Zach said anything.

"Yes, I do think it's true."

"What if I never can find my father? I'll be more of a Boggele then, forever."

"Your father is the most powerful scripture maker alive. He's out there."

The village appeared almost completely empty. There were some people staggering along the sidewalk frantically looking for somewhere safe, but the rioting seemed to have come to an end and the mobs of people filling the streets had vanished.

"Where is everyone?" I asked, confused. A cold breeze blew litter across the ground and made the only noise that could be heard through the streets. A dark fog settled over the village that only shadows could penetrate.

"The storm riders must be gone, too. The fog is the only thing left from them."

"All the Charmers though, where would they have gone?

"The Boggeles must have been growing weak from staying in Charmer territory for so long. They must have fled to the underground networks below the village where they thought they were safer. I'm sure some of the Charmers followed, and others went to seek shelter is my guess."

My heart started to beat quickly as we stepped over a puddle. It was blood. "How many people do you think were..," I stammered.

Zach knew what I was trying to say, "A lot. Mainly the Boggeles were killed I would expect, but there's no doubt we lost some of our own."

As we walked I started to notice people huddling in alleyways, panicked and afraid and some wounded. Zach's attention was focused on something up ahead. There were no cars on the roads, no noises in the distance, nothing but a desolate, ruined village.

"What are you looking at?" I asked, panicked.

"What is that?" He said pointing ahead.

"There's nothing there," I said defensively, scared. The fog over the village was still too thick to see through.

"There's someone up there," he said. He pulled me over to the side of an alley and we crouched down.

"Zach you're scaring me." I still saw nothing.

"They're getting closer."

Then I saw it. A hunched figure broke through the haze, steadily walking towards us. They had walked in front of the turnoff to the alley where we stood and I could now make out that it was a lady, old and weak-looking, but with a scepter held firmly in her hand. She turned and walked towards us. She was tracking us; a small ball of light floated towards us and dimmed when it reached where we stood.

"Stop there," Zach warned, making himself noticed. We both rose to our feet and Zach cautiously walked forwards.

The lady stopped and stood with her hand reaching out, holding something out to us.

"Drop your scepter," Zach ordered.

She bent down and dropped it to the ground. Zach went closer. I didn't know why the lady was obeying him so obediently.

"Who are you?" Zach demanded.

The lady offered Zach what I could now make out as a slip of paper.

"Auck sent me."

Zach didn't seem afraid any longer. He took the paper from her cautiously. The lady reached for her wand again and Zach quickly held his scepter to her. She rose back up, empty-handed, and watched as Zach read.

Zach reached for the woman's scepter and gave it back to her after he finished reading.

"Sable, it's okay," he said back to me. Then he turned back to the lady, "Where is my father? When did he give this to you?"

"I have not been in contact with him since yesterday morning. We met at the shipyard at the far end of the island. He said he had somewhere urgent to be, but that he needed someone to deliver this to his son. I've been trying to locate you ever since."

"Did you know who he was when you saw him?"

"I'm sorry?" The lady didn't seem to understand.

"Did you know that he was Auckmonrahado, the scripture keeper?"

"Who wouldn't recognize him? There's a wanted poster of the man on every street corner."

"Why did you help him, if you knew he was a felon?"

"I have never thought your father was guilty." Zach listened intently as she continued to talk. "The Boggeles have ways of murdering a man's stature without even touching him."

Zach nodded sympathetically. He seemed to sense that the Boggeles had done more than simply sided a different way than the lady. It seemed as though there was something else that happened to her because of them.

"Thank you," Zach said. "I don't know if we would have known what to do next if it wasn't for you."

The lady walked away without saying another word, quickly disappearing into the fog.

"What did the letter say?" I asked when we were alone again.

"My dad said that he was safe; but that was yesterday, something could have happened to him since then. He wouldn't have sent those warnings to my scepter if he was still okay."

"We can go to look for him now," I said.

"He was able to contact the people who he thought might have the last three scriptures. He wants us to find them." He showed me an address scribbled at the bottom of the paper. "He wants us to get the scriptures before we go looking for him."

"Is that what you want to do?" I asked.

"We should stick to his plan. That's best," Zach said reluctantly.

We walked up and down the streets looking for an open shop to ask about the directions we were given in the letter, but everything was sealed closed. Finally we found a kiosk that wasn't locked. Everything was on the ground, destroyed. Loose papers and magazines floated around the inside of the newsstand and a single map was lying on the floor in a shallow puddle of water. It was the only one I could find, the ink was blurred, but it was still readable.

Zach pointed to the street when he saw it on the map.

"Do you know where it is?" I asked, struggling to keep up with his brisk pace.

"Not exactly," he said, twisting the map from side to side as we moved forwards. "I don't go to this end of the village often."

We wove through the city streets and towards the mysterious building in silence. Everything seemed so grim; darkness from the fog still overtook the sky and the quiet set in from all around. I knew there were still Boggeles around, I just didn't know exactly where. Every movement made me jump, and every slight noise made me jolt my head in its direction.

The closer we got to the address the more I worried that we were given false information. Graffiti was etched into the wall, I assumed from the use of scepters, and clothing linens that looked as though they had been torched by scepter fire hung from each side of the narrow walled streets. I looked at Zach, concerned, but he didn't seem to notice the uncertainty in my expression.

Finally we found the building we were looking for. We made a complete circle around the outside of it and neither one of us saw any doors to get inside. Not even a window blemished what appeared to be a solid mass of brick.

"This has to be it," Zach said, puzzled.

Zach craned his neck back, looking up to the top of the building. He seemed certain that there was some way of getting inside.

In the distance something caught my attention. A small break in the wall seemed to be carelessly boarded up.

"Look at this," I said pulling at one of the boards that had become soggy from gutter water spilling onto it.

Zach came over to look. He punched at the wet boards and finally made a hole large enough to peer through. I curiously strained my eyes to see what was inside. It was dark, as was the rest of the street, and I couldn't see what lay beyond. Zach used his scepter as a light and cautiously started to crawl through the small space. I watched nervously as he stepped inside. Within moments of stepping inside he jolted back in a frenzied motion, tripping over the wood pieces he had ripped from the wall.

"There's someone in there," he said, startled.

I stepped back panicked.

"What do you mean there's someone in there?"

"I saw a face," he said, pulling me away from the hole and over to the far side of the building.

The quick-beating thud of my heartbeat pulsed against my throat. I looked back to see if we had been followed by whomever loomed in the tiny dwelling.

"Who were they?"

"I didn't see a Matiasima. It must have been a Charmer, still hiding out from the fighting."

I leaned against the wall, trying not to let my trembling body be noticed by Zach. I was scared. "Are you sure we are in the right place?"

Zach nodded to the street sign in front of us. "This should be it."

I walked away from my place against the wall and went to look at the sign for myself. As I looked closer I saw that one of the signs pointed left, while two overlapped one another pointing straight, to our street.

"Zach." I motioned him towards me. "There are two signs here."

He couldn't seem to tell.

"Look," I said, lifting the front one, realizing that is was loose.

Zach looked closer at the strange arrangement, running his hand along the pole that held the signs in place.

"This sign came loose."

"What do you mean?"

Zach grabbed hold of the sign and studied it closely.

"There's a screw missing from this sign. It should connect up here," he said, pointing to a small hole further up on the pole. "This one points up."

"Up?" I questioned, turning my attention to the open skies above.

Zach didn't answer. I looked back down from the sky. He wasn't there.

"Zach," I whispered at first, "Zach!"

"Over here."

I looked to the voice and saw Zach standing back over by the building.

"This is it," he said. He was staring at the side of the wall, seeming to notice something that I still wasn't. Then he took out his scepter and held it to the building. What looked to be small streetlamps suspended in the air illuminated the side of the building and revealed a metal staircase winding around the side of the building until it hit the roof.

"Up," I nodded.

Zach grabbed hold of the railing and started to climb.

"My scepter illuminated this, a *Charmer* scepter. This has got to be right."

I looked out into the dark street below us when we made it to the top. The rooftop was farther up than I had originally thought. I felt secure, so high up, for only a quick moment. The sound of someone tripping on the stairs we had just ascended broke the calm. I jumped and felt goose bumps run along my skin. Someone was running. I couldn't tell in what direction, but I started running too.

I could hear the footsteps now on the gravely rooftop. I didn't know where Zach was any longer, and I couldn't tell what direction the footsteps were coming from. A depression in the roof made me trip, my foot catching it by surprise. As I went to stand back up I realized it wasn't any sort of pothole, but an opening to another set of stairs, this time leading down into the building. The footsteps were getting faster, closer. I could nearly make out a shadowy image in the dark. I was almost at the opposite end of the rooftop now, I had nowhere else to run; I would be cornered. I took the steps down into the darkened hole, not looking back, praying that they wouldn't lead to a dead end.

A thick metal door sat at the bottom of the steps, I pulled it hard and it slowly opened. Once I stepped inside it shut on its own, slamming loudly as it hit the metal brackets that held it into place. It startled me. I tried to pull it back open, but it had locked behind me. I had just become aware I was still holding onto the scripture and I drew it close to my body, thinking that perhaps that was why I was being chased. The footsteps had been those of a Boggele, I was sure of it; and I had left Zach out there with them.

I grabbed hold of the door handle and pulled, yelling for Zach, hoping he was still okay. Finally I gave up, just then noticing that it was no longer completely dark. A dimly lit hall stretched out in front of me with sconces on each side lit by fire. I silently released the door handle, realizing I had already been too loud not to have been noticed if there was someone else there.

I paused, trying to see if I could hear a sound or sense some sort of movement, but nothing was detectable. After a moment I heard something, the repeated thud of slow moving feet.

I quietly tried the door one more time. Nothing. The

footsteps grew louder and I tried to hide my face from the light of the flames. I still couldn't see anyone standing on the other side of the hall, but their presence was undeniable.

I again took a step back from the hall, my back now pressed against the locked door. Someone was getting closer to me. My hands got sweaty and the scripture dropped to the ground. I pried at the exit and prayed that no one would come any further. It was too late. I looked back up to the light of the hallway and a face, glowing in the flames.

"Who are you?" I could now tell it was a man.

"I came for the scripture sections," I said nervously, looking down at the man's hand wrapped firmly around a scepter.

He took another step into the light and I was able to see his entire body, impressively tall and built for his age. He looked down on me, curiously, melancholic. I stared back, afraid, but intrigued. My forehead wrinkled and concentrated hard, thinking of where I had seen him before.

"Where did you get this?" he said holding the scripture I had dropped, finally breaking eye contact. He was trying to figure something out, I just didn't know what.

"I've been hunting for the sections."

"Come," he said, walking down the hallway, the scripture still in his hand. I hesitantly followed behind him, keeping a few steps away from him as a precaution. "Can you open it?" he asked me.

I looked at him, puzzled. I wasn't sure yet if he was a Charmer or not.

"Can you open it?" I asked.

He laughed, pulling out his scepter, watching as the scripture unfolded. Then he touched his scepter to it again and the scripture snapped closed. He handed it over to me and nodded.

I knew I couldn't open it without harnessing Boggle magic.

"I'm sorry. I can't."

The man looked at me again, with the same curious expression.

"Try."

I was confused. It wasn't going to work. The man continued to look at me, and I felt pressured to do something. He held his scepter by his side, but I still felt slightly threatened.

I looked at the scripture and opened it. It unfolded just as it had for the man, but I knew that when I went to try and read the pages the book would start to enact its counter spells on me. He would think I was a Boggele. I stared at the pages, waiting for the words to fade out, or something to happen, but nothing did. I turned to another page, and then another. I kept reading, studying the images and the words and the poems and calligraphy that covered the borders of each page.

"What did you do?" I asked curiously, finally looking up from the scripture, to the man. Slowly the man's hair was turning from a faded grey to brown, his back straightened, and his complexion took on a sturdier form. It was then, when his shoulders broadened, that I finally noticed a pendant hanging from his neck. The Greek eye, but it was different than the others. Only half showed the

Boggele worship pendant while the other shone soft silver.

Now I was afraid. I took a step back, clutching the scripture tighter in my arms, slowly moving for the exit, eyeing the man's scepter, his pendant, him.

"Isabella," he said, stretching his arm out towards me.

I hadn't told him who I was. It was too dangerous for a stranger to know that. I turned my back on him now, running towards the door. He stopped me, blocking the hall with a transparent seal.

I turned back to face him again, breathing hard, unable to conceal my terror.

"Please," the man said. He saw me glance to his scepter and dropped it to the ground. "You can trust me."

I studied his face as he walked towards me. It was not only his appearance that seemed familiar, there was something else about him.

"Do I know you?" I asked.

"No, but I believe I know you." He thought hard before he spoke again, "I am one of the scripture creators."

One of the creators. Both the man and I stayed still now, both thinking the same thing, both seeming to know something that neither one of us could muster the words to say out loud.

I remembered something else now: a picture, perhaps a dream. I was young, and the man was with me. He took me through a field, until we reached a tunnel of trees. I hugged him, I knew him quite well.

I stared at him again, tracing the outline of his body, face, nose, with my eyes.

It wasn't a dream that I was remembering; it was too real to have been a dream. The leaves on the trees had started to blow, lightly at first, then stronger, so violently that they were uprooted from their branches. The man had said something to me. I couldn't remember what.

"I will never truly be gone," the man said again, after all these years.

My skin was christened with goose bumps and hair stood up on my neck. He had been recalling the same memory.

"You're my father."

He nodded.

"You left me," I said, trying to remember the rest of the vision.

"No, Isabella, I was forced to leave you. I had to hide you, somewhere where you could never be found, or hurt. I had no choice."

"Why am I able to remember you all of the sudden?"

"I was never really gone. I watched over you, from a distance. Then one day, I snuck you back into the Charmer world. I thought that tension among the Charmers and Boggeles had subsided, but it hadn't. Wizards found you, almost as soon as I brought you back and they took you back to the human world. They stripped all your memory of the Charmers again and hid you somewhere they believed I would never find you."

"But I do remember you, I can remember that day, when you brought me back."

He looked up at me silently for a moment, "Some

memories can never truly be lost."

"Why was I taken?"

"You were powerful, and it scared people."

"What do you mean?"

"You have the blood of the Charmers and Boggeles, powerful ones at that."

It was true. After all this time, I finally knew, Duchura was my mother and this man was my father. I was adopted. I was related to the leader of a genocide against the humans, and a bloodline that caused war.

"Duchura is my mother then, isn't she?"

"I am a powerful man, Isabella, but I have made mistakes. And I am smart, but I have been fooled more than once before."

"Until now you had only been in contact with your Boggele bloodline; the scripture knew it. Now the scripture can sense both, a balance of loyalty between the two that gives you access to two different kinds of magic."

I didn't know how to respond, so I changed the subject.

"You became young when I opened the scripture," I said.

"Ever since the scripture's creation it has taken tremendous amounts of energy from the seven scripture makers to help protect them. When the scriptures were taken it took all of my energy to keep Duchura from opening them, and when she found you..." he stopped and looked at me with sad eyes. "Oh, I was worried. If you had decided to side with the Boggeles you would have been able to give Duchura just enough extra strength to take back the scriptures and switch the power over to the Boggeles. I grew weaker each time you saw her. It made me grow older much faster, but when you opened the scripture just now, it could sense your Charmer allegiance and I was able to regain my youth, my strength."

Talking about Duchura, I remembered that Zach was still outside with the Boggeles.

"I need to find someone. I will come back. I promise."

He nodded, walking down the hall to the locked door and casting a spell towards it. I left without saying another word, emerging back onto the rooftop alone in the dark, completely dumbfounded.

CHAPTER XVIII

I felt like an open target on the empty rooftop. I was the only one there. I took the stairs back down to the ground and looked for Zach in complete silence, not wanting anyone to know I was out on the streets alone.

I realized that I had left the scripture with the man, my father, I hoped. I tried to ignore the slightest bit of paranoia I had knowing that the scripture wasn't still with me.

I heard a scuffling noise from somewhere around me. I stayed quiet, hunched in the corner of an alleyway. A shadow cast on the wall nearest me. I heard someone trip and quickly get back up. I jumped and felt goose bumps run along my skin.

I aimlessly ran forwards, finally ducking into an alley to catch my breath. I scanned the streets and tried to remember what way I had come from. I was safe with the scripture keeper. I needed to remember how to get back.

I stepped out from the alley and into what I thought was an empty street. I heard the sound of footsteps again and before I was able to get back to the alley and away I saw a glowing light float towards me. Then a hand reached out and grabbed me in one swift motion as they continued running. I screamed and refused to run along with the stranger.

"Sable, come on!" It was Zach.

I breathed in like I had almost had a heart attack. "Oh, my God. Zach, where did you come from?"

"Someone is following me, the same person from up on the rooftop. We've got to get out of here," he panted.

He started pulling me farther away from the neighborhood.

"No, Zach, we can't leave."

"I have no idea who is following us, but everywhere I go I keep seeing the same person lurking a ways back. We have *got* to go!"

"We need to go back."

"Where's the scripture?" he said, still running forwards.

"I don't have it."

Now he finally stopped. "What do you mean?"

"I found my father," I said, realizing how irrational it all seemed, "it's with him."

"You found your father?" he asked, intrigued.

"Yes. I can't just leave now."

"Are you sure?"

I wasn't certain, but there was something about the man that felt comforting. The vision of the two of us should have been proof enough. "Yeah, I'm sure." I lied.

"Okay. You're right then. We've got to go back," he said, looking up and down the streets with strained eyes for the person following him. "He could restore your Charmer magic."

Zach looked over his shoulder one last time before

turning back towards the scripture keeper's building.

"I don't know who this person is that's following me, but we can't let them get inside that building with us."

I nodded.

Zach moved with great speed and stayed almost entirely silent as we ran. I was unable to keep such a low profile, my footsteps were much louder and my breathing heavy.

I followed Zach up the stairs and onto the rooftop, and then ran towards the dip in the ground where more stairs led down to the doorway.

"How do we get in?" Zach asked, trying to turn the knob to the door.

"It wasn't locked last time"

The presence of the stalker was undeniable; he had followed us. Zach let go of the door and looked up the dark staircase. Whoever was up there, they were hiding themselves well.

"You're sure he's a scripture keeper, Sable?" Zach whispered.

"Of course I'm sure," I said sternly.

He must have known he shouldn't have asked that question right as he said it.

"I'm sorry."

I was about to speak again when Zach held his finger to his mouth. He slid his scepter out of his pocket and pointed it up the stairwell.

"Sable, you've got to get us inside."

The person finally made themselves known. They stepped out of the complete darkness and into the shadows and then took another step down where the light from Zach's scepter illuminated their face. It was a woman, with the Matiasima dangling from her neck.

"Sable," Zach warned.

"Zach, I don't know what to do," I said helplessly.

The woman cast a spell towards us. Zach was caught off guard. She then cast another and right before it reached us a counter spell was cast from somewhere behind us and the lady staggered back. The door to the entrance had been opened and Zach pushed me through, following close behind.

The scripture maker was standing on the other side of the door. He sealed the door behind us and led us down another staircase that sat at the end of the entrance hall. Once we had all made it down to the next floor he set fire to the floor above us.

Zach looked at me, concerned.

"Follow me," the scripture keeper said, motioning us down yet another flight of stairs and setting fire to those as well, as we made it to the bottom.

"I don't have much time," he said.

"What do you mean?" I asked.

"The Boggeles must have found out where I am."

The man walked over to a desk and sifted through the drawers. Zach and I stood watching.

"These are the last three," he said, setting down the scripture sections on the desk. He then grabbed the scripture sections I had left with him and cast a spell connecting all of the pieces back together.

"This is all of them?" Zach asked.

"This is it," the man said, handing the scripture over to Zach.

"Thank you."

"There are going to be more Boggeles coming. They travel in groups," he said. "We have maybe a minute or two left before you've got to get out of here. You know what to do with this?" he said to us, holding out the scripture for us.

"We'll secure it back at the Prism," Zach said.

"Good. Now I've got to get you two out of here. I can stay back and hold off the Boggeles." He took out his scepter and held it up to us.

"Wait," I said, pushing his scepter back down. "Come with us."

"The Boggeles will find a way to follow you back."

"Please."

"Isabella, this has to be goodbye." I heard a loud noise coming from the first floor of the building. The Boggeles were in.

"They are going to kill you. Let me stay instead, you and Zach go," I cried. "Restore my Charmer magic and then I will be stronger than the Boggeles. I can fight them myself," I pleaded.

The first Boggele of many had managed to jump from the second story to the third, where we stood. My father quickly grabbed my hand and I could feel a rush of energy surge from him into me. He had given me my Charmer magic back. Another Boggele had made it to the third floor and cast a spell at us, knocking my father to the ground. He was weak after restoring my magic.

"No!" I screamed. I tried to run to him, to help him, but Zach held me back. The room was now flooded with Matiasimas. My father cast a spell at us and before I could stop him we were no longer in the room.

"No," I cried. Zach held onto me tightly, keeping me from fighting the spell.

"Zach, let go!" I yelled, but it was too late. We were back in the Prism.

"Sable, it's okay. He's going to be okay."

I broke free of his grasp and took a step back from him.

"I didn't even know his name, Zach!"

Zach handed me the scripture.

"Look," he said, forcing the scripture into my hands. "All the sections are still here. He wasn't killed. If he was his section would be gone."

I started to calm down. I looked at the spine and counted seven distinct titles: Gregg Abbott, Peter Blanch, Cosmo Galvinson, Edison Rhodes, Charles Winters, James Devenon, and Marcus Lakes. One of them was my father.

"He's safe," Zach said, grabbing my hand again as he walked up the staircase.

"Do you know which one is my father?" I said, showing him the spine of the scripture with the seven names.

Zach read each name intently.

"I'm sorry," he said, shaking his head.

"What are we going to do with this now?" I said holding up the scripture.

"We've got to get it back where it belongs again,

where it will be protected. Then we have to go and find my dad."

I followed him back to Elchyard's office where he started overturning the already destroyed room.

"Look around for the sanction," Zach said to me.

"Sanction?"

"You don't know what that is?" he asked, confused.

"No."

"It should look like a sort of glass display case. Once the scripture is back in there it will be safe and the spells can be restored."

We tore off each shelf and piece of furniture, pulled the paintings from the wall, and removed the floorboards, but nothing was there.

"Are you sure the sanction is here?" I asked.

"I don't know," he said, discouraged. He looked out the window, and I noticed it was getting light outside again. "We need to get this scripture secured. My father has been missing for days and we can't start looking for him until we know the scripture is safe."

"Your dad never mentioned where the sanction was?"

"No. He thought it was safer if I didn't know."

"Never even a clue to where it was?"

Zach thought for a moment, opening his mouth to speak, but then thought again.

"There is one other spot," he said, making his way to the office exit. He wandered further into the building and I followed reluctantly. He finally stopped at the end of the hall where a lone table sat in front of a stained glass window.

Zach walked forward towards the window and I watched.

"Are you coming?" he asked.

I was confused. Then he opened the window. Behind it was another set of stairs.

"My dad's office," he explained.

I followed him up the stairs and into the room. We started searching and finally I gave up, sitting down in the office chair by Auck's desk.

"Zach, why is there no one else here, in the building?" I had just become aware of the intense quiet.

"It's still too dangerous right now."

"What do you mean?" I said, sitting up straighter, feeling more alert.

"The Boggeles are still here, they are just weak; but I'm sure some are still stationed around the Prism building, ready to torture information out of the workers here."

Zach went back to searching the room. He didn't seem concerned about a Boggele encounter. I was still uneasy. Every time Zach made a loud noise I could feel my muscles tense, and I looked to the door to make sure we were still alone.

"It's not here." Zach stopped his search and leaned against the back wall of the office. He looked exhausted.

"What if we take the scripture with us while we look for Auck?"

"We can't risk it."

"Let's look in Elchyard's office again, we could have missed it," I offered.

Zach was insistent on continuing his search around his father's office for the sanction, so I left him alone in the room and went back to Elchyard's on my own.

The sun was just now peeking above the mountains and rays of light pierced through the window in Elchyard's office. I held my hand above my eyes to block out the sun and realized that an oblong shadow was cast on the ground from the windowpane. It took me a moment to realize, but I finally discovered that the window was double-paned somehow so that it wasn't even noticeable. That was the sanction. I was sure.

I had made it partially up the stairs to Auck's office when a piece of glass went straight through my shoe and pierced into the bottom of my foot. I cringed and jolted my foot up into the air, pulling the glass out of my skin.

The glass was part of the stained glass window. I looked back down the stairwell and saw that the window had been broken and glass shards had been strewn all the way to the top of the staircase.

"What," I whispered to myself, confused. I listened for any noises and heard nothing. Then I ran, taking two stairs at a time, until I got to the top. Zach was there, plastered to the side of the wall by the entrance and when I walked in he shot out a burst of light to my head, barely retracting it in time before it hit me.

I jumped back in surprise and tripped on the stairs.

"Sable!"

"Zach, what's going on?"

"We're not the only ones here," he said, distraught, as he pointed to a body beside the desk.

I gasped. "Zach what did you do?"

"I thought someone was coming after the scripture; it just became instinct after all this time, to kill them."

"This is bad. There are already wanted posters of us everywhere!"

"I know."

"We've got to get out of here before more people come."

"But we still haven't found the sanction. We have to."

"I already did, come on," I said urgently.

I quickly led Zach back to Elchyard's office and walked over to the window.

"This is it."

"What do you mean?"

"The window, it's double-paned, the sanction has got to be in between there."

"I don't see anything, Sable," Zach said, standing right in front of the windowsill.

"What? Zach, it's so noticeable."

"Sable, I have no idea what you are talking about."

"Give me your scepter," I said. Zach looked at me with uncertainty. "I'll open the sanction up for you."

"John!" We both heard a woman cry out from above. "John, no! What happened?"

"The man I killed. John," Zach panicked. "He worked at the Prism, and I killed him." His hands shook and his face went pale.

"Quickly, give me your scepter."

Zach did as I asked and dropped his scepter in my

hand. I wasn't even sure how I knew what I was doing, but ever since my father gave me back my Charmer power I felt different, more knowledgeable about magic.

I held the scepter up to the window frame and cast out a spell, not even conscious of what I was saying.

Zach watched with anticipation. The glass forming the window started to ripple and then, as if it was water, it rushed down the wall and disappeared before breaking on the ground.

"This is it," I said. Zach handed me the scripture and I placed it inside. The glass re-formed over the window and the scripture vanished behind it.

"You think that's all?" I asked.

Zach was still beside himself about what he had done. He didn't answer.

"Zach."

"Yeah, that's it," he finally said.

"Okay," I nodded. "Where do we start looking for your dad then?" I asked, wasting no time.

"The lady who gave us Auck's note said she last saw him at the harbor. We'll start there I guess."

Before leaving the office we checked for anyone who might have come after the lady, and John. Zach walked out first and motioned me to follow behind him. I knew that all he wanted at that moment was to get out of the building, and away from the man he had killed.

Zach's pace started to quicken. We turned corner of the hall and were met by a lady's grim face.

"You," she said to us, "which one of you killed him?"

I was startled and jumped back into Zach. Zach and I both looked at each other, unsure what to do.

"Which one of you killed him?" she screamed, holding her scepter to our heads.

"I don't know what you're talking about," I stammered.

She drew her scepter away from our faces and pointed it to something around the corner that I was unable to see. Then she drew it back in towards us, levitating the man Zach had killed in front of us.

"Which one of you?"

Zach discreetly drew out his scepter and was ready to point it at the lady in front of us, but she was faster than he was. Before he could cast a spell the lady dropped the man's body to the ground by our feet and shot Zach's scepter out of his hand. She cast a spell at us. All I felt was pain, and I screamed.

I sank to my knees as the spell worked its way deeper into my body. I gathered all my concentration for one split second, just long enough to reach out and grab Zach's scepter. I forced myself to get to my feet, and held the scepter up to the lady. I countered her spell faster than I ever thought I would be able to, absorbing it into my wand, and with an overwhelming anger consuming me, released it back out at her.

"Sable, stop," Zach urged. I paid no attention. I barely even heard what he was saying. "Sable!" He tried grabbing the scepter from me, and without thinking I cast the same spell at him. "Sable, please!"

It finally registered with me what I was doing and I

stopped the spell.

"That was crazy, Sable," Zach said, hunched over, the pain still moving through his body.

I looked at the woman who I had originally cast the spell at. She lay motionless by the man.

"Zach, what did I do?" I said, dropping his scepter to the floor and leaning down by the woman, trying to feel for a heartbeat. I couldn't find a pulse. I backed away from her, not knowing what to do.

Zach and I both stood over the two people, staring at them in silence. Finally, the lady gasped and started vigorously coughing. I sighed with overwhelming relief.

"Thank goodness," Zach breathed.

We left the building before the lady was fully conscious again. The streets were now dotted with people, forcing us to keep our heads low because of the wanted posters.

The harbor was crowded with boats, but I saw no people around. We kept walking, looking for anyone who might have seen Auck, who we could ask about his whereabouts. Neither of us saw a single person as we walked further onto the docks.

"I should have been able to control my magic." I wasn't sure if Zach had known I cast that spell at him by accident.

"It will take time. You've got a lot of power now; it's not going to be easy to control. The rage you feel from the Boggele magic can sometimes mask all other emotion."

I didn't like hearing that I didn't have control. I didn't like knowing that I had Boggele magic either, but I would find a way to conceal it; I had to.

We continued down the docks in silence. All that I was able to hear was the sound of the waves under the boats and vessels in the harbor.

"Zach, look." I pointed at a sailboat that had all of a sudden been untied from the dock and was heading out the mouth of the harbor.

"Stop!" Zach yelled through cupped hands. The boat kept moving. Zach ran down to the end of the pier and shot a spell towards the entrance into the open ocean. The sailboat slowed to a stop and a man emerged on its deck. I watched as he drew out his scepter, not towards us, but to the opening to the ocean. He was attempting to break the spell down.

"Damn," Zach said, irritated. He took off his shirt and undid the belt to his pants.

"Zach, what are you doing?"

"I've got to get out there before he's able to leave. There's no one else here to ask about my father," he said, diving into the water.

I stood watching Zach swim out to the sailboat and checked to make sure I was still alone on the docks. I was paranoid that the lady from the Prism might come looking for me and when I heard a noise coming from the other side of the docks I jumped into the water and followed Zach out to the boat.

I remembered that the last time I had been out in the ocean was back on the island where I had first met Zach, where I first saw a Boggele. I swam faster, exciting my imagination with fear.

"Zach!" I yelled as I got closer. "Pull me up!"

He leaned over the edge and reached out to grab my arms.

"Where did that man go?" I panted as I treaded water. I had no idea how Zach had managed to get on the boat with no help. He still reached out for my hands, and attempted to strengthen his grip before he pulled me up.

"I don't know, when he saw me swimming he..,"

"Move!" I yelled to him. The man had snuck up behind him with his scepter at the ready. Zach ran out of the way, but it was too late, the man pushed him overboard.

"Who are ye'!" he demanded as he peered over the side of his boat.

"We're Charmers!" Zach yelled over the waves.

"Who. Are . Ye'. Is what I asked."

"Sable Writhm," I said, barely able to tread water any longer.

The man squinted at me and then looked over to Zach, "And ye'?"

"Zach Etan."

The man didn't seem to recognize us from the posters around the village. He lowered a rope down for us and allowed us on board. We climbed up and once we made it to the top the man yet again greeted us with his scepter pointed our way.

"Now, what business do you have on my boat?" He was still skeptical.

"We're looking for a missing man. We think he was at the docks a few days ago," Zach explained.

"Who?" The man was jumpy and I sincerely

questioned his sanity.

"My father, Auckmonrahdo. Do you know of him?"

"I've met 'em."

"Here?"

"Yes here. Where else?"

"Well, do you know where he might be now?"

"Looking for a boat to take him out t' here last I heard."

Zach sighed, "Do you have any idea *where* he wanted to go?"

"And why should I tell you?" he said, leaning in closer to Zach's face.

"He's my father. I told you, I'm looking for him."

The man seemed to find amusement in knowing that we needed his help. He stared at us for a moment longer through squinted eyes, with a stark grin on his face before he began to speak again.

"Asked me for a lift to the island nearby. My boat was in rough shape then, been fixing it for the past week, getting it ready to sail north away from this war zone."

"So he didn't get off the island then?"

"Said all the others told him the same, couldn't give him a ride."

Zach looked at me for help. I wasn't sure if the man was being stubborn or if he still didn't understand what we wanted from him.

"Look, if you know where he might be now, please tell us," I urged.

He man didn't seem to be paying attention to us anymore. He was back to work attempting to break the spell Zach had placed at the opening to the harbor.

"Can't we just use a seeker spell to find him?" I asked Zach.

"I already have. It's not working."

"What do you mean?"

Zach sighed. "It means he's dying."

"No, you're over-thinking things, Zach."

"I'm not," he jabbed. "The only way a spell binding two people's magic wouldn't work is if one of them surrenders their magic. That's what Auck did. He must be too weak to control it."

"Try one more time," I urged.

Zach looked at me with an expression of defeat.

"Try again."

He did. The light was faint and moved only slightly before dimming out. As it moved my attention was brought back to the man, still trying to break Zach's barrier. I didn't have the patience any longer.

"Give me your scepter, Zach."

"Sable…"

Before he could say otherwise I took it from his hand and walked up to man, knocking his scepter to the ground.

"If you know where Auck is, tell us now," I demanded.

Zach seemed disappointed in what I was doing, but he watched as I continued to question the man. "What do you know?"

He held his hands up in the air and tightened his shoulders to his sides.

"He told me not to tell anyone."

"Well, you can tell us. He's probably looking for us anyway."

The man looked up and I could see the full whites of his eyes. He still didn't say anything. I got closer to his face and as my anger grew it became harder for me to maintain control again.

"Sable, he's one of us. Stop," Zach said.

"Like he said, we're all Charmers, just tell us where he's gone."

"Okay," he said, backing up from me. I lowered the scepter and waited for him to start talking. "He mentioned going underground where some of the Charmers were killing off all the weak Boggeles who had fled there. That's all I know. He could have moved by now."

Zach came up behind me and took his scepter back.

"Thank you," he said as he took down the spell in the harbor.

I offered the man back his scepter and he snatched it with a grunt.

"Now get off 'e my boat."

The man started sailing out the mouth of the harbor with no warning and Zach and I were forced to jump from the boat.

"Sable, you've got to stop doing that," Zach said as we swam.

"I'm sorry. I couldn't help it."

"You've just got to learn to control your magic," he said as we strode over a wave. "I know it's not easy, but you've got to make an effort."

"I'll figure it out. I just need more experience," I said a little too defensively.

We were finally back on the dock, and there was still no one else around. "Can you get us to the underground hideouts?"

"Yeah. I've been in them before."

"And I'm sorry, Zach, I'll try harder, I promise."

"You've just got to be willing to learn, Sable, and I don't know if you are right now."

"I am. I will learn, and you can teach me."

He smiled.

The underground tunnels weren't far. We got to them within minutes.

"Do you think there are still Boggeles down here?" I asked, a little nervous as we entered inside.

"I don't know, but we're stronger."

The further inside we got the more people we came across. Some looked like they had been in the tunnels for days -- dirt covering their clothes and faces and exhaustion setting in on their faces. No one said anything to us as we walked by; they only stared. Some quickly put out the lights from their scepters and lamps and waited for us to pass.

"Do we ask someone about Auck?"

Zach looked around and saw a woman and her daughter huddled in a corner of the tunnel, and when we walked in their direction they too turned off their lights and I could hear them walk further away from us in the darkness.

"No," he said. "They're all too scared of strangers

right now. We can look on our own."

"How long is this tunnel?"

"There's a network of them. They go for miles, under the whole village; but I'm assuming if Auck was at the harbor before he came here then he wouldn't have gotten far."

We wandered deeper into the tunnel system and I continued to see more shaken Charmers, but no sign of Auck. Zach must have seen something. He ran ahead of me and brightened the glow coming from his scepter.

"Sable, he's here!"

I ran over to where Zach was and squatted down beside him. Auck looked terrible. He was even thinner than before and covered in dirt and blood.

"Dad, Dad," Zach said, shaking his father. He wasn't responding. Zach took his scepter out and pulled a silver cup out of the air and then he used his scepter again to fill it with water. He dumped it over his father and Auck began to stir. "Here, drink this," he urged him, handing him another cupful.

Auck drank the entire thing and handed it back to Zach for more.

"Thank you, son," he mustered.

"How long have you been down here?"

"I have lost track, my boy."

"I wasn't able to bind my magic to yours," Zach started.

"I had to give it up. It was taking too much of my energy," he said shaking the cup as he held it to his lips.

Zach looked at me with watery eyes.

"Sable, I need you to go and do something for me."

"Anything. What is it?"

Zach leaned in close, out of Auck's earshot before talking,

"He's not going to make it if we aren't able to get a healing potion for him; you've got to ask around for one. Someone in the tunnels is bound to have one."

"I'll find one."

Zach grabbed my hand when I went to stand up.

"Giving up your magic is the first phase of death," he whispered.

I walked up to as many people as I was able to see, but nearly all of them turned their lights off before I had time to talk to them.

Then I heard a familiar-sounding voice further down the tunnel. "Oh, dearie, it's okay now. There are no more Boggeles."

I was almost sure it was Thonet and I ran towards her voice. It was dark and I was running much too fast. I slammed into someone in front of me and I felt my nose start to bleed. Light from a scepter shone on me and blinded me from seeing what I had just hit.

"Sable?"

The light from the scepter was lowered away from my face and I was now able to see that it was Jake.

"Jake, how did you get here?" I said wiping the blood that had dripped onto my lips.

"We've been helping the Charmers who were caught down here ever since there were Boggele sightings."

"What are *you* doing here?"

I had been so relieved to see him that I had forgotten what I was supposed to be doing.

"Zach and I have been looking for Auck, and we found him here. We need to get a healing potion for him."

"How bad is he?" Jake asked.

"He gave up his magic."

He looked back in the direction Thonet's voice was coming from, "mom! We need you fast."

I could hear Thonet hustling towards us.

"Oh, my God, Sable!" she said, hugging me. "What are you doing here?"

"We need a healing potion for Auck."

"Auck's here?"

"He's given up his magic," Jake said gravely.

"Where is he?" Thonet said pulling out a bottle of liquid from the air with her scepter.

We took her back to where Zach was and she quickly knelt down to see Auck's condition. She took the silver cup that Zach had used from the ground and we all watched as she stirred liquids into it.

"Is that Thonet?" Zach whispered.

I nodded and Jake waved from beside me.

"How did they..?"

I shrugged, not knowing how I had been so lucky to run into them.

We all watched in anticipation as Thonet finished the potion and gave it to Auck to drink.

"Come with us once Auck's better. We're going back to restore the spells on the scripture," I said to Thonet.

She didn't say anything back. She only brushed the

hair from Auck's face.

"Thonet?" I asked, concerned.

"I'm afraid you'll have to leave us behind," she said. I wasn't sure what it was that she wasn't telling us. Then she spoke again. "The Boggeles managed to find a way back to the human world. We have to get there as soon as we can."

My heart started to pound.

"The news is claiming it was an act of terrorism," she continued.

"What are you talking about?"

"We have to go and help. More Charmers are needed there."

"Where did the Boggeles manage to get?"

"Greece was where the first sighting was then they spread through the Mediterranean. The Charmers were able to stop them before they got any further."

A wave of heat instantly rushed over me as Thonet told me this. I looked to Jake with a pale complexion and fear in my eyes.

"My parents are in Turkey right now."

Thonet pursed her lips and her eyebrows rose. She looked concerned. "I'm sure they are okay, dearie."

"I have to come with you when you go," I pleaded.

I looked to Zach, who was still closely watching over Auck.

"Zach," I said, putting my hand on his shoulder, "I have to go back with them. I have to make sure my parents are alright."

Zach looked up and I was now able to see that Auck

had fallen unconscious again. I didn't want to leave Zach there, alone, but I had no choice.

Velvet appeared out of nowhere and whispered something to Thonet.

"We must leave now," Thonet said to Jake.

"I don't know what to do." Tears pooled in my eyes and dripped down from my chin to my neck before falling to the ground.

Zach stood up and wrapped his arms around me, holding my head tight to his chest.

"You need to make sure your family is okay," he whispered to me. "Thonet has done all she can for Auck."

"Auck's going to make it." I looked up to Zach, my eyelashes nearly touching his.

He breathed in deeply and tightened his grip before letting me go.

CHAPTER XIX

Greece was in ruins when we arrived.

"We've got to get to Santorini before we go anywhere else," Thonet said. "We can ask Leo, the innkeeper, what he knows." Thonet then turned to speak directly to me. "If it's safe enough we can let you travel to Turkey on your own, Sable, otherwise we'll have to go with you."

I had forgotten about Thonet's connection with Leo. He was one of the only Greeks who knew about magic. He would be able to tell us more about what had happened.

The ferry to the island of Santorini barely seemed to be moving forward. I just needed to get to a phone and call my parents, or read the paper -- anything that could give me more information on the Boggele attacks in the Mediterranean.

The ferry finally docked and Thonet hurried us up to the top of the hill where the inn sat. The extent of the damage was much worse than I realized. Entire bridges had been crushed and walls of buildings had broken off into the streets. Police stood in rows on the corners of intersections and walkways were blocked off by heavy machinery being used to reconstruct the infrastructure of shops and apartments. There were few civilians out, and the ones who were visible had the same expressions as those back in Zach's village: terror.

"Velvet," I whispered, "The Boggeles are gone now, right?"

She looked overwhelmed by everything that was going on.

"Yes. And we can be sure of it when the spells are restored on the scriptures."

I was silent for a moment. I didn't know how to ask about Auck.

"What if the spells can't be restored?"

Velvet turned to face me.

"They have to be."

I swallowed hard, and felt my hands warm, "What if Auck is dead?"

Velvet didn't say anything back.

The inn was in view now, and Thonet stopped us before we approached it any further.

"We need to find out from Leo if there is anyone on Santorini who still remembers what really happened. Then we can find them and change their memory. None of these people can know the truth."

The steps to the front entrance had been destroyed and we were forced to tread through the rubble to get inside. As I stepped through the gravel I saw that a greenish rock stood out from the others: a Matiasima. I looked to Thonet, but she hadn't seemed to notice.

We entered the building with caution, the door swinging open with ease when we tapped it. Jake went inside first. He stood in the doorway, unmoving for a while, looking intently at the room in front of him; then he finally looked back and motioned for the rest of us to follow him in. The building had been scavenged through. Furniture was overturned and papers from file cabinets covered the floor and clung to the edges of the walls where wet dew from the sweltering heat covered them.

Thonet looked nervous.

"Leo," she whispered, wandering further into the room.

We followed Thonet as she walked down the hallway that led to Leo's office. The sound of feet stepping over wet papers and the drone of the city noise from outside of the inn blocked out all other sound. It was nearly silent; everything was still.

The paperwork was all the same, all bills and time logs of the renters, crinkled and dirty, but one was different. It was small, the size of a wallet photo, halfway tucked under a door. I slid it out from the crack and wiped the dirt from the front with my thumb. It *was* a photo, warped from water, and the cracks filled in with mud where it had ripped apart; but I could still tell that it was of a woman.

Thonet reached for the handle to the door above me and I stood up, moving away so that she could get inside. It was the door to Leo's office. The maps of Santorini he had been using to track Boggeles were draped across the floor; hundreds of new points where sightings had been made covered them.

I looked back at the photo. It had to be his father's wife, the one he had spent his life trying to find. A tear in the paper blocked out the side of her face, but when I went to brush away more of the dirt, the wet flap was pushed back into place, revealing the woman.

I stared at her image. I *knew* her.

"What is it?" Jake had come up from behind me and looked over my shoulder at the photo.

"I've met her," I said. "She gave Zach and me a letter. She helped us get to my father and the last scripture sections."

Jake looked confused.

"This is the woman Leo has been trying to contact. She's the reason for all of these maps, so that he could find a way to the Charmers and tell her that his father never stopped looking for a way back to her..." I looked to Jake with disappointment, "he wanted her to know that he never stopped loving her."

Jake took the photo from my hands.

"He never told me any of this."

"She spoke of the Boggeles as if they had taken something from her," I said, referring to the lady in the photo. "They took her family."

"And this is where her family has been, right here," Jake said in shock, "all this time, that's what Leo has been doing with the maps. I never knew."

Thonet had been crouched behind Leo's desk for a while now, completely out of sight.

"Mom, what are you doing?" Velvet questioned.

We heard Thonet sniffle and I walked behind the desk. I could feel the vessels in my heart crumble, and the blood rush from my face. My hands went cold almost immediately and every hair covering my body rose to form a thin protective layer around me. Leo lay under the desk, unmoving, dead.

"Leo," Thonet said, wiping her eyes, hugging his limp body. A Matiasima pendant had been placed around his neck and Thonet tore it away from him. "The Boggeles found out he was harboring Charmers. I know it," she whispered. "I'm so sorry, Leo."

Every part of me shook with fear and anger. I felt lightheaded, taking hold of furniture and grabbing for the wall as I ran out of the office. I had to find a phone. I needed to call my parents. There was one at the entrance of the building, connected to the wall. I could barely focus my hands enough to dial the number. It rang over and over. I held the phone tight to my face, and felt my mouth go dry and my lips start to crack.

"Hello?" someone answered.

"Mom, Mom?" I called back.

"Sable, what is it?" she laughed.

I felt my heartbeat slow. The Boggeles must have never reached Turkey. "I just wanted to check on you."

"It's good to hear your voice, let me put your father on."

My father, I thought to myself.

I could hear my mom pass the phone off to someone else.

"Sable, how are you?" I closed my eyes and visualized them both. So many more days had gone by in the wizard world that I couldn't remember how long it had been since I had actually seen them.

"I'm alright." I leaned my head against the wall as I spoke, still with my eyes closed.

We talked for what felt like a long time before they finally said they had to go. I hung the phone back up on the wall mount and slid to the ground with relief. They were safe and happy, and they had seen the meteor shower just as they had planned.

I had to get back to Zach now. I didn't know what was going on back with the Charmers or the scripture, or Auck. I still hadn't allowed myself to think about what could have happened. I felt that I already knew the truth, but I couldn't let it into my thoughts. I had to block it out.

There was still no noise from Leo's office. I opened the door to Thonet and Jake sitting around the room in silence.

"You called your parents?" Thonet asked.

"Yes."

"Are they safe?"

I sighed with relief. "They are okay. Are you?"

"Leo lived a long life, and now that we know the reason behind the maps, we can find his father's wife. His life's work will be completed."

"You have to go back to the Charmers, don't you?" Velvet said.

"I need to get back to Zach, and make sure the scripture has been secured."

"We understand," Thonet said gently, "we can get you back to him."

"Are you going back too?" I asked.

"We must stay to help repair the city. It is the

Charmer's duty to watch over Greece."

"When will you be back?"

"Oh, it won't be long until everything is back to normal. We just need to help with reparations and change memory patterns of the civilians. We will see you again soon." Thonet hugged me before leading me through the front door and down to the beach.

"When the flash comes, this spell will allow you to switch worlds," she said as she cast a burst of light out towards me. "Will you manage on your own?"

"I'll be fine," I said, looking out into the distance waiting for the flash. "Thank you, Thonet."

CHAPTER XX

I found myself back in the tunnel that I had left Auck and Zach in, but now they were gone. Everyone was gone. I made my way back out into the light of the morning and found that the village streets were unusually busy. I had never seen the village anything like that. People were everywhere, all cleaning the streets and rebuilding what had been destroyed. All of the Boggele pendants that had been left behind were being destroyed with scepters and throw into vats of fire that were stationed all around town. Something had changed since the last time I had entered the village.

I walked towards the Prism. It was the only place I could think of where Zach might have gone. I saw the wanted posters of us being stripped from the walls and no one seemed to be suspicious of me any longer. The scripture had to have been restored. I just didn't know by whom.

I walked past groups of people sitting on the steps to the Prism and opened the doors to inside. The building was busy. I had never been inside when other people were around. I moved around people walking by with stacks of boxes piled above their heads and avoided crates that were being levitated through the air.

I walked up to the second story where Auck's office was without being questioned and entered through the stained glass window into the room. I heard the mumbling of voices from above and stopped in the stairwell to listen. I couldn't make out who it was. I walked up another step and looked up, face-to-face with Zach.

Without saying a word he hugged me.

"Zach, you're alright, thank goodness."

"Are your parents okay?" he asked, taking my hand and guiding me into the office. I didn't get a chance to speak before I saw Auck, sitting in his desk chair. He was alive.

"Auck!" I went over to greet him. "You're here, you're alright," I said, surprised.

"The potion worked," Zach said. "I thought it was too late, but after you left," Zach shrugged, "he started to get better."

I smiled. I was too relieved to say anything else.

"What about the spells?" I finally asked.

"Auck was strong enough to restore them; but in order to bring back those who went missing because of the break in their spells on the scripture, we'll need help from their family members. It will take a lot of magic."

"And my parents," I had finally composed myself enough to answer, "They are alright. The Boggeles never made it to Turkey."

Zach smiled. "Good."

Auck got up from his chair and walked over to the entrance where Zach and I stood.

"I have to get in contact with a few people, check

up on things," he said, "I'll meet up with you later."

Zach let Auck part ways with us. He led me out of the Prism and through the streets. We were headed into a part of the village I had never before seen.

"Where are we going?"

"You'll see."

The townhouses in the heart of the village began to thin out and larger, self-standing homes took their places. We walked for what seemed like miles, where nothing but fields lined the road. I thought about what was going to happen now that everything was over. Now that everything was back in its place, except for me. I couldn't imagine leaving the village, and magic, for what now seemed like an even stranger place than the village.

Zach must have sensed my uneasiness.

"What's wrong?"

"Nothing, I'm just thinking."

"Come on," Zach said, "I want to show you something."

He grabbed my hand and led me through the fields. We walked through the middle of a herd of grazing cows and into a tunnel of trees.

The tree line seemed familiar. It took me a moment to realize why. This was the same place my father, my *real* father, had taken me. This was the place where my one memory of him resided.

"This is where I have always come when I need to think," Zach said.

"It's peaceful," I said as I wandered further into the opening, letting the tunnel of foliage engulf me. I didn't know whether I should ask how he knew of this place so I stayed quiet, enjoying the sound of only the wind and remembering what had happened in this exact place so many years ago.

CHAPTER XXI

We made it to a gated compound a little ways past the pasture and Zach held his scepter up to the wrought iron gates. I watched as they opened and I saw a gravel driveway leading up to a brick estate. Auck was already there, opening up the front doors to us.

"You're back," Zach said, surprised.

"My meeting was cancelled." Auck said blatantly.

"Why?"

"It seems that some of the men had gone missing."

"From their spells?"

Auck looked uncomfortable, "We believe so."

"Well, they'll be brought back then, won't they?"

"Let's hope." Auck shifted his body to the side to let us in and walked away without saying anything else.

I hadn't realized how close to the edge of the island we were. As I walked in I saw the ocean through the windows on the other side of the room. "Zach, this is amazing." I tried to take his mind off of what had said. I wasn't sure if there was something he wasn't telling us.

Night was drawing in and it was getting colder. Zach opened up a wood box to get wood for a fire but it was empty.

"I'll go get some more from outside."

Zach went out the back door and I waited inside for him to come back. I looked around the house while he was gone and wandered farther away from the living room. I stumbled across a family portrait hanging from the wall. I saw Zach as a young boy standing with Auck and a woman that I didn't recognize. They were in the tunnel of trees.

I hadn't even noticed that Zach had come up behind me.

"Sorry," I said, startled.

He smiled and looked at the picture. "It's okay."

I followed him back to the living room where I sat and watched him build the fire. We were both tired and I leaned against him, with my head on his shoulder, watching as the fire stained the air with a smoky smell.

"Zach?" I asked, not sure if he was asleep or not.

"Mmm?" he said, groggily.

"Who was that lady in the picture?"

He sat up a little straighter, "That's my mom." I waited for a minute for him to say something else, "She went missing when I was nine, when her spell on the scripture was broken. It was reinstated years ago, but she still never did come back."

"I'm so sorry."

"We are going to find her one day, I know it. Auck has been restless ever since she went missing."

"Is that why he seemed so anxious about those men who went missing?"

"Partially." He looked around to see if Auck was nearby before continuing, then he began to whispered, "When Auck went to reinstate the spells it didn't go well.

He almost wasn't able to. He thinks there are still some Boggeles passing themselves off as Charmers and that they are conspiring to bring Duchara more power. If it's true, bringing back those who went missing could be hard to do."

"But he did reinstate the spells, so shouldn't the Boggeles be gone?"

"They should be, but we already saw it with Edgar, they sometimes have ways of staying. Auck is worried that with the amount of Boggeles that made it past the barrier that there are bound to be some that weren't caught."

"Do you believe it?"

"I'm not sure. I'm not worried like he is though. If any really did manage to stay they would be weak. They would never have the magic it would take to relay Duchara information."

We sat in silence after that, listening to the fire crackle. Zach must have carried me to a spare bedroom after I was already asleep; the next morning I awoke to a light knock on the door and an envelope being slipped underneath it.

I went to get it and when I opened it up I realized that it was an invitation to a banquet at Mr. Lule's store, where the spells on the scripture were to be officially reinstated, and where families would finally be reunited.

I walked out into the living room and searched for Zach. He was outside on the deck.

"Morning," he said, handing me an empty coffee mug.

"Morning."

He took out his scepter and held it up to the cup. I watched as warm coffee filled it to the brim.

"Did you get one of these?" I asked, holding up the letter.

"It's tonight," he said, anxiously.

I knew that he was thinking of his mother, and our conversation from last night.

"We're going to get to go back to Mr. Lule's." I tried to distract him from thinking of the possibilities of the restorations.

The day went by quickly as we got ready for the banquet. Auck left curiously early in the morning without saying where he was going and Zach and I went into town to look for clothes to wear that night. He left me alone in a dress boutique as he wandered the streets for a men's suit store.

Dresses hung on uneven racks all along the walls and tables with clutters of shoes and jewelry hid under the stacks of clothing. I ran into one of the purse displays as I tried to move further into the store and knocked the entire thing to the ground. It was a loud crash and I looked around to see if anyone had noticed. As I knelt down to start picking up the display, I saw the purses one by one lift off the ground and stack themselves back up. It made me nervous for some reason. I suppose I was still so used to bad magic that when someone used a spell around me I became slightly frightened.

I looked up to see who had fixed it and noticed an old lady standing on a set of stairs above me. Strangers began to make me feel uneasy after what Zach had told me about the Boggele conspiracy.

"Sorry," I said to the lady. She had a grim look on her face as she fixed the display.

"What are you here for?" she questioned.

"A dress."

She tilted her head to the side and stared at me for a moment. "You're the Writhm child, aren't you?" she asked.

I nodded, "Sable."

She pushed her glasses up her nose for a better look.

"Well, my God. Never thought I would see you walk into my store. Come," she said to me.

I found the staircase she had been standing on behind a rack of dresses in the corner of the room and followed her further and further up the floors. I stood smashed against the lady in the narrow room and I watched her as she floated dresses down from racks higher above. A stack of dresses had formed and she instructed me to try them on, showing me a fitting room before she left.

After I found one that fit I went to find the lady but she was nowhere in sight.

"Hello?" I hollered up the floors. She didn't come. I didn't like not knowing where she had gone. I had a weird feeling that she was going to sneak up on me. I'm sure I was just paranoid after everything that had happened, but after a while the quiet started to bother me and I panicked.

Then I heard the bell as the door of the store opened and I peered over the railing on the second story to see who it was. Zach came in with a tux slung over his shoulder.

"Sable?"

I walked down and found Zach among the mess of

dresses. I sighed with relief, "right here."

"Did you find something?"

"Yeah, but I can't seem to find anyone to buy it from."

Zach looked around the store confused, "That's odd. Hello?"

When no one answered he looked at the price tag on the dress and left the money on a table in the front of the store. "We've got to get back to the house soon, its later than I thought."

I decided not to tell him about my panic attack in the store. Zach didn't think too much of the lady suddenly disappearing so tried not to think about it either.

I had still not gotten used to how fast the days went by here. It was already dusk outside and by the time we got back home it was dark.

Zach was waiting for me at the bottom of the stairs while I got ready for the banquet and he watched with wide eyes as I made my way to the bottom. He walked up to me and I looked into his deep blue eyes.

"You are gorgeous," he said, taking my hand and walking me outside to the car. Zach opened the door for me and got in on the other side. Auck was sitting in the front, still seeming slightly apprehensive, and we made our way to Mr. Lule's store.

When we got there we realized that the spells were to be reinstated outside, in a pavilion out back from Mr. Lule's, before we actually went inside.

Zach and I stood in the front of the crowd and watched as Auck opened the scripture and summoned the first family up to the pavilion. The family members stood around the scripture in a circle with their scepters each touching in the center. Auck drew from their magic and cast a spell on the scripture.

Everyone waited in silent anticipation. Then, a figure started to shimmer in the center of the circle where the scripture had been. The first spell had been restored. It seemed so easy; the conspiracy must not have been true.

The family sobbed and hugged the young boy who now appeared in front of them. I looked to Zach and smiled sympathetically. He was still looking forward and a tear dripped down his face. I knew he was thinking about his mother. Her spell had already been restored, and still, she hadn't ever appeared.

I looked forward and watched the rest of the ceremony, reaching for Zach's hand. He grabbed onto it tightly, and out of the corner of my eyes I saw him wipe his cheeks.

When everything was finally over and the outside started to clear out, Zach and I went and sat in the pavilion in silence. He took out his scepter and cast a spell on the pavilion's covering. The wooden roof vanished and we were able to look up into the stars. There was a meteor shower here, too. I stared up, wondering if my parents were seeing the same night sky as I was.

I knew that beyond the stars was another home and I would have to choose. I had already chosen what I was going to do after tonight, and the choice I had secretly already made broke my heart, but it was the only way.

"Zach, your mother is still out there," I said. He

refused to show much emotion in front of me, but I knew he was upset.

Inside the feast was about to begin and Auck came out to find us. Most everyone else had already taken their seats around a large table that sat in the center of the store. The store was bursting with the desires of those who sat at the table. As I walked in behind Zach I felt like something was wrong. I felt an unexplainable rage building up inside of me, like what always happened when I was drawing from Boggele magic. I tried to calm myself, but I couldn't.

"Sable, you okay?" Auck asked.

"Yeah," I said casually. I made my way to an empty seat beside Zach and waited for the feast to start.

The anger, the power, was building up inside of me. The lights in the store started to dim, and slowly the room started to thin out of the desires of the others. I wasn't consciously doing anything, but I knew I was the cause of what was going on. The people at the table started to grow restless and a low murmur arose as everyone looked around.

The lights went completely out and everyone used their scepters as a light source, shining them around the room and up against the walls.

"Zach," I whispered, I think I'm doing this," I said, panicking.

"Just concentrate on Charmer magic," he whispered back.

"I'm trying. I don't know what's happening." In the darkness I saw the outline of a man, and the soft glow of a Matiasima that no one else seemed to notice. I closed my eyes, fighting every thought I had and holding myself back from drawing from any more Boggele magic.

"Keep your focus," Zach urged. "concentrate."

I opened my eyes and the lights had come back on. People were still stirring, but the desires of everyone else were back.

We were sitting close to the council and I strained my ear to hear what they were arguing about.

"She *cannot* stay," one member said.

"She is going to choose our side. We just need to give her time to learn how to manage her magic," another argued.

"Giving that girl a scepter could be the end to us!"

Before the other was able to argue again, the man sitting at the head of the table rose and silenced everyone for a speech. The uneasiness started to settle and he began to speak.

"Everyone, please be seated!" He yelled over the crowd. "Everything is under control."

"That's Mayor Elchyard," Zach leaned in whispered to me. "Some of the Charmers managed to figure out where he was being kept. They got him back while the Boggeles were weakened."

The silence became stronger as everyone started to settle back into their chairs.

"We have been joined together under the power vested in the scripture of spells before us," he started, holding the scripture up for all to see. "We have many brave wizards to thank, and we have many wizards to remember that were lost."

Everyone started to clap and they all sent up the same sparks from their scepters into the air to honor those who were killed.

"There are a few Charmers in particular who have made it possible for your loved ones to be brought back, for the Charmer's magic to be secured, for the safety of the future of our world to be secured. The Etan family, please rise." Zach and Auck stood for applause. "We have much to thank them for, and we can only hope that they can forgive us for our mistake in the assumption of where their loyalties lie."

I saw Zach and Auck smile to each other from across the table.

"There is one last wizard I would like to recognize," Elchyard said, hushing the crowd: "Sable Writhm."

As I stood up next to Zach and watched as those at the table stood with us to applaud us, I couldn't help but notice that all of the council members except for Elchyard and one other stayed seated.

"There is much to celebrate," Elchyard said as he summoned for food to be brought to the tables.

Throughout the dinner strangers came up to me, wanting to meet me and ask me questions, but I was only half listening to what they were saying. All I could focus on was the council arguing over whether or not I was welcome to stay in the Charmer's world.

"We will vote then," one of the members said.

"You know how the vote would turn out. The girl is going back to the human world. It is what must be done."

"She will make the choice herself; we owe it to

her." It seemed to be an ongoing argument.

When the night was over Auck drove Zach and me home in silence. I knew that he and Zach were only silent out of exhaustion, but I on the other hand had too many things to think about to hold a conversation.

Zach and Auck went to their rooms when we got back to the house and I quietly snuck out onto the deck. I sighed and thought about what the council had said. If I stayed I wanted to be welcome. I wanted a scepter and the freedom to practice magic. If I left I didn't want to have to remember all I had been a part of here, and all that I would be leaving behind.

I heard someone slide open the door to the deck and turned around. Zach walked over to me.

"Couldn't sleep?" he asked.

"No."

"What is it?"

I looked to him with teary eyes, "Zach, I had made my decision, I wanted to stay here," I told him.

"Good," he said with a sigh of relief, hugging me tightly in his arms.

"But Zach," I started again, running my fingers through his hair, "I don't know if I can anymore."

"What do you mean?" he said, releasing the grip of his hug slightly.

"The council doesn't want me here."

"Sable, we can find a way around them, they don't matter."

"What if it's a sign?" I said, now facing out towards the water. "Maybe I belong with the humans."

"Don't think that. It is your choice, Sable," he said, putting his arms around my waist from behind me.

"I couldn't help but to draw magic from the Boggeles. I've caused so much destruction here as it is."

"No, Sable you have helped the Charmers in ways not possible by any other person. Your magic has helped us, and if you stay you can teach yourself to block out the magic you don't want. I can help you."

"And if I go back," I started, "would I still keep the memories of this place?"

"That would be your choice."

We didn't say anything more that night. The meteor shower was still raining down through the sky and we both watched in silence.

ABOUT THE AUTHOR

Meg Price resides in Northern Nevada and is currently a student at the University of Nevada, Reno. Meg is pursuing a dual major in Business and Creative Writing with a minor in entrepreneurship. This is Meg's first book and she plans to continue writing throughout her college education.